The Trans...

Th... ... ...
thr... ... ...y ...fferent destinies!

Meet Meg, Bella and Celina—
three loving sisters, desperate to escape the iron rule
of their fanatical rector father...

One by one they flee the vicarage—only to discover that the
real world holds its own surprises for the now-disgraced
Shelley sisters! How will they get themselves out of the
scandalous situations they find themselves in?

Find out in...

Practical Widow to Passionate Mistress
August 2011

Vicar's Daughter to Viscount's Lady
September 2011

Innocent Courtesan to Adventurer's Bride
October 2011

The Transformation of the Shelley Sisters

Author Note

Welcome to the world of Margaret, Arabella and Celina Shelley. Brought up by a harsh and repressive father, all the sisters wanted from life was love—and by looking for it, they found themselves branded as sinners and parted from each other.

Early nineteenth-century England was an unforgiving place for fallen women. Dreamy Meg, practical Bella and innocent Lina fought back against society, and their own fears, to rebuild their lives and find their true loves, transforming themselves in the process.

This is the story of Meg, the middle sister. Dreamily romantic, she eloped with her childhood soldier sweetheart and found herself learning to be practical and realistic in the brutal world of the war-torn Iberian Peninsula. Now, alone and virtually penniless, she must find her way back to England—and her only hope is dark and brooding Ross Brandon, a man wounded in body and soul.

I hope you enjoy Meg and Ross's journey as much as I enjoyed discovering it.

**Look for these further stories in
The Transformation of the Shelley Sisters**

LOUISE ALLEN

PRACTICAL WIDOW to PASSIONATE MISTRESS

TORONTO NEW YORK LONDON
AMSTERDAM PARIS SYDNEY HAMBURG
STOCKHOLM ATHENS TOKYO MILAN MADRID
PRAGUE WARSAW BUDAPEST AUCKLAND

Recycling programs
for this product may
not exist in your area.

ISBN-13: 978-0-373-29652-1

PRACTICAL WIDOW TO PASSIONATE MISTRESS

Copyright © 2010 by Melanie Hilton

First North American Publication 2011

www.Harlequin.com

Printed in U.S.A.

Prologue

'North Wales?' Celina repeated blankly as Meg finished pouring out her news. 'But that's hundreds of miles away. We will never see you.'

'That wouldn't be so bad if we knew you were happy,' Arabella ventured. 'But Great-Aunt Caroline? She's a recluse—'

'She is mad as a hatter,' Meg Shelley retorted, biting back the tears. 'You only have to listen to those horrible letters she sends Papa. She is worse than he is.' She reached out and took her sisters' hands, wincing and letting go as the grip tightened on the livid weals across her palms. 'I would rather be here with you both and be whipped every day, than go there.'

'Perhaps if you promised Papa you would not read novels again?' Arabella suggested, picking up the worn shirt she was darning for the poor box and then dropping it back into the basket with a sigh. Meg felt the affection surge through her; at nineteen, her elder sister tried so hard to be dutiful, to do what was expected, despite constant carping and coldness from their father. How did she manage it? Meg wondered. Could she ever be as good, as submissive?

'Or anything else but the Bible?' she demanded. 'If it is not books, it is going for walks, or trying to grow flowers, or talking to people or singing—I cannot do it. I cannot promise to stop thinking, stop doing *everything* that gives me any pleasure. I will go as mad as Great-Aunt Caroline. I don't mind the housework and the laundry and the mending and the praying. I don't mind working hard, but to be punished for wanting joy and beauty...'

'And I don't understand what he said about Mama,' Celina said with a frown. 'How can he say we all carry her bad, sinful, blood? Mama wasn't a sinner.'

'He has not been right since she died.' Arabella glanced towards the door, as though expecting the Reverend Shelley, switch in hand, to stalk in at any moment. Meg shook her head impatiently. They had discussed this so many times, and still could not fathom what, beyond natural grief, had turned a naturally serious and strict father into an embittered and suspicious domestic tyrant.

'He says Great-Aunt Caroline's health is deteriorating and I must go and nurse her and be a companion. She could perfectly well hire a dozen nurses and companions, she is wealthy enough,' Meg said. 'It is just an excuse to punish me. We would all be better off in a nunnery.

'You, Bella, are to look after him in his old age, you, Celina, will marry the curate—if he ever finds one dour and puritanical enough to suit him—but I am just a nuisance and, this way, he will be rid of me.'

'But what can we do?' Celina whispered. Meg shook her head. Celina was too sweet and too pretty for coldness and drudgery, but her seventeen-year-old sister always seemed unable to rebel.

All three glanced at the sampler hanging over the cold grate. Arabella had worked the first line, Margaret had stitched the second and Celina had managed the plain cross-stitch border. It was a favourite saying of the Reverend Shelley, one he fervently believed to be true.

> Woman is the daughter of Eve—
> She is born of sin and is the vessel of sin.

'Is that a horse in the lane?' Meg pushed open the window: any distraction was welcome. From high in the eaves of Martinsdene's vicarage, the old schoolroom had a clear view down to the church and the village green.

'Oh, don't!' Half-lying across the sill, Meg ignored the nervous plea from Celina. 'You know how angry Papa was last time he saw us hanging out of the window, like common hoydens, he said.'

'It is James!' How very strange she felt inside. Was it love? It must be. 'He's come home at last and he's in regimentals! He has joined the army as he said he would, despite Mr Halgate forbidding it. Oh, but he looks so handsome. Bella, don't you think he looks handsome?'

'James Halgate may look like Adonis…' Arabella countered. Bella's common sense was a predictable as Lina's nervousness. Meg glanced back into the room. 'And he might be a very pleasant and well-bred young man,' her sister continued. 'But you know Papa would never let him call and I shudder to think what would happen if you tried to get out to see James again. Remember before he went away? Papa had you locked in the attic for a week on bread and water. Really, Meg—'

Meg leaned out precariously and waved. 'He must see me!'

Celina joined Meg at the window.

'Look at him.'

Lina's pretty mouth curled into a smile, but she glanced over her shoulder at the door before agreeing. 'Oh, yes, he does look very fine. The Squire is going to be so proud of him. Surely he will forgive him for going off enjoying himself in London for almost a year?'

'He has seen me,' Meg whispered. Something inside her contracted, as though her heart had faltered for a moment. All those long nights dreaming about her childhood sweetheart, and now here he was and she still felt as she had when he had left. She was in love with him, she knew she was, and the fields of buttercups still stretched out in the sunlight where they had run hand in hand and exchanged soft, innocent kisses. Although perhaps, in retrospect, James's had not been so very innocent.

Even as he reined in, taking advantage of the tall hedge to doff his shako and wave it to the two young women in the window, he was casting a careful eye around. Every one in Martinsdene knew the Reverend Shelley's views on the upbringing of girls and how closely he guarded his three motherless daughters.

'Now what is he doing?' Celina wondered as James made gestures towards the stream that ran on the other side of the lane.

'He means to leave a message in the old willow, just like we used to do before he went away.' Meg clutched her hands to her bosom, although it did not stop her heart thumping. 'He means to meet me.' It was just like the fairy stories. Her knight in shining armour had come for her, he would scale the castle walls, cut through the hedge of thorns that surrounded her, carry her off to a lifetime of happy ever after.

Meg watched as the bay mare walked on down the lane and out of sight, then there was nothing to do but go back to the table. She kicked the mending basket out of sight.

'Oh, Meg. Do you truly still feel affection for him?' Arabella asked, her expression the familiar one of mingled sympathy and exasperation. 'You know Papa will whip you if he finds out.'

'I don't care.' Meg sank down on her chair, perilously close to tears again. It was not the thought of the switch. It hurt and was humiliating, but she went away in her head while she was beaten or lectured, off into her imagination. 'If he would only treat us with some trust then I would not have to sneak out. I am eighteen, I know my own mind. And I love James. I always have. We are meant to be together. I love James and he loves me, so where is the sin in that?'

What was so wrong with love that it was classed with crimes like theft or murder? She had asked that once, when she was fifteen, and had hardly been able to sit down for a week.

'Only in the defiance of Papa's authority,' Bella said, with a thoughtful frown. 'Otherwise it is a perfectly eligible match, I am sure—for anyone else. Lina, would you be very kind and go and ask Cook if we might have some lemonade?'

There was something in Bella's placid tone that had prickles running up and down Meg's spine. Hope?

Bella waited until the door closed. 'You are the one he punishes most, because you are such a dreamer, so romantic. And being shut away with Great-Aunt Caroline would be dreadful for you. If James truly loves you, means to marry you—then I'll help, somehow. We mustn't say anything to Lina, then she can swear she was ignorant, and

I *never* do anything wrong—Papa will not suspect that I had anything to do with it.'

More than hope. A plan. A surge of feeling, of joy and anticipation and fear, and with it the realisation of loss. But this would not be like losing Mama. Bella and Lina would still be there, she would be with them again one day. 'Bella, thank you! But to leave you both—'

'In any other household but this we would have to part soon anyway, because we would become betrothed and move away. We will miss you, dearest, but it will be more tranquil without your constant friction with Papa, so perhaps Lina will become less nervous.' Arabella reached for her hand, her own warm and strong. 'And I want you to be happy. James will have to swear you have Papa's permission for a licence, of course, but once you are married, even Papa is not going to object—think of the scandal if he did!'

'It is a good match. Provided we are married there will be no scandal.' Meg's mind was racing. 'James will be going overseas. I sneaked a look at Papa's *Morning Post* yesterday and it says they are sending troops to the Peninsula. If he does go to Portugal, I will go with him. But—oh, Bella, it could be years before we see each other again!'

It felt like goodbye already, the fierceness of Bella's hug. 'It would be years if you are sent to Wales. I want you to be happy. Let us see if he proposes first. If he does, then love will find a way. Somehow.'

Chapter One

@@@@@@@@@@

20 April 1814—Bordeaux

The breeze funnelling down the Gironde estuary from the sea was chill, Meg told herself, snuggling her shawl around her shoulders. And it was a long time since she had eaten much and the bag containing her pelisse was somewhere on the battlefield of Toulouse with an abandoned wagon train. That was all these shivers were, not fear.

A group of people were coming along the quayside, making for the England-bound ship moored further along. She put her shoulders back and her chin up. It was important to look respectable, competent and not at all needy. One of them, surely, would welcome a willing pair of hands to help on the voyage in return for her passage? That did not seem a very certain plan, but it was the only one she had now.

A tall gentleman with a lady on his arm, a valet and maid, a stack of baggage—they most certainly had no need of her. A plainly dressed middle-aged man with a valise in one hand, a clerk at his elbow. A businessman, no doubt. Then more luggage. The porters shoved a loaded cart to one side to reveal another passenger and shock had her stepping back in superstitious dread.

Death was striding—no, limping—along the quayside in the bright spring sunlight. *For goodness' sake!* Meg took a grip on her nerves. He was a flesh-and-blood human being, of course he was. *Just a man.* But very much a man. He seemed to dominate the long quayside until there was nowhere else to look.

Tall and strongly built, clad in the dark green of the Rifle Brigade uniform, he was bare-headed, his sword at his side. His red officer's sash was stained and blackened and, unusually for an officer, a rifle was slung over his shoulder. The right leg of his trousers had been slashed to allow for the bulge of a bandage just above his knee and flapped around the long black boot with each stride.

His hair was crow-black, a stubble beard shadowed his jaw and his dark eyes squinted against the sun beneath heavy brows as he scanned the quay with the intensity of a man expecting enemy sniper fire.

His scrutiny found Meg. She forced herself to look back indifferently, letting her glance slide across him. Her experience had taught her to size men up fast, a habit that was no longer one of life and death and which perhaps she should lose. Not that she had ever had to assess anyone who looked quite this dangerous.

Not only was this dishevelled officer big, dirty and obviously wounded, even cleaned up he would not be a handsome man. His big nose had been broken, his jaw was brutally strong, his expression grim and those dark eyes had a slant to them that was positively devilish under the thick brows. No wonder she had thought of Death when she first saw him.

Then he was past her, a porter following with a trunk and a few battered bags stacked on his barrow. Meg had heard yesterday that now that Napoleon had surrendered they were sending part of the Rifle Brigade straight off to America. But this man was obviously not fit for the rigours of that war; like her, he was heading back home.

To England, she corrected herself. Was that home? It was so long since she had seen it that it felt more alien than Spain. But it was where her sisters were and she had to find them.

More passengers. Forget the grim officer and focus on this group. In front was precisely the sort of person she had been hoping for: a well-dressed Spanish or Portuguese lady with three—no, four—children and a maid with her arms full of the fifth, a squalling baby. Meg fixed a respectful smile on her lips and stepped forwards to approach the harassed woman.

'Whee!' A small boy rushed past her, following his hoop as it bounced and clattered over the cobbles. How good to see a child happy and safe after so much death and destruction.

'José! Mind that lady—come back here!' The woman's voice was shrill with an edge of exhaustion. She would welcome help, surely?

'*Signora*, excuse me, but may I be of assistance?' Meg asked in Spanish. 'I see you have a number of children and I—'

'*José!*' There was a splash. Meg spun round to see no child, only the hoop teetering, then falling to the ground by the edge of the quay.

She picked up her skirts and ran. There might be a boat… She looked over the edge at the brown swirling water fifteen feet below her and realised that not only was there no boat, but that the tide was flooding out, the level was falling by the second and there were no steps down. She couldn't swim in this, no one could. A small head bobbed up, then vanished again. She ran along the edge, trying to keep up with the child in the water. Where was everyone? Where was her pitiful French when she needed it to call for help?

Then a dark figure brushed past and launched into a long, flat dive that took him slicing into the river just behind the boy. *'Aidez-moi!'* Meg shouted as men began to run to the edge of the quay. *'Une corde! Vite!'*

He had him. She was panting with the effort of keeping up, the need to somehow breathe for all three of them. The black head turned as the man struck out for the quay, the child in his grasp. But he was slowing, hardly making any way against the ebbing tide. It was the darkly sinister officer, she realised. With his bandaged leg, the heavy, painful limp, it was a miracle he could swim at all. Ahead she saw an iron ladder disappearing down the stone face of the quay and measured the angles with her eye. Would he make it to there? Could he make it to the edge at all?

The breath rasped raw in his throat; his right leg had gone from burning pain to a leaden numbness that dragged him down. Ross shifted his grip around the child's chest and fought the muddy current, angling towards the sheer cliff of the quayside. Diving in with his boots on didn't help. And only one leg was obeying him anyway.

The boy struggled. 'Keep still,' he snapped in Spanish. He wasn't going to let this brat drown if he could help it. He'd seen too much death—caused too much death: he couldn't face another. Not another child.

Then the sheer weed-slimed granite wall was in front of him without a single handhold up the towering face except perhaps... 'Boy!' The child stirred, coughed. 'See that metal ring?' They bumped hard against the stone, the water playing spitefully with them as he tried to keep station under the rusty remains of a mooring ring. It was big, large enough to push the boy's head and shoulders through.

'*Si.*' The brat had pluck. He was white with terror, clinging with choking force to Ross's neck, but he looked up.

'Let go and reach for it.' He boosted the child up, the force of the lunge pushing him completely under the surface once, twice, and then the weight was gone. He surfaced, spewing water, and saw the boy half through the ring, wriggling into it like a terrified monkey. 'Hold on!' The child managed to nod, his little face screwed up with determination as he clung to the rusty metal.

But something was very wrong. Ross's vision was blurring, his shoulders burned as though his muscles and tendons were on fire and his legs were too heavy to kick.

Hell. So this is it. Thirteen years of being shot at, blown up, frozen, soaked, half-starved, marched the length and breadth of the Iberian peninsula—we win the war and I die in a muddy French river. Everything was dark now. Ross tried to kick, tried to use his arms, more out of sheer bloody-mindedness than any real expectation that he could swim any further. *Doesn't matter. Didn't want to go back anyway... Duty. I tried.*

He hit something with the only part of his body that wasn't numb—his face—put up his hands to fend it off and found himself clutching a horizontal metal bar. *Hold on... Why? No point...*

'Hold on!' The words echoed in his head, very close to his ear. In English. A female voice? Impossible— which meant he was hallucinating. *Not long now.* Someone took hold of him, gripped one arm, and the blackness claimed him.

* * *

When was he going to come round? Meg pushed her hair out of her eyes and stood up to pour dirty water into the slop bucket. Her soaked skirt clung unpleasantly to her legs, but that would have to wait. She had just the one other gown left and she was not going to risk ruining that. Time enough to do some washing and make herself respectable when she had dealt with her patient.

She stood back, hands on hips, and studied the man on the bunk with some satisfaction. It had taken four dock-hands to get a rope round him and haul him out of the water, not helped by having to do it with Meg bent double, still hanging on to his arm, twined into the rusty ladder as the river surged around her knees. He was big; with him unconscious and soaking wet, it had felt like trying to shift a dead horse. She rubbed her aching shoulders at the memory.

The crew of the *Falmouth Rose* had not asked who she was when she walked up the gangplank in the wake of the men carrying his body on a hurdle. She was with Major Brandon and that, as she had gambled, was enough to gain admittance to the ship. Fortunately he had his name on his luggage, and she could read uniforms as easily as her prayer book by now—she had removed enough of them over the past eighteen months.

The men who had lugged him down to the cabin had been obliging enough to strip him for her, otherwise she supposed she would have had to cut his clothing off. It was dripping now, hung on nails that some previous occupant of the cabin had driven into the bulkhead, and he lay with just a sheet covering him from upper thigh to chest.

Meg had washed the scrape on his face where he had hit the ladder. Now she poured fresh water into the basin, opened the sturdy leather bag that sat beside her valise and took out scissors to cut away the sodden bandage on his leg. 'Aah!' The breath hissed between her teeth. This was battlefield surgery, rough and ready, and then he had neglected the wound. The edges of the messy hole in the side of his leg just above the knee were raw and puffy.

Lead had been dug out with more speed than finesse, and not very long ago by the look of it. No doubt he had been wounded at Toulouse. It was hard luck to take a bullet in the leg during the last battle of the war, almost within hours of the news of Napoleon's surrender and abdication.

She would have expected them to amputate the leg— that would have been normal practice. One glance at the jaw of the man on the bunk suggested that perhaps he had refused; he looked stubborn enough. He must be either immune to pain or quite extraordinarily bull-headed to be walking with it like this. She suspected the latter. Perhaps the scowl was not natural bad temper but a way of dealing with agony. She could only hope so.

Meg sniffed the wound. It was infected, her sensitive nose told her that, but there was no sickening sweet smell of mortification. 'Which is more than you deserve,' she informed the unresponsive figure. 'It is a good thing you aren't awake because I am going to clean it up now.'

The leather bag with the initials *P.F.* had all its contents intact still. She supposed it was theft, taking Peter's medical bag, but he was beyond using it now and she had seen no reason to leave it for looters. The surgeon had taught her well in the months she had shared his tent and worked at his side amidst the blood and the pain of the battlefield casualties, but neither of them had been able to do anything about his own sudden fever.

Now she washed her hands and studied the wound in front of her, trying to see it as a problem to be solved, not part of the unconscious man. She sponged and swabbed, then probed, first with her fingertips around the swollen edges and then into the wound with fine forceps, her lips compressed in concentration.

Eventually she sat back on her heels and flexed her tight shoulders. She had never learned to relax as a good surgeon should, now she would never have to. This was the last wound she would probe, thank God.

There was a satisfaction in viewing Major Brandon's leg, neatly bandaged, and the jagged splinter of metal and several bone chips that lay on a swab. Now it might have some chance of healing, if he would only show some common sense and look after it.

Finally she let herself look at her patient. She had done what she could to clean him as she helped strip away his clothes, detached as a good nurse should be. Now he lay sprawled on his back. His chest and shoulders were tanned and the black hair that made a pelt on his chest and dusted his legs and arms only compounded the impression he gave of darkness. How old was he? It was hard to tell—those strong, harsh features made him look older than he probably was. Thirty-two?

Meg spread the sheet out to cover him from collarbone to toes now that she had finished working on his leg. It was warm in the cabin, even with the tiny porthole open, and she had to keep the lamps burning to see what she was doing, which added to the heat. He would not need a blanket, not unless he began to run a fever, but the thin sheet did little to conceal what lay beneath it.

Her gaze ran slowly down the long body and she found she was biting her lip. A heat began to build low in her belly and her mouth felt dry. He was a magnificent male creature, despite his harsh, forbidding face. All smooth, defined muscles, sculpted bulk, scarred skin she wanted to taste with her fingertips. Her lips. He was a patient and she should not be looking at him with those thoughts in her mind. Yet he was stirring feelings in her that seemed so much more acute, disturbing, than any she had felt before.

Surely after five years of living with James she had learned that sexual satisfaction for the woman was a fleeting thing at best? She had never wanted to touch him in the way that she wanted to touch this man, a way that had nothing to do with hoping for a comforting cuddle or the protection of a sleeping male body at night.

Meg gave herself a little shake. If he regained consciousness and made any sort of move to touch her in that way, she would probably flee screaming. Her intimate experience of men so far had not included anyone so big, so grim—so thoroughly frightening.

It took a while to tidy the cabin, pack the medical bag, dispose of the dirty water and soiled cloths. There would be just room to unroll blankets on the deck to sleep on and she created a tiny private space with a sheet across one corner and more of the convenient nails. She was used to living in tents and in huts; neatness had become second nature, settling in was somehow soothing. Meg paused, put her hands to the small of her back and stretched. What would her sister Bella say if she could see her now? Romantic, dreamy Meg with her sleeves rolled up, sorting out the practicalities of nursing a wounded man at sea.

The big man's breathing seemed to fill the cabin and her consciousness. It was steady and deep despite the amount of water he had thrown up when they had dumped him on the quayside. His lungs would be all right, she felt fairly confident of that. There was no excuse to check his pulse or lay her head on his chest to listen. No excuse to touch him at all.

And then she realised he was awake. His breathing did not change, his eyelids did not flicker, but there was a personality in the cabin with her now. She put down the cloth she had been folding and watched his face. His nostrils flared, like an animal scenting the air. He had come round, not known where he was, or with whom, and he was warily assessing the situation before betraying that he was awake.

Interesting, she mused. That took a lot of self-control, a highly developed sense of self-preservation and a very suspicious nature. Then she remembered those watchful black eyes; he had stayed alive so far by using all those attributes.

Cautiously his right hand flexed on the mattress as though seeking an object.

Her self-control was less good than his, she found. 'Good afternoon, Major Brandon. Would you like something to drink?'

His eyes opened then and she found it an effort to stare back, unflinching. 'Where is my rifle?' he demanded without preliminaries. When she did not respond he snapped, 'Who are you, how do you know my name and where the hell are my clothes?' He levered himself up on his elbows, swore as his leg moved, and looked round the cabin.

'I am Mrs Halgate.' It seemed important not to allow him to dominate her. Could he tell that inwardly she was quaking? 'I know your name because it is on your baggage and your rank is obvious from your uniform. Your clothes are drying and your rifle is in that corner.' It was with his sword, but he had not asked about that as she would have expected an officer to.

'And why is my leg hurting like the devil?' He hauled himself up further with no attempt to catch at the sheet. It ended up draped across his thighs within an inch of indecency. Strange how dry one's mouth became when one was frightened. And aroused.

'Possibly because the wound still had bone chips and

metal in it,' she suggested, running her tongue over her lips. His eyes followed the movement. 'It no longer has. You have neglected it and you have just immersed it in muddy water and over-exerted yourself. It is no wonder it hurts. I do have some laudanum if you find it troublesome.'

Brandon narrowed his eyes at her. Probably she would need six men to sit on him if she wanted to get an opiate between those strong teeth. He did not deign to answer the offer. 'And who undressed me and dealt with my leg, Mrs Halgate?'

'Two sailors helped me undress you. I imagined, given the paucity of your baggage, that you would not want me cutting your uniform off you. I cleaned and dressed your leg.' Meg sat down on his small trunk at the foot of the bunk. Her legs were not feeling very strong. Had they cast off yet? She wanted to go and look through the porthole, but did not dare risk alerting him in case he still had time to throw her out.

'I see. You appear to be a woman of talents, Mrs Halgate. I thank you. And where is Mr Halgate, might I ask?'

'Lieutenant Halgate was killed at Vittoria,' she said tightly, not wanting to discuss it. Certainly she did not want to explain that, in truth, she was not Mrs Halgate at all, that her marriage certificate was not worth the paper it was written on.

The major nodded. She was grateful that he did not launch into meaningless expressions of sympathy. 'And Master José Rivera is safe, you will be glad to hear, although he is much subdued.'

'Who in Hades is José Rivera?' Brandon demanded, flipping back the edge of the sheet, reducing its coverage to little more than a loincloth in the process as he glowered at his bandaged leg. Meg fixed her gaze on an upper corner of the cabin. Looking at his naked body when he was an unconscious patient was disturbing; staring at it now with the muscles bunching and stretching beneath the skin and the dark hair arrowing down to the sheet was nothing short of disconcerting.

'The small boy you saved from the Gironde. Do you remember diving in after him?'

He frowned more deeply. Did he have any other expression? 'Yes. Most of it. I thought I was drowning—who was it who caught my arm?'

'A group of sailors pulled you up.' For some reason she did not want to admit to scrambling down that ladder and plunging half into the water to hold him. Meg got up and went to twitch his uniform into a different position on the nails.

'That was not what I asked you.' She turned and his eyes narrowed as he looked down her body to the wet skirts clinging to her legs. Without his expression changing she sensed he was seeing the form beneath the clothes. Or perhaps it was her own, mysteriously feverish, imagination. 'It was a woman. You, I presume?'

'Well, yes.' Meg shrugged, turned her back and fidgeted unnecessarily with the wet clothing again. 'I was nearest. I could not let you drown.'

'I am in your debt,' he said shortly. It was hardly fulsome, but it was sincere. It gave her some hope that he would agree to her proposal.

'Would you like a blanket?' Out of the corner of her eye she saw the realisation dawn on him that he was virtually naked and that she was a lady. *Of sorts.* Major Brandon swept the sheet over his legs and pulled it up around his waist. He did not appear bashful about his body, there was not a hint of a blush under the tan. Even with his lower body covered, the sight of his bare torso with its interesting array of old scars and fresh bruises should be enough to send any gently bred female into hysterics. It was lucky that life recently had knocked any pretensions to gentility out of her. And this strange hunger was not hysteria.

'Thank you, no. As soon as you are returned to your own cabin, ma'am, I will get dressed.'

Oh dear, now it begins. Her smile was more to bolster her own courage than in any futile effort to charm him. 'No, Major, you will stay in bed and keep the weight off your leg for at least another day, perhaps two, if there is to be any hope that you will not end up with a severe and incapacitating limp. Even then, you must take a good deal of rest. And I do not have a cabin; I am sleeping here.'

'You are *what*?' It was an effort not to take a step back, to retreat from the scowl and the harsh voice.

'I am staying here.' Her hands were knotted together. She unclenched them and congratulated herself on keeping the smile in place. The last thing she wanted now was to touch him.

'And what does the captain say about a stowaway?'

'Nothing at all. I told him I was your wife.'

Chapter Two

'**Y**ou told him you were my wife?' Brandon repeated softly. She certainly had his full attention now and Meg was not at all sure that lying on a bunk with his leg in bandages made him any less dangerous. She had heard officers use that tone before, followed by a bellow of rage and some most unpleasant orders.

'Yes. I need—'

'Whatever *you* need, *I* do not need a wench, however good natured she is.'

The blood rising in her cheeks was either fury or shame—perhaps both. She knew what a good-natured wench was: one who would lie down with a man for a few coppers. This battered ingrate would have to offer a good deal more than coppers before she became even mildly amiable, let alone good natured, however disturbing his muscles were.

'Indeed? And I do not *need* a man—of any description, Major. You possess only one thing I desire—a cabin on a ship bound to England. I will pay for it by nursing you;

perhaps preventing you from drowning will give me a little credit in the ledger. But I will not pay for it with any other coin, let us be quite clear about that.'

There was a long speculative silence. He was used to hiding his thoughts behind those dark brown eyes, but the process was thorough. 'Vittoria was ten months ago.'

It was not an inconsequential observation. She had not remarried and she had obviously not starved, so how else could she have survived in the midst of an army, he was thinking, unless she had prostituted herself? 'The battalion surgeon took me under his protection and I assisted him in his work. He taught me a lot about surgery.'

Major Brandon would assume she had been Peter Ferguson's mistress as well as his assistant. Everyone else had assumed it too. All that mattered was that he did not expect her to sleep with him in return for the shelter of his cabin.

'I do not require a nurse.' He was certainly a man of few words. Whatever he was thinking about her now, he did not feel the necessity to express it out loud, which was most irritating. She wanted to put him and his suppositions about her morals right, but he had to voice them first.

'Yes, you do—or you will need a surgeon to take that leg off. And believe me, I can do that if I have to.' In theory. She found her hands were fisted on her hips as she frowned at him, which was no way to ingratiate herself with the man.

He snorted. 'Can you make it strong enough to take me back into battle?' he asked.

'No. I can make it heal properly, if you do what I tell you, and I can show you how best to exercise it. But you have lost bone—it will never be strong enough for an infantry officer. And I have seen the Rifle Brigade march—you will never be able to maintain that pace again.'

Some trace of emotion passed across his face, then it was unreadable again. 'Very well, Madam Surgeon. You appear to know what you are talking about, and you are honest enough to tell me the truth. You may stay.'

'Thank you.' Meg turned her back and fussed with her medical bag while she blinked away the stinging sensation at the back of her eyes. How wonderful to sit down and indulge in a nice bout of weeping, just out of sheer relief. An impossible luxury that would weaken her in his eyes. 'Which of your bags has your nightshirts?'

'I sleep in my uniform or my skin, Mrs Halgate.'

If you think you are going to drive me blushing from this cabin, Major, you had best think again. 'This is not some Spanish bivouac, so you must sleep in a shirt. Which bag are *those* in?'

'The larger one.' Was that a thread of amusement in his voice? Surely not? She was not at all convinced he really was human, let alone had a sense of humour. 'Haven't you explored them already?'

'No.' She snapped the catch open and began to lift out his meagre supply of shirts. Major Brandon might be earning seventeen shillings a day, if her recollection of rates of pay was correct, but he was not spending it on his wardrobe. 'I had no intention of wrestling your unconscious body into a garment, however much civilised living might require that you wear one. You are about as easy to move as a dead bear.'

He made a wordless noise, something between a hum and a growl that resonated, not unpleasantly, at the base of her spine. Apparently he found the idea of her wrestling with his naked body interesting. She did not even want to think about it. A cat's-tail flick of heat inside signalled that her body did not require her mind's permission. This was ridiculous; she had been with James for five years, she knew perfectly well that sex for a woman was overrated.

'Here you are.' She handed him the most worn shirt, lips still tight. 'I will go and find out about food. There is a chamber pot under the bed.'

'And who will deal with that?'

'I will, Major. And if you are seasick, I will deal with that also. Nurses cannot afford to be missish.'

'I am beginning to appreciate that,' he said, his face without a trace of expression. Meg stalked out. Either he was utterly humourless or possessed a gambler's control of his face and was secretly laughing his head off at her. It was uncomfortable not knowing which. 'And see what there is to drink,' he called after her. Meg closed the cabin door with exaggerated care. If he thought he was going to get overheated drinking rum or brandy and inflame that leg, Major Brandon was in for a surprise. Ale, and perhaps some claret when the wound was less inflamed, was what he was going to get.

Ross waited until the brisk click of her heels faded away, then delved under the bed. He could not place his nurse—his *wife*—he corrected himself with a grimace. She was not a whore, even if she had been a camp follower of some sort, and her voice was that of a well-bred woman. Her clothes, although worn, were decent and modest, shielding a trim, curved figure, and she moved like someone used to physical work. If she had held his waterlogged body against the pull of the river until help came, then she was stronger than she looked.

Perhaps she was just what she said she was—a widow who had been forced to accept the protection of another man, one who did not see fit to marry her. He frowned. Why not? He shrugged, pushing the battered pewter pot back under the bunk, and lifted his legs back with wincing care. As he drew up the sheet he hesitated. She might be reduced to nursing, but she was no drab from a dockside tavern to have to perform the most menial tasks for him. He put his feet back on the deck and stood up, the long shirt flapping around his thighs as he hobbled painfully to the door, cracked it open and leaned against the frame while he watched the passageway.

'Here, boy!'

The skinny lad stopped, eyeing him warily. He was used to that reaction to his saturnine looks and size. Looking like a killer was useful on the battlefield, less so in everyday life. 'Aye, sir?'

'You part of the crew?'

'Aye, sir. Cabin boy, sir. Name's Johnny.' He tugged his forelock, his expression changing to an ingratiating smile. 'I'll do odd jobs, sir.'

'Then you can empty the slops from this cabin and fetch hot and cold water every day.' The deck pitched and Ross had to grab at the doorframe, cursing his weak, throbbing leg. The damned woman had been in there with an entrenching tool by the feel of it. 'Are we at sea yet?'

'No, sir, still the estuary. Do you want hot water now?'

'Yes. Now, and get a move on. There's three pence a day for you if you're sharp.' He'd wash and shave himself before she came back. He had a pretty fair idea that he looked and smelled like the dead bear Mrs Halgate had likened him to, not that he was ever much to look at, shaven or bearded.

The boy shot off and Ross cursed his way back to bed. He hated being unfit, loathed the vulnerability of it and the loss of control. It was easiest to carry on as though nothing was wrong. Eventually most things healed if they didn't kill you first. To find himself relying on a woman, for anything, was the outside of enough.

The lad came back with a steaming bucket and dealt with the dirty water and the pewter pot so fast he was probably overpaying him. When he was gone Ross wedged the door closed and stripped off his shirt.

It was perhaps half an hour later, while he drew the razor in a satisfying glide down the last strip of foam, that the handle rattled. 'Major Brandon! Open the door, if you please.'

'I'm stark naked.' He wiped the razor and packed away the things with a casual efficiency born of long practice, waiting for the explosion from outside.

Ross counted in his head while he pulled the shirt back on and dragged a comb through his hair. *Nine...ten.*

'Then kindly put your shirt on and open the door.' So she had decided on sweet reason, had she? Ross grimaced. He was not used to having a woman underfoot, certainly not a halfway respectable one. The women in his life were for one purpose only, were paid well enough for that and then left.

His body stirred at the thought of those purposes. No need to frighten the poor woman with the evidence of what she was sharing a cabin with, although she did not seem alarmed by the sight of him. He limped back, got on to the bunk under the sheet and reached out to pull the wedge out of the latch.

'You've been out of bed,' she accused the moment she was inside, balancing a precarious assortment of objects. For some reason the bossiness amused him. A bottle fell on to the bunk and Ross scooped it up: claret.

Mrs Halgate put down a small pail with a lid, a bundle that looked loaf-shaped, a flagon and two beakers, then turned and twitched the bottle out of his lax grasp while he studied the seal. Perhaps bossiness was not so amusing. 'Tomorrow, if you have no fever. Ale now, and stew and bread. You deserve to have a fever,' she added, peering at him. 'I told you to stay in bed.'

'I needed to shave.' She continued to stare, probably wondering if he looked any better without stubble, or perhaps she thought she could cow him into apologising. Hah! Still, it gave him a chance to study her. Oval face, tanned, with freckles across her nose that should send any lady into despair. Dark brows and lashes—darker that the heavy plait of medium brown hair that lay across her shoulder or the sun-lightened curls that softened her forehead. A firm, determined mouth that betrayed strong will and courage. Candid blue-grey eyes that seemed to reflect her changing mood. A lance of lust had him hardening all over again.

'Where did the hot water come from? And where has the dirty water I used gone?'

'I have hired a cabin boy. His name is Johnny, I'm paying him three pence a day and don't be cozened out of any more.'

'I could have done all that.' She dished up the food, managing it neatly in the confined space. There was a vertical line furrowed between her brows and she glanced again at the pile of worn shirts.

'Just because I do not choose to spend my money on linen does not mean I cannot afford to pay a servant,' he observed, seeing the colour touch her cheeks when she realised her thoughts had been so obvious. She was used to making ends meet, it seemed.

'I beg your pardon.'

'And it ill befits the wife of a major to be carrying the slops,' he added, interested to see if he could provoke her.

'Yes, of course,' she agreed gravely. 'We must preserve

your dignity at all costs. James was a mere lieutenant, so I must be more aware of your status.'

Ouch. That was a nasty dig. 'I was thinking more of yours, *Mrs Brandon,*' Ross said, then remembered that if she was his wife, she would not be plain *Mrs* at all. He really was going to have to get used to the title and life awaiting him in England, now it appeared that Fate was not going to drown him in the Gironde or allow a French sniper to kill him. He could stop worrying about whether his leg was ever going to work properly again: he wasn't going back to the army, however much he might try to forget the fact.

The darkness deepened in the major's eyes, turning them black. Best not to answer back, perhaps. Just because he had not savaged her with his tongue or the back of his hand yet did not mean he was not capable of either. There was something beyond his wound that was troubling him and whatever it was, it was hurting him deeply. And in her experience men who were hurt, in body or mind, were more than likely to lash out.

Was it as simple as the fact that he would no longer be fit enough to serve in the Rifle Brigade and had lost his occupation? But he was a gentleman, however impossible it was to imagine him in a London drawing room. Did he need the employment?

Speculation was pointless, her dratted imagination had drawn her out of the present and into daydreams again. The task at hand was to serve out the stew on to the platters she had stuffed into the cloth with the bread. She passed one across with a horn spoon and a hunk of bread and received a nod of thanks.

'The other passengers—the ones who have not taken to their beds with seasickness already—are eating at

communal tables down the centre of the next deck up.'
The arrangements were interesting, she had found, and
very different from the discomforts of the troop ship on
the way south, six years before. 'They strike the tables
between meals and it becomes the public salon. We're
almost at the mouth of the estuary, but the captain is going
to drop anchor for the night. He says the news about the
peace will not have reached all the enemy ships yet and
he would rather wait until daylight before venturing into
open waters.'

The major was demolishing the stew as though he had
not eaten in days. Perhaps he had not. Or perhaps he always
ate like a bear; there was certainly enough of him to keep
nourished.

'We do not have to pay separately for the food.' She put
down her own plate, ladled more on to his and cut another
wedge of bread. 'It is better than I thought it would be and
all included in the passage.' She finished her portion and
poured ale. The major's vanished in one swallow, so she
topped up his mug again.

'We are a very strange assortment of passengers.' Meg
peered into the pan. 'There's more stew if you are still
hungry.' He held out his plate so she scraped the rest on
to it. 'And not as many people as I thought there would be.
Officers' wives and children, merchants, someone I think
must be a minor diplomat. No military men, unless they
are out of uniform. I did wonder—'

'Mrs *Brandon*, do you never stop talking?'

The major was regarding her with an air of exasperation.
When she fell silent he went back to his food. Presumably
he was even less sociable over his breakfast. If that were
possible.

'Yes, I do occasionally fall silent. Especially in the face

of an indifferent conversationalist. As we are going to be spending several days—'

'And nights,' he interjected, apparently intending to make her pay fully for inflicting herself upon him.

'And nights together—' *I am not going to blush* '—I thought it would be more pleasant to make conversation and to get to know each other a little.'

'Did you?'

'Yes, I did. I am Meg Halgate. I am twenty-four years old. My…James was a lieutenant with the 30th Regiment of Foot and he never returned from Vittoria. I had followed the drum with him for five years. I told you what happened after he died.'

At least, she had told him all that she was prepared to reveal. Certainly not the shocking fact that had been revealed when James was killed, the truth that meant she could not go to her in-laws as everyone expected her to do. Their curt letter had made it clear that they would not welcome the arrival on their doorstep of a woman who had lived in sin with their son for five years, even if she had genuinely believed James had been free to marry her.

She had seduced their son from his duty so that she could escape from her home, they believed. Or so she told herself; it was too bitter to think that they were simply unfeeling and uncharitable.

And returning home to the vicarage had never been a possibility, not then, even if she could have found the money for the journey. Sometimes she wondered whether it would be worth it, just to see her father's face, but it would be a petty revenge for the misery he had made of her childhood. Besides, he would probably say that he expected nothing better of her.

'Only twenty-four?' Major Brandon was infuriating,

but at least he presented a practical problem she could deal with: get his leg healed. 'You seem older.'

The dark eyes rested on her face. Was he was referring to her tanned skin, or the roughness of her hands? Perhaps she just had an air of experience from the life she had led. She was not going to ask him.

Meg tidied the dirty plates and spoons away into a pail and stood it outside the door for the boy. Then she wrapped the remains of the loaf up in its cloth, stoppered the ale and went to sit on the trunk, hands folded demurely in her lap.

'Are you waiting for me to reciprocate with personal revelations?' Major Brandon lay back against the planked wall, his big hands clasped, apparently relaxed. Yet he still exuded an air of barely controlled impatience. He must hate being cooped up in here with her.

'What I told you were hardly revelations. But if I am to pretend to be your wife I should at least know your name and how old you are and where you were wounded.'

'Ross Martin Brandon. Thirty. Battle of Toulouse. If you preserve some distance from the rest of the passengers, that is all you need to know.'

'Thirty? You look older.' She echoed his own remark, but he reacted as little as she had. 'Why should I keep a distance from them? It is only sociable to talk and it helps pass the time.'

He shrugged. 'Nothing in common. Civilians.' The word seemed to give him pain, for the corner of his mouth contracted in a fleeting grimace.

Meg stared at his lips, then dragged her eyes away. His mouth was one of his better features. It was generous without being fleshy, mobile and expressive in the rare moments when he let his guard down. What would it be like to be kissed by that mouth? Would it slide over her skin, licking and kissing, or would it be brutal and demanding? But the mouth went with the man, and she had no desire at all to be kissed by Ross Brandon, however much some foolish feminine part of her quivered when she met those brooding eyes.

'It is dark,' he observed. Meg got up and picked her way to the small porthole. If she stood on tiptoe she could see out. There were distant lights from the shore.

'We must have anchored. The motion of the boat is different. Shall I leave the porthole open?'

He nodded when she turned to look at him, his face eerily shadowed now by the swinging lanterns. 'Are you tired?'

It was the first sign of any concern for her that he had shown. The tears swam in her eyes again. Yes, she must be tired if she was so close to that weakness. Bone weary, if she was truthful. And frightened of the future. Damn him for being kind. Sparring with him was keeping her going.

'Yes.' She managed a smile. 'It is such a relief to know I am going back to England that I seem to be quite drained.'

'Nothing to do with hauling dead bears out of the river, setting this cabin to rights and doctoring me, then?'

'Oh, no, Major Brandon. That is all in a day's work.'

'Call me Ross,' he said abruptly. 'If you would go and take the air on deck for a few minutes, I will get ready for bed.'

Meg drew her shawl around her shoulders and went out. The euphemism produced a smile, despite a nagging discomfort at the thought of spending the night together in such enforced intimacy. She had tucked another pewter pot and a jug of water behind the curtain in one corner and she would just have to make do with that; she could hardly throw an injured man in his nightshirt out into the passageway while she undid her stays. There were some odorous little cupboards for the passengers' use—*heads*, the sailors called them—but she could not undress in those.

When she came back only one light was burning and Ross was lying on his left side facing the wall, the sheet pulled up to his shoulders. *Ross.* She moved past softly. *I'm thinking of him as Ross.*

Meg wriggled out of her gown, unlaced her stays, took off shoes and stockings and let down her hair from its net at the nape of her neck. The water was cold, but refreshing, and the simple fact of being clean was a source of pleasure. When she crept out in her petticoat and sat on the edge of the trunk to comb out her hair and plait it, the cabin was quiet with just the slap of waves on the ship's side, the creak of wood and ropes and the familiar sound of a man's breathing. Peace. No more war, no more alarms and trumpets in the night. No more death and maiming.

She unrolled her blankets on the deck, found the pillow and the sheet and settled down, blowing out the lamp. It was hard under her hip bone and shoulder, but she'd slept in worse places. This was warm and dry and safe…

'What the devil do you think you are doing?'

Meg sat bolt upright, clutching the sheet to her petticoat bodice. There was not much light to see by, but Ross was sitting up and sounded as though he was glaring at her.

'Trying to go to sleep, of course!'

'On the floor?'

'Well, yes. Obviously. There is only one bunk and you are injured and I am perfectly fine down here.'

'Get into bed.' The sheet flapped as he tossed it back.

'I will do no such thing! I thought we had dealt with this—I am not sleeping with you, Major.'

'You most certainly are. I'll not have you lying on the floor and I'm damned if I see why I should.'

Meg huffed, lay down and drew the blanket up to her shoulders, her back to him. She was not going to argue with him. Overbearing man. Sleep in the same bunk with him, indeed! She knew what would come of that: men were not to be trusted. She punched the pillow and wriggled down. Behind her there was a muffled thump on the deck. She ignored it.

Then a hand took hold of her shoulder and rolled her on to her back, another slid under her knees and she found herself rising through the air as Ross Brandon, apparently unhampered by his wounded leg, lifted her and deposited her on the bunk.

Chapter Three

'Put me down!' Indignation won over the stab of fear and the arousing awareness of strength as she landed unceremoniously on the hard mattress.

'I have.' Ross climbed in beside her and adjusted the sheet over them both. Perhaps fear had been the right emotion after all. Trapped against the wall, she tried to wriggle down the bed and was stopped by one outthrust foot. 'Stop panicking, Meg. I might look like a brute, but I do not force women. If I wanted you flat on your back under me, you would be by now, believe me.'

'You, sir, are outrageous. And you don't...' Reassuring him about his appearance was the last thing she should be doing. And as for being flat on her back...it was precisely what her imagination was conjuring up. And her imagination was not as horrified as it should be.

'Why outrageous? For not ravishing you?'

'For even alluding to such a thing.' He was still sitting up, looming over her, and Meg was beginning to feel hot, bothered and definitely panicky. If he decided to force her, she could not hope to stop him. She was not certain she really wanted to stop him, and that was the worst thing of all. It must be his size, she thought. She was frightened at going back and she wanted to cling to him.

'It was what was worrying you, was it not? Best to have it out of the way.' Ross seemed completely unembarrassed by the discussion.

Shameless man, Meg thought, lingering fears of rape retreating. Which left the thought of willingly lying under him, the pair of them naked, about to make love.

'Understand this,' he continued when she did not respond. 'I will not lie in a bed while a woman has to make do with the floor. If there was only room for one, then I would take the floor. As it is, it is ridiculous for one of us to be uncomfortable.'

'You might be comfortable like this. I can assure you, I am far from being so.' He was hot. And so close that one of them only had to take a deep breath for their bodies to touch. The disturbing pulse she had been attempting to ignore became insistent.

'I give you my word, you will be safe.' He sounded irritated now. Obviously she was keeping him from his sleep with her worries and scruples. It was a mercy he could not read her mind.

'While we are awake, of course I trust your word.' Not every officer was a gentleman, but her instincts were telling her that this one was. 'But when we are asleep we might…touch.'

'Meg, have you been following the drum with not one, but two, men for the past five years or have you been locked up in a vicarage?'

That was so near the knuckle she almost gasped, but the question was obviously rhetorical. The major lay down

again, turned on to his right side with his back to her and
gave every indication of falling immediately asleep.

If she lay with her elbows tight against her sides, her legs
straight, rigid as a board in her half of the bunk, she could
pretend they were not both in the same bed. Eventually,
when he showed no signs of leaping on her, she turned over
cautiously so her back was to him. Their buttocks touched.
Recoiling, she tried the other side so she faced him. That
was better, she could curve her body now to avoid his.

But what she could not avoid was the scent of him, she
realised once she had managed to relax sufficiently to
breathe. Man. He'd had as good a wash as he could under
the circumstances and had got rid of the worst of the river
water and the grime and sweat of his journey, but in a way
that was even more disconcerting. There wasn't a great
deal of distraction from the natural scent of hot male. She
bit her lip and tried not to fidget. Tried, very hard indeed,
not to remember what it was like to be held, just held, in
strong arms for a while. Safe, secure, trusting.

Not that James had ever been trustworthy, exactly, even
at the start of their scandalous runaway marriage. But he
had been strong and young and handsome and, when it
was no trouble, kind to her. And often fun. At least, he had
been fun while things went his way. His sense of humour
did not hold up well, she soon discovered, under adversity.

But she had believed herself in love with him when she
married him; she had made promises, even if he had been
lying to her all the time. Despite the pain of the memory
Meg felt her limbs grow heavy as sleep began to fog her
mind. She gave a little shuffle back to press tight against
the wall and drifted off, exhausted.

Ross half-woke to find himself lying on his back on
a bed that was moving. *A ship.* Yesterday's events began

to present themselves, still confused, to his memory. The child, the river, a woman's voice.

He stretched out his legs, opened his eyes and came fully conscious as a jolt of pain stabbed down through his right knee. Several things were apparent all at once. It was daylight, the ship was under way again and beside him was not his rifle but a warm, sleeping, woman.

In fact, it was amazing she had not been the first thing he had been aware of. Her head was on his shoulder, her right arm was across his chest and she was snuggled up close down the length of him. At some point he had got his arm round her while they slept so she was cradled in a way that was positively possessive. She was so tight against him that he could feel every swell and dip and softness of her body. His became instantly hard.

It was a remarkably pleasant, and novel, sensation, if he ignored the ache in his groin. His life had never been lacking in women to satisfy his needs, but he was not in the habit of spending the night with them. That was a reliable method of waking up to find the woman gone and with her, his money.

This woman, his temporary wife, was not after his money. She was a strange creature, expecting conversation and confidences as though their chance alliance was actually a real relationship, and yet not asking anything in return for saving his life and tending to him beyond her passage back to England.

Had he thanked her properly? He rather doubted it. Yesterday he had been feeling like the devil when he had arrived at the docks and had been in no mood afterwards to analyse whether he was actually grateful for having been fished out of the river at all.

Today… Today was time to get a grip on himself and stop kicking against fate. He was wounded, he was never going back to the Rifles, he would probably limp for the rest of his life and that life was going to be something utterly alien. He had run away from it when he was seventeen, but it was catching up with him fast now.

There was a tap on the door and he reached out, careful not to wake Meg, and unjammed the wedge from the latch. The door opened a foot and Johnny's tousled head appeared. 'Hot water, Major?'

'Yes. Bring coffee and take away the slops. Quietly, now.' But Meg was awake. With a gasp she recoiled from him until she was tight up against the wall.

'Wha—?' Her eyes were wide, fixed on him with a mixture of shock and fear that was like a kick in the guts. Her lack of fear last night had obviously been an act; now, shocked awake, she was showing what she really thought of him. She looked terrified and she was drawing breath to scream.

'The boy is here, my dear,' Ross said, putting one large hand hard over her mouth, his body shielding her from Johnny. 'I've asked him for hot water and coffee.' She struggled against him and he tipped his head towards the door. 'That's all, boy, nothing else at the moment.'

He managed to hold her, one handed, until the latch clicked home, then she wrenched her head away and came at him with fists and nails. 'You brute! You lying, lecherous—'

'Hey!' Ross swivelled round, ignoring the pain in his leg, and pinned her to the pillow with both hands. 'Don't you dare scream,' he threatened. 'What the devil's the matter with you? I told you, I don't force women.'

'You said I would be safe,' she panted. 'You gave me your word and I wake to find you groping me, you—'

Ross slapped his hand over her mouth again, coming down on to his elbows over her as he did so. His leg hurt, he wanted his coffee and the blasted woman had called him a liar. Under him her body felt slight, soft, feminine, yet she was tensed to fight him even though he was crushing her.

'Listen to me,' he said between gritted teeth, his face so close to hers that he could have counted the lashes that fringed her wide, defiant eyes. Under his hand she was trying to find the purchase to bite his palm. 'I do not lie. I do not break my word. I woke up and you were cuddled up to me, your arm was over my chest and I had one of mine around you.' She stopped trying to bite. 'And that is all. We had passed an uneventful night and if you take a moment to think you will find I managed to not ravish you.'

He had not thought it possible for her eyes to open wider, but they did, with such a look in them that he felt as though he had hit her. 'Has someone…did someone hurt you?' He took his hand away.

'They tried.' Her lids closed to cut off his scrutiny. 'Three of them. I was trapped. I knew what they wanted, what they were going to do. James had only been dead two weeks.'

'They tried,' he repeated. 'What happened?'

'Peter—Dr Ferguson heard me scream. He took me back to his tent. The next day the news came that his lover had died. He was heartbroken. Beside himself. So I stayed.'

'Just two weeks after your husband was killed?' He did not make a very good job of keeping the judgemental tone out of his voice.

'Peter's lover was a man,' Meg said, staring him out defiantly. 'A young lieutenant.'

'But that's—'

'A hanging matter at worst, a dishonourable discharge at best,' she finished for him. 'Peter was in too bad a state to be discreet. By staying with him I could cover things up—I told everyone he had a contagious fever. In a few days he could function again and his pallor and depression were put down to the illness.'

'So you were never his mistress?'

'No. But I was safe and so was he. We were protection for each other. Major Brandon, do you think you could get off me now?'

His legs bracketed hers, his groin and what he could feel was a fairly impressive erection was grinding into her in all the right…in the worst possible place and her breasts were flattened under his weight.

'Hell!' He rolled off to his side of the bed and sat up. For a few moments it had seemed so good to be that close to her. Beside him Meg sat up too, the sheet rumpling around her. 'I'm sorry. I just wanted to stop you screaming.'

Meg put up both hands and pushed the loose strands that had escaped from her plait back from her flushed face. 'I woke and didn't know where I was. I didn't recognise you at first.'

At least he was under no illusion what she thought of him as a man. Ross turned a shoulder to give her a little privacy as she slid from the bed. The rejection and fear on her face as she had stared at him told him all he needed to know about that.

'You can credit me with controlling my wild animal passions, then.' Easier to make a bitter joke of it.

Meg gave a little gasp, but when he looked at her she smiled and came back at him with the tart retort he was coming to expect from her. 'If you can sustain wild animal passions after exhausting yourself saving that child, being half-drowned and having your wound probed and redressed, then I am full of admiration for your stamina, Major Brandon. I should have realised you were in no fit state to be any kind of threat to me, without needing your word.'

Don't count on it. Apparently she had not noticed the erection, or it was less impressive than he thought it was. Or perhaps as a lady she was above noticing such things. He should look away as the light from the porthole struck through the thin material of her petticoats, outlining her body. He did not.

An unfamiliar muscle twitched in his cheek, then he realised he had almost smiled. How long ago had it been since anything had seemed worth smiling about? And how long since he had felt any passion—or desire that went beyond the need to satisfy a basic urge, come to that? The way she stood up to him was refreshing, amusing—and stimulating. He caught himself; the state he was in was just the normal morning arousal, best to remember that and not think this woman held any special attraction for him.

The mental darkness that seemed to be his constant companion these days swirled back and he saw her recognition of it in her eyes. The light seemed to go out behind the blue-grey pupils, but her chin came up and she gave him back stare for stare.

For some reason the stubborn face cheered him a little. If nothing else, she gave him something to kick against, a counter-irritant to the nagging thought of England and what it held. An intelligent, practical woman, his temporary wife, and one who did not appear to have a great deal of respect for male authority, to boot.

'What are your plans today, Meg?'

'I do not recall giving you leave to use my name, Major,' she said.

'I gave you leave to use mine, and I somehow do not

think we are such a very proper married couple that we would not use first names when we are alone.'

'Perhaps.' Meg said. She looked flushed and tousled. He wanted to make her even more so. Not just the usual morning erection, then. 'I will wash and dress and then have a look at your leg to see if it needs redressing. You will then please remain in bed. I will find something to occupy myself in between tending to your needs, I am sure.'

Ross found he was on the point of asking her whether she intended catering to *all* his needs, then closed his mouth with a snap. Bandying words with her would take them both where it was dangerous to go.

Now what is he glowering about? Meg threw her shawl over her shoulders in an attempt to render her petticoats more decent. If it was the prospect of staying in bed for the day, then that was just too bad because she would hide his trousers if that was what it took to keep him there. He really ought to rest for at least a week, but she was a realist—he would have to be tied to the bed and she doubted the captain would lend her anything substantial enough to tether this bear with.

Her heart was still pounding from the terror as she had woken to find the big male body trapping hers, the dark, shadowed face with its heavy morning beard that for one terrifying moment she had not recognised. And then his strength as he had pinned her down.

Meg shivered and found to her shame and shock that it was partly a shudder of sensuality. What on earth was the matter with her? Perhaps it was simply the unfamiliar shipboard world, the freedom, for a little while, from disapproving stares and whispers.

A tap on the door. Johnny with the hot water. Meg

ducked behind the curtain, glad of a distraction from her thoughts.

'Put that can by the screen so Mrs Brandon can reach it,' Ross instructed the boy. 'And pour me some coffee. You can come back in half an hour with more hot water.'

A wash in hot water was a pleasure. In water someone else had heated and carried, it was luxury. By dint of contortions that would not have been out of place in Astley's Amphitheatre, Meg managed to sponge herself all over and felt her spirits rise. Her water-soaked gown had dried, the worse for wear, but not looking as bad as she feared.

When she emerged Ross was propped up in bed, one large hand enveloping a mug of coffee. The aroma curled rich and strong through the air.

'I'll go and have my breakfast with the other passengers. And get Johnny to bring you some food down with the hot water. When I get back we can look at your leg.'

'Can we?'

'Yes, *we* can. I want you to have a good look at the wound so you understand my concerns. Perhaps you will take care of yourself better, then. You really do not deserve to keep that leg.'

Irritated with him now, she stuffed her hair into a net, tied her shawl around her shoulders and went out, telling herself that she misheard the muttered, *It scarce matters,* that she caught as the door closed.

It seemed a long time since that stew last night and the prospect of exchanging civil conversation with the other passengers was pleasant out of all proportion to the occasion. Just the brief contact last night as she had been greeted, had mingled while she collected their supper, had been enjoyable.

How long was it since she had behaved like a *lady*? Since just before Vittoria, of course, when, as a junior officer's wife, she had a certain status. After James's death, she became merely the scandalous woman who had lived in sin with a man. A few of the regimental wives had believed that she really did not know her marriage had been bigamous, but others were prepared to believe she knew perfectly well. They had all shunned her. And when she had taken refuge with Peter Ferguson and had lowered herself to nursing wounded common soldiers, then of course she was utterly beyond the pale.

It had seemed strange to her then, and still did, that it was as shocking that she tended to brave men in pain and distress as it was that she was apparently living in sin. Perhaps the sense of betrayal, the shock, had been so great that their attitude had hardly hurt. It was James's betrayal that wounded her, kept her using her married name in a desperate attempt to deny this had happened.

Signora Rivera, surrounded by three of her older children, beckoned her to a place opposite them at the long table and she made an effort to shake off the ghosts of the past and smile. 'How is young José, *signora*?'

'Much recovered, I thank you, Signora Brandon. In fact, I am having much trouble keeping him in his bed. Fortunately my maid can watch him while she tends to little Rosa. And how is your brave husband?'

'Quite well, *signora*, although he must rest today. He has a wound in his leg.'

'You have been married long?' Signora Rivera buttered toast, her eyes bright with curiosity. Meg told herself that she was unaccustomed to female company and that it was only natural that Signora Rivera would want to gossip to pass the journey. She controlled a natural impulse to recoil from the probing.

'It seems like only yesterday,' she said with a laugh and the other woman laughed too, accepting the reply as a jest before pouring out the story of her journey to England to join her husband, a wine importer.

Her meal eaten, Meg took a turn around the deck. She had to clutch her shawl against the brisk wind and her eyes watered as she squinted to try to catch a glimpse of coast. But they were well out into the Bay by now and perhaps would not see land again until they passed Brittany.

When she judged that Ross would have safely finished washing and shaving and eaten his breakfast Meg went back below decks. The cabin door was unlocked and when she entered she found him standing by the porthole, his legs encased in the loose white cotton trousers the sailors wore and wearing one of his better shirts, open at the neck and with the sleeves rolled up.

The purely visceral jolt of desire at the sight of broad shoulders tapering to taut hips and the sheer, powerful size of him brought her to a standstill. And then, before she could completely recover herself, he turned and it was the same dark, dangerous face, the same cold eyes, and the desire turned to something more like anger.

'What the devil do you think you are doing?' The door banged behind her as she marched in to confront him. 'I told you to stay in bed and rest and here you are—'

He raised one brow and the slant of his eyes looked even more satanic than usual. 'Your language shocks me, Mrs Brandon.'

'And you shock *me*!' she retorted, finding in the excuse to lecture him a refuge from the decidedly contradictory feelings that were unsettling her. 'Take those trousers off and get back to bed.'

With an obedience that was patently provocative his hands went to the fall of the trousers. It seemed that just as she had got over her fright, so he had moved from worrying about her fears to actively provoking her. No doubt it appealed to his dark humour. As he undid the buttons the trousers started to slide from his hips. It was not funny.

'No! Let me go out first, for goodness' sake.' *If he so much as chuckles,* she thought grimly, *I'll...* But, of course, he did no such thing. Major Brandon did not smile, let alone laugh, she remembered when she was out in the passage, her back flat against the door.

It was shocking how arousing the sight of those trousers sliding down had been. Yesterday she had seen the man stark naked, and although she had certainly been able to admire his fine physique, it had not disturbed her half as much as what had just transpired.

It was because he was conscious now and fully aware of what he was doing—which had to be provoking her, punishing her for having him at her mercy when he was already seething with frustration over his injury. It was not attempted seduction. There was no heat in that dark stare, no amorous intent in his gestures and she believed him when he explained what had happened that morning.

The wood was rough under her knuckles as she tapped on the door. 'Are you in bed yet?'

'Yes,' he said, amiably enough as far as one could tell through half an inch of panelling.

'Where did you get those trousers?' She walked past him without a glance to open her medical bag. She would not give him the satisfaction of looking at him. 'From Johnny, I suppose.'

'Yes. They are practical,' Ross said indifferently. 'But it hardly matters.'

The contents of the medical bag blurred out of focus. Four words, yet they told her so much. His indifference was not about trousers, or her presence or their cramped accommodation. Anyone else might read merely annoyance at her interference or weariness after a bad night in the way he said those few words. But they betrayed something else, something that explained his dark mood and unsmiling face.

She had heard that tone before in the voices of men who were exhausted from battle and pain, men who would not have taken action to end their own lives but who were beyond minding if someone else did. It was the voice of a man who hardly cared whether he lived or died and it was all of a piece with the way he had neglected his leg, the darkness in his gaze. But it was not battle fatigue that had brought him to this, nor the pain of his leg. Something deeper had wounded him.

She spread a towel on the trunk and laid out what she needed, filled a bowl with water and set it by the bed, her hands steady, her thoughts reeling. It was not just his leg that needed saving, it seemed. If helping drag him from the river yesterday was to have any value, then she had to hope he could find something to live for as well.

'It has not bled.' She lifted back the sheet above the bandage, laid her hand on the bare skin just at the edge of the linen bindings and felt his flesh contract at the touch. 'It is not inflamed, or over-hot.' Ross made no reply as she undid the knots and unwrapped the bandage, finally lifting away the pad directly over the wound.

'That looks better,' she said, bending her head to sniff discreetly, hoping he did not realise what she was doing. 'Look now, it is less swollen. It is important to keep it clean and to exercise very gently. Apparently the blood must continue to flow in the muscles all around in order to help it heal.'

'No sign of mortification, then?' Ross asked, as casually as if he was enquiring what was for dinner, not establishing whether she was going to deliver a death sentence or, at the very least, tell him his leg would have to come off.

'No.' Meg sprinkled basilicum powder over the wound, laid on a fresh pad and began to bandage it again. 'I will leave this for a couple of days now and tomorrow you may begin to walk on it again.' He made no comment so she risked a little more. 'I suppose we will be at sea three or four days. By the time we dock it should be much more comfortable, although you should not ride even then.'

'No doubt I would have hired a post chaise in any case,' Ross observed, as though he had given no thought at all to the practicalities of his arrival in England.

As if he expects there to be no future. The thought made her shiver. For herself, she had everything planned out: a cheap but decent lodging in Falmouth for a night or two while she recovered from the journey and accustomed herself to England. And then she was going straight to Martinsdene and Bella and Lina. But her imagination would not take her beyond that, beyond that first embrace, the tears. They had to be all right, she told herself as she had every time she had thought of them, day in and day out. The silence was because Papa destroyed her letters, that was all.

Ross Brandon, it seemed, had looked no further than getting on to this ship. And a ship was the perfect mode of transport for a man who did not want to make decisions. You got on it and it took you where it was going—no opportunities to change your mind, vary your route or interfere with its direction until you arrived in port.

'Is it a long journey to your home from Falmouth?' She tied the final knots and pulled back the sheet.

'A long way home?' Ross turned his heavy gaze on her as though she had asked a deeply philosophical question that he must ponder with care. 'Thirteen years,' he said at last.

56 SOMETHING SOMETHING

At one any longer Ross turned his never mind to her
Although he had asked a rather philosophical question
her he must comply with Ross... Thirteen years... it said
to her.

Chapter Four

Meg was staring at him as though he had said something
strange. 'Thirteen years,' she repeated eventually. 'But
how long by road?'

Ross shrugged. He was not going to explain his choice
of words. Until they had left his lips he had not realised
what he was going to say. 'Not far, although the roads are
narrow.' It was not miles that separated him from the place
where he had been born, it was guilt and loss and the man
he had become because of that.

'And where is your home?' Meg persisted. She was
packing away her bag again, apparently engrossed in the
task. But the question had not been casual.

'I am going to a village some distance outside Falmouth,
on the Roseland Peninsula.' It was easier to answer her
than to evade her questions. Social conversation seemed
difficult, as though he were speaking in a foreign language
that he had not quite mastered the grammar for. And yet
he had never been an unsocial man, not until the last few
months when the reality of his future had begun to close

in around him as a duty as heavy as chains. A bullet in the leg had removed any last lingering illusion of choice that he could stay with his beloved Rifles. His fate was plain: go back to where he had been bitterly unhappy and take over the reins from a father he disliked while surrounded by the ghosts that would never leave him.

'How lovely that sounds.' Meg straightened up and scanned the cabin, apparently looking for trifling signs of disorder as she folded his new trousers, put away the towel and twitched the corner curtain into place. 'I am looking forward to arriving in Falmouth. I have always wanted to see the West Country and the coast, ever since I found a ridiculous novel about pirates and smugglers in the charity box.' She smiled, apparently amused at the memory of her youthful self. 'I read it secretly at night, straining my eyes and filling my head with tales of adventure and secret coves.'

'I was seventeen when I left,' Ross said. 'Hardly an age when the beauties of the countryside are of much interest. But I did explore caves and climb cliffs and learn to swim in the sea.

'But escape and the army were all that had truly interested me then. I knew I could shoot better than anyone for miles around despite my age. I'd haunted the footsteps of my father's head keeper Tregarne by day, and I sneaked out to spend nights with Billy Gillan, a poacher.' He closed his eyes, recalling the thrill; it had not all been unhappiness. 'I could bring down a pheasant or a pigeon and I could stalk game unseen and evade Tregarne's men as easily as the crafty old rogue who taught me.'

'It will be good to return to the peace of the countryside, then, to be away from war and noise and killing.'

'No.' The thought of the quiet, the lack of the purpose he understood, appalled him. 'The Rifle Brigade was what I dreamed of, a chance to use and hone my skill. The countryside taught me, that is all.' The thought of the silence and the memories made him shudder. Strange that he had never anticipated that, far from becoming hardened to death as he had expected, it would come to haunt him. Other young men started out shaken by their first experience of battle or of killing the enemy by sniping from cover. Gradually they became used to it, indifferent. But for him it seemed as though it was the other way around and the horror had grown, slowly, insidiously until he felt as though Death himself walked constantly at his shoulder and sighted along the barrel of his rifle whenever he took aim. But then he had left a legacy of death behind him in England.

'I suppose young men are interested in other things,' Meg agreed. 'Do you have a large family waiting for you?'

'No one.' He said it matter of factly and was unprepared for the sadness that transformed Meg's face.

'I'm so sorry.'

'There is no need for you to be. My mother died eighteen months after I joined the army. My younger brother six years later. My father four months ago.' Said flatly like that it betrayed no embarrassing emotion at all.

'I have two sisters.' Meg sat down and began to shake out his shirts, checking each for tears or loose buttons. Ross contemplated telling her that she should not be valeting him, but if she was busy it kept that clear gaze off his face and he could watch her, which was curiously soothing. 'I am the middle one. Celina, the younger, is sweet and biddable and very good. Arabella, the elder, is practical and kind and sensible.'

'Like you.' It was a surprise to see her blush.

'I had to learn to be practical.' Meg tugged at a button and then apparently decided it was secure. 'I used to be the dreamer, the romantic one. I was always in scrapes, always in trouble with Papa.' As he watched she put down the shirt for a moment and spread her right hand, palm up, looking at it as if seeing something that was no longer there. She shivered and picked up the sewing again.

'But you married your true love in the end? Your childhood sweetheart, no doubt.' *How charming. How very romantic.*

'Yes.' Meg nodded, her head bent over her sewing roll, apparently not noticing the sneer in his voice. 'I eloped. Bella helped me, which was brave of her.' She apparently found the cotton she was seeking and began to thread a needle, squinting at the eye in concentration. 'But I am sure Papa would never guess she would do anything so dreadful, so I do not think she would have suffered for it. I do hope not.'

'Suffered for it? Your father was very severe?'

'Oh, yes, although it was usually me who got the whippings. Bella was too sensible to annoy him and Lina too timid. One thing that convinced me to go was that I was sure life would be much saf…quieter for my sisters with me not there to infuriate Papa.'

Safer, was what she almost said. And the tyrant whipped her? A young girl? It was his right, of course, in law. A father was lord of his household. He could still recall the bite of the switch on the numerous occasions when his own transgressions had been found out. Boys were always being chastised and he bore his father no ill will for that. But the thought of someone taking a switch to that slim frame, that tender skin, sickened him. What sort of man beat a woman? A girl?

'And they are all right now? They have married, left home?'

'I do not know. I wrote, often, but I never heard from either of them. I expect Papa stopped the letters.'

'But that is where you will go as soon as we land?'

'I—ouch!' Meg dropped the needle and sucked her thumb. 'Yes. But I will not arrive on the vicarage doorstep, begging to be taken back.' Her voice held a hard edge he had never heard before, not even when she had been angry with him. But when Ross looked closely at her face all he could see was concentration as she whipped a section of torn hem into place.

'Why not hire a reliable man, a Bow Street Runner, perhaps, to go and make enquiries?' Ross asked. 'That will put your mind at rest without you having to undertake the journey.'

She folded the shirt and added it to the pile, shaking her head. 'No. I want to go myself, at once.'

'But your in-laws, surely they will help you?' Ross found he was becoming positively outraged over the fact that Meg was on her own. Which was ridiculous. She was an independent adult woman and what she did was no affair of his.

'I had eloped,' she said simply, although her eyes were dark with emotions that seemed to go far beyond her words. 'And they blamed me for leading James astray.' Ross felt a stirring of puzzlement. It was a long time since he had been in England, but surely the fact that she had married would have squashed the little scandal of a vicar's daughter eloping.

'They made their position very clear when I wrote to tell them what had happened,' she continued with a shrug. 'I couldn't even bring them a grandchild. Now, of course, I am quite beyond the pale with everyone, although I am not sure whether it was sharing a tent with Dr Ferguson or soiling my hands by tending the wounded that most scandalised the ladies of the regiment. No, I must make myself a new life.'

The day passed slowly. It was hard to accept inactivity, to have the comparative silence of the ship after the bustle of camp and, perhaps most of all, the absence of duties to keep him focused on the here and now, to give some purpose to life. And without something to keep him occupied all he had to think about was the alien English world and its inescapable responsibilities and memories that waited for him.

Meg seemed to find plenty to keep herself busy, although he suspected their meagre combined wardrobes would not hold enough mending to occupy her for another day. She came and went, leaving him tactfully alone for half an hour at a time. He must get up tomorrow, whatever she said, and give her privacy. It must be hard, managing modestly behind that scrap of curtain. But she never once complained—not at the confined space, the gloom of the cabin, the insidious smell of the bilges. Or his dark mood.

Meg returned in the late afternoon to report heavier seas—which he could feel in the roll of the ship and the creaking that seemed to come from every part of it. 'But the sun is shining and apparently we are making good time,' she added as she worked on the last of his deplorable shirts. 'There.' She shook it out, looked at it critically, then folded it up. 'You now have five shirts that are halfway decent. I'll just put them back and then I will see what I can do with your uniform now it is dry.'

Ross found himself staring at the undeniably attractive sight of her rounded backside as she bent over the open trunk, and shifted his gaze to the deck over his head. The

lust he had felt when he had woken that morning to find
her in his arms had not lessened and he was not going to
add fuel to its flames by ogling Meg's figure. It had been
hard enough getting to sleep last night, with her warm in
the bed next to him; tonight would be worse, now he knew
how good she felt against him.

'Oh! You have books!' She was on her knees, staring
into the bottom of the trunk. 'Lots of them.'

'Take one if you want to read.' Someone might as well
enjoy them.

'May I?' She was lifting them out before he could reply.
'Gulliver's Travels—I have always wanted to read that.
Would you like one?'

'No.' Reading military tactics would be rubbing salt in
the wound, the thought of classical texts made his head
ache and poetry and fiction held not the slightest charm. He
had carted those books with care the length and breadth of
the Iberian Peninsula, had read them with passion whenever he could, and now he found he had not the slightest
desire to see them ever again. The urge to discover all
the literature he had spurned as a youth had suddenly left
him. 'Thank you,' he added, aware that he was probably
sounding like a lout and not really caring much about that
either.

'I'll read to you.' Meg opened the book carefully on her
knees.

'I want to sleep.'

'You cannot possibly be tired and if you sleep now you
will not rest well tonight.' She sounded remarkably like
his old nanny when he was five. Ross rolled his eyes and
settled back, resigned to his fate.

*'Travels into several remote nations of the world in four
parts by Lemuel Gulliver, first a surgeon, then a captain
of several ships. Part the first, a voyage to Lilliput,'* Meg

read. *'My father had a small estate in Nottinghamshire; I was the third of five sons....'* Her tone deepened as she realised she was reading a first-person account by a man, and Ross closed his eyes, caught immediately by the fluency of her clear voice. Perhaps, after all, he would not sleep.

'...and lie at my full length in the temple.' Meg closed the book and sighed, revelling in the luxury of a book and the time to read it in. 'Oh! Have I put you to sleep after all?'

'No.' Ross opened his eyes. 'No, I was quite lost in the story you were recounting—you have the knack of reading aloud very vividly.'

'Thank you.' *He almost smiled.* Meg closed the book and set it aside, careful not to stare at Ross directly, as though the fleeting look of pleasure on his face was a wild animal she might scare away by confronting it. 'I am agog to know what happens next, but that is the end of the chapter and time, I think, for dinner. I'll send Johnny down with yours.'

It was more difficult to move about now the ship was well out into the bay and receiving the full strength of the swell. Meg found herself putting out both hands to fend off from each side of the passageway in turn and smiled to find herself staggering about like a drunk.

When she reached the stairs—*companionway*, she remembered to call it—she took a firm grip of the rail and then slipped as her foot skidded on the worn wood. Immediately a hand cupped her elbow and steadied her.

'Ma'am. Have a care.' There were two gentlemen standing behind her; one had reached to steady her.

'Thank you, sir. I have not yet got my sea legs, I fear.' He kept hold of her arm as they climbed and Meg glanced up at him, recognising his face. He and his companion were merchants, she had decided when she had seen them at breakfast. They certainly did not appear to have wives or families with them. Both men were well dressed, in their thirties, perhaps.

'Thank you,' she repeated when they reached the next deck where the food was being served, but it took a pointed glance at his hand before he released her.

'Gerald Whittier, ma'am. And this is Henry Bates.'

'Mrs Brandon.' Meg began to feel uncomfortable at the way they stood so very close. She scanned the long tables between the hanging lanterns for Signora Rivera or some other lady. 'If you will excuse me, gentlemen, I must organise dinner for my husband.'

'Oh, yes, he is a cripple, is he not?' Whittier observed. 'We saw him being carried on board. Difficult for you, ma'am, being all alone with him in that state. Perhaps you would care to join us for dinner?' His smile made her uneasily aware of the warmth in his eyes. 'We would be delighted to entertain you.'

I am sure you would. 'My husband, Major Brandon,' Meg said with all the frost she could inject into her voice, 'is not crippled, but wounded.' She glanced up and down their immaculate civilian clothing. 'My *husband* is an officer and a hero.' Whittier flushed at the scorn in her voice, but stepped back as she swept past him.

There, the colonel's lady could not have been so haughty. She found a seat between a clerk who had a book propped up on the table before him and a fat woman and her husband whose occupation she was quite unable to guess.

As she ate she kept a wary eye out for the two men, but, when they made no move to join her and took a table on the far side, she gradually recovered her equilibrium. Perhaps she had been over-sensitive and had read more than a somewhat unconventional invitation into Mr Whittier's words. But she was still angry at the way he had described Ross.

'Anyfink wot you want, mum?' It was Johnny, standing at her elbow.

'Yes, you may carry some food down to the major, if you will. I am not very steady on my feet in this sea.'

'Wot would the major like, mum?'

'Everything, and lots of it, he has a good appetite,' she said, smiling at the boy. 'And ale.'

'He's a big 'un, he is,' Johnny said. 'My ma would say she'd rather feed him for a day than a sen'night.' He scurried off in the direction of the serving table.

Meg was so amused by that she decided to save it up to tell Ross. Perhaps she might tempt that elusive half-smile out again.

She lingered a little, then went up and out on to the deck to give Ross some more time alone. He was probably thoroughly tired of her company, although if he was up and about tomorrow he would probably find some congenial male passengers and would not need her efforts to entertain him. If he did, then perhaps it would prove her wrong about his dark, fatalistic mood. Perhaps, after all, he had merely been exhausted, in pain and bored.

She wandered up towards the bows and leaned her elbows on the rail. It was quiet on deck, most of the passengers apparently preferring the stuffy, poorly lit communal stateroom to the stiff breeze and salty air. The sea was liberating after years of heat and dust and danger. Somewhere out there beyond the darkening sea, where the vanished sun still made a glow on the horizon, were Bella and Lina. Would they be happy and well? Would they have found—?

'Still alone, ma'am?' It was Whittier, his friend Bates

smirking behind him. 'That won't do, a young lady like yourself. You need some lively company; no wonder you don't want to go back below to your wounded hero.'

'I am alone, Mr Whittier, because I choose to be. Thank you, but I do not wish for company.'

'Come now, there's no need to be standoffish.' They moved in close, far too close for comfort. The rail pressed into her back, no escape that way. Panic began to catch at her breath as she glanced around the deserted deck. Not even a deckhand was in sight. 'We are much more fun for a lady like you than that cripple of yours below decks.' Bates put his hand on her arm, his fingers hot through the cotton of the sleeve.

Where was their cabin? Could they bundle her down there without anyone realising? She looked around for a weapon and saw none. It was up to her; no one was going to save her this time.

'Mr Bates, if you do not remove your arm, I am going to scream—very loudly.' Someone, surely, would hear? The threat did not appear to alarm them. Still, she must try. Meg dragged down a deep breath, opened her mouth and—

'But not as loudly as you will scream, *Mr Bates*, when I rip your testicles off and throw them to the sharks,' said a cold voice from the shadows of the rigging. *Ross. And sounding like Death.* An hysterical giggle rose in her throat at the sight of the men's faces as they swung round to confront the threat in the shadows.

Ross was wearing his stained, filthy uniform, his sword at his side and a pistol pushed into the sash. He looked as if he had just walked out of the swirling smoke and bloody carnage of the battlefield—or straight from hell. He looked, Meg thought, as she sagged back against the rail, big, dangerous and utterly wonderful—provided he was on your side.

'Who the hell are you?' Whittier demanded. 'This woman is with us.'

'This *lady* is my wife.' For the first time, Meg saw Ross smile. And then wished she hadn't. 'I believe she expressed the desire to be left alone. Are you hard of hearing, perhaps?' His sword ripped out of its scabbard as the men backed away. 'Are you as attached to your ears as your friend is to his balls?' He had them trapped now, pressed back against the rail with nowhere to go. It was time to intervene.

'Major Brandon.'

'My dear?' It was hard not to be distracted by the warmth in those two drawled words.

'The captain would dislike blood on his deck.'

'So he would.' There was a thoughtful silence while the sword point remained unwavering. 'And the men work so hard holystoning it. Did these scum touch you?'

She knew what he meant and shook her head. 'No, they were merely offensive.'

Ross kept the sword up while Meg and the two men eyed it like rabbits in front of a stoat. 'Very well. You two—undress.'

'What?' Bates's voice wavered between fear and incredulity.

'You heard me. Every stitch. Avert your eyes, my dear. This will not be a pretty sight.'

Meg hastily turned her back. Amid sounds of spluttering indignation it was apparent that Bates and Whittier were obeying Ross. She could hardly blame them for giving in, not once they had seen his smile and looked into his eyes.

'Now throw it all over the side. Good. And now, walk back to the companionway and down the stairs.'

'But that's the public saloon! And we're stark naked!'

'Yes, indeed. And hardly a vision to inspire an artist, I fear. Off you go. I'll be right behind you.'

As he passed her, Ross murmured, 'I thought I told you to avert your eyes, wife.'

Meg dragged her gaze from two pairs of pale, goose-pimpled buttocks retreating towards the companionway and laughed. 'And, as always, husband, your judgement is entirely correct. I have never seen a more revolting sight.'

Chapter Five

Meg stayed where she was, listening as the outraged shrieks from below died down. Her knees felt wobbly now as her amusement ebbed away. That had been a nasty little incident and it had left her more shaken than she expected. Uneven, limping footsteps on the deck made her look up. 'What happened?'

'They snatched up platters from the serving table to cover their modesty so most people were spared the worst of it. But they won't dare show their faces for the rest of the voyage.' Ross stood close, looking down at her. 'Johnny saw them follow you and came to me. Are you all right, Meg?'

'Yes, of course,' Meg began, then found her voice cracking. 'No...not really. It is very foolish, I just feel rather...'

And then he stepped forwards, wrapped his arms around her and pulled her to him. It was rather like being hugged by the bear she had compared him to, one smelling of river-soaked, badly dried cloth with a lingering whiff of gunpowder and smoke, but it was marvellously comforting. And utterly improper. Meg wrapped her arms around Ross's waist and clung, her cheek pressed against the dark green broadcloth of his jacket, her toes bumping his boots. How long had it been since she had been hugged?

He was big and strong and beautifully male. Appropriate female parts of her tingled disconcertingly at the realisation of just how good he felt.

His chin was resting on the top of her head. He was certainly a very thorough hugger, but that was all this seemed to be, thank goodness. *Thank goodness*, she repeated rather desperately to herself as her body soaked up his warmth and the strength of his arms stirred the feelings that were nothing at all to do with relief and entirely to do with the effect of being held close by a very masculine man.

She really should step away, now, before his thoughts began to run along the same path. Meg wriggled and said, muffled, into his chest, 'I'm all right now, thank you.'

'Mmm?' Ross opened his arms a little, enough for her to lean back against his embrace and look up. It was hard to see in the light of the swaying lantern and she frowned, trying to make out his expression. It did not occur to her that this position, or the length of time she held it, was an invitation—not until he lowered his head and kissed her.

It was not a subtle kiss, but it was a satisfying one, tingling right down to her toes. And it was a surprising kiss, not least because she was hazily aware that Ross was as taken aback as she was by what was happening. She wrapped her arms around his neck and kissed him in return and he seemed to emerge from his shock and put his mind to what he was doing.

And at that point the movement of his mouth over hers became subtle, intimate and far more assured and arousing than Meg could deal with. She much preferred him confused. And besides, she was not used to kissing like this.

James had not been much given to preliminaries. 'No.' She pulled back. 'Ross, we should not be doing this.'

He did not release her abruptly as he might have done, finding himself rejected, but opened his hands and his arms so they still supported her. 'No?'

Meg found she could not reply. It was difficult, just at this moment, to remember why falling into bed with a troubled near-stranger she did not understand was not a perfectly rational thing to be doing. Then the ship rolled and she was back in his embrace, her hands reaching up to slide into the thick hair at the sides of his head. Oh, but this was good, this closeness, this heat.

This time it was Ross who stopped. 'Downstairs.' He strode towards the companionway, one hand clasped firmly around her wrist. She allowed herself to be pulled along, half-excited, half-afraid, wholly incapable of resisting him.

The buzz of conversation that rose to greet them as they emerged into the public stateroom showed that the scandalous entertainment Ross had provided earlier was still exercising the passengers.

'Mrs Brandon!' Meg turned, with the flustered realisation that she was beginning to answer rather too readily to that name, and found the large woman from dinner at her side. 'Did you see that outrageous sight just now! Two men, stark—I mean, in a state of nature!'

'My goodness! How utterly shocking. They must have been drunk, don't you think?'

'Or insane,' the other woman said darkly. 'Oh, and here is dear Major Brandon, young José's brave rescuer. The *signora* told us all about it. How are you now, Major?'

'Quite recovered, ma'am.' Ross sounded as though he was facing a court-martial. 'But if you will excuse us—' He guided Meg through the stateroom and away towards their cabin, his hand firm on her arm.

When the door closed behind them they stood look-ing at each other. The cold realisation that they had acted very imprudently was beginning to creep over Meg. Ross looked as though the court-martial had resulted in a death sentence.

'Bed,' he snapped.

'I don't think—' she began, aware as never before of the size and the strength of the man. She had provoked him—inflamed him—and now she had no idea how to stop him from taking what she had so rashly offered. Did she even want to stop him? *No*, was the honest truth, but what happened afterwards?

'Neither of us thought. Go to bed.' Ross reached for the blankets she had folded on the trunk. 'I will sleep on the floor.'

Meg sat down on the edge of the bunk, her knees giving way. He did not intend to finish what they had begun on deck—either by force or persuasion. She supposed it was relief that was making her feel so light-headed. Now she did not have to make a decision.

'You will not sleep on the floor.' Guilt overcame the relief. 'We will both sleep in the bunk. If you lie on the deck, it will hurt your leg and I will not sleep for worrying. If I take the deck, then you will not sleep fretting about that.'

The sound Ross made in response could only be described as a snort. 'You expect me to sleep easily next to a woman I have just kissed? Held in my arms? You have been married, have you not, Meg? You know what happens.' He found the pillow and tossed that down too.

Well, that was certainly frank, Meg thought, knowing she was blushing. Of course she knew the effect that kiss-ing a woman had on a man and if that was followed by both of them getting into bed together and doing nothing about it she was sure it would be downright uncomfortable for him.

She could trust the promise that he had given her the other night; she would be safe with him even if he did spend the night in discomfort both from his wound and his body's own reactions. Now she felt guilty. And embarrassed. And more than a little frustrated herself.

'And if we both get into that bunk we will be lying like planks, one on each side,' Ross added. He stood, hands on hips, regarding the mattress with disfavour.

'I don't believe either of us would be any less uncomfortable with you on the floor. I apologise; I hugged and kissed you out of sheer relief. It was too much like that time before Peter rescued me.'

'I kissed you first,' Ross said with the air of a man who was going to be fair if it killed him.

'And it was not just relief,' Meg admitted. 'Let that be a lesson to us not to give way to our, er, animal passions, as you called them,' she added briskly, with more resolution than she felt. 'We are adults, with the will-power God gave us, I trust, not undisciplined adolescents.' That sounded very fine, but it did not stop her feeling seventeen again, before experience taught her that romantic daydreams dissolved in real life.

Look at him. He isn't handsome in the slightest, he's dour, dark and mysterious and thoroughly out of temper, so what is the matter with you? But it was no good—the fact remained that Ross Brandon was overwhelmingly masculine, he excited her unbearably and she wanted him. She, Margaret Shelley, who had sworn never to allow her emotions to lead her into trouble again.

'Animal passions,' he repeated, looking even more saturnine than before. 'Will-power. Right. You undress behind that curtain and I will get into bed. If you extin-

guish the lantern before you emerge you may pretend I am
that large dame we have just met and I will pretend that
you are.'

'That might work,' Meg conceded. She retreated to
wrestle with hooks and eyes behind the screen. She could
not decide whether Ross had a sense of humour or was
being deadly serious. She pulled the gown over her head.
'This is a momentary awkwardness, after all,' she observed
to the unresponsive silence in the cabin. 'In the morning,
after a good night's sleep, we will hardly regard it.'

Ross lay in the gloom deliberately flexing his thigh
muscles so the pain would provide a distraction from the
ache in his groin. He shifted on to his side to ensure the
evidence of the effect of that kiss was not visible through
the thin sheet. What was the matter with him? He'd
kissed the woman when she needed comfort and she had
responded, that was all. He had not thought for a moment
of it leading anywhere and he was certain Meg had not.

But it was easier to tell his mind that than it was for his
body to understand. He was not an undisciplined adoles-
cent, according to Meg. It was a good thing she could not
see the proof that he was responding to her like a randy
seventeen year old. He did not even have the excuse of a
long period of abstinence; up to the eve of the battle he had
kept any frustration at bay with the willing camp followers
who were the army's constant companions and sources of
comfort. It occurred to him that he had been aroused by
her since he met her.

The curtain flapped and the light went out. Even Meg's
soft *huff* of breath as she breathed on the wick was provocative. Her lips, soft and pink, would have formed a circle
as she blew, pouting...

Stop it. Ross conjured up the fat woman's round, rather

foolish, features, her thin lips and her nondescript brown eyes, her inconsequential chatter. That was better. The sheet was tugged as Meg wriggled up from the bottom of the bunk into the space between his back and the wall. The *narrow* space. *Wriggling.* The image of the other woman vanished as the scent of warm female and plain soap reached him.

Ross controlled his breathing and resigned himself to a long night. He had lain still and endured silently when the surgeon dug the bullet out of his leg—once the shouting match over the man's intention to cut the limb off had been won—he could endure this torture now.

But this was a stimulating kind of agony, he had to admit that, he thought as he resisted the urge to get out of bed and pace about on the deck. Meg Halgate was a frustrating, opinionated, infuriatingly commonsensical thorn in his side, but she was giving him something to think about besides his own woes. Eyes open in the darkness, Ross admitted that he had thought about little other than himself from the moment he had been carried off the field and into the surgeon's tent, with the battle and his men entirely out of his hands and the future he had been trying to ignore inescapable in front of him.

He woke in the morning in exactly the same position as he had fallen asleep, which was a miracle. He had slept, he had managed to stay still and Meg had not unwittingly wrapped herself around his suffering body in the night. He felt, in fact, quite calm and in control of himself.

Ross turned over and found himself nose to nose with her. Her eyes were open, the dark pupils dilated. She looked nervous. His own reflection stared back at him. She had every reason to be uneasy. His feeling of calm control vanished, leaving him wanting nothing more than to reach out for her, take her, lose himself and the darkness in her softness and light. Bury himself in her, make her scream with needing him…

'Good morning,' she remarked with caution. 'You slept well?'

'I slept.' He felt like a randy bear with a sore head. 'I am getting up today.' Let her protest, then they could argue to clear the air.

'Of course.' Meg slid down to the end of the bed and disappeared behind her curtain. 'A little light exercise will help your leg now.'

'Aren't you going to wait for the hot water?' Ross thought about his preferred form of exercise, then caught a glimpse of himself in the scrap of mirror she had propped up on the trunk to help her plait her hair. Now there was an effective antidote to lust. No wonder she was wary of him—Beauty and the Beast just about summed it up. Last night she had been frightened and needed some affection— that was all. The last thing a woman like her wanted was a maimed, ugly killer like him.

'No. This is fine.' There were sounds of splashing and the curtain billowed. Ross closed his eyes and endured. For some reason his body would not give up as easily as his mind. 'I'll get dressed and go up on deck until you are ready—if you come and find me we can take breakfast together.'

'You do not want to check my bandages?'

'Not unless the discomfort has become worse. But I can if you like.'

'No.' He had only asked so he had fair warning to get his unruly body under some sort of control before she laid hands on his bare flesh again. 'No, thank you.'

They were both speaking as though that kiss had not happened. Perhaps that was for the best. He was not used to living with a woman, and he did not understand this one's moods and the way she dealt with awkward situations. But Meg was used to living with men—two, at least. She had been a wife and a close companion, so perhaps she understood him a lot better than he understood her. Or thought she did. If Meg could see inside his head, she would take her bag and go and sleep on the upper deck for the rest of the voyage, he was quite certain.

Is he feeling any better or is he just learning to hide from me? Meg walked up and down the deck, pretending a lively interest in Signora Rivera's children and their characters, fads and charms. José, who was being made to suffer for his accident, was held firmly by the hand and his constant whining had given Meg a headache half an hour since.

Ross, seated on a hatch cover, continued the systematic assault he had begun that morning on the pocket books of any of the male passengers who would play piquet with him. Fortunately he set low stakes—*chicken stakes*, one man had grumbled before proceeding to lose hand after hand. He had stopped complaining about the stakes after the second hand.

Winning did not, however, seem to please Ross any more than the sunshine on the waves, the occasional school of dolphins playing in the bow wave or the blue sky. His play was ruthless, efficient and merciless. Meg began to wonder if he insisted on the low stakes because he expected to be accused of cheating if he played for anything higher.

James had tried to teach her the game, but her incomprehension of the complex strategy involved would always drive him to frustrated irritation with his inability to drum even the essentials of discards into her head.

'*Repique,*' Ross called as the ladies' strolling walk brought them past once again.

'Your husband is an excellent player,' the Spanish woman observed.

'Indeed. I think piquet appeals to him because it is so strategic.' Meg watched Ross's narrow-eyed concentration. The good players in the regiment had been the strategists, she recalled, and the major was fighting each game as though he were commanding troops in battle.

Playing cards was never going to be a substitute for the army life he had lost. She only hoped that whatever challenges the home he seemed so reluctant to reach held for him, they would satisfy him. Somehow she was coming to doubt it.

Ross put down another winning hand and money passed between the two men before the merchant he had just trounced got up and walked off, trying to put a gracious face on his losses.

'Excuse me.' Meg recalled an excuse to remove herself from Signora Rivera and her grizzling son. 'I must ensure the major takes his exercise.'

Ross looked up as she approached him and raised an eyebrow. 'Yes, my dear?'

'Time for your walk,' Meg said with wifely sweetness for the benefit of the nearby passengers. 'Dear.'

'I am not a lap dog requiring a stroll around the deck,' he retorted, low voiced, as he gathered up the cards and his winnings.

'More like a mastiff needing a run in the park or looking for a bull to savage.' Meg maintained her smile. 'Frequent gentle exercise is what that leg needs now; besides, if I leave you to clean out every mark on this ship we will find ourselves dropped overboard before we sight land again.'

'You think I am prigging the cards, do you?' Ross asked. But he put the pack in his pocket and got to his feet.

'I am sure it is all your skill and there is no sleight of hand involved,' Meg assured him, falling into step beside him and deliberately dawdling to restrict his limping stride. He needed to slow down, control his impatience as he had controlled the need to take her last night. He had been aroused, however well he thought he could hide it. And that in itself was arousing her, an effect that unfortunately did not seem to be wearing off.

Meg reminded herself, yet again, that she could not afford an entanglement with a man she would never see again once they landed. For him it would be a matter of satisfying a physical urge. For herself, she did not think she could deal with it quite so simply. Perhaps it was her old, foolish romantic spirit again, but the thought of that intimacy without a mutual affection, without emotion, frightened her.

They got to the bows and were halfway back on the circuit that she had decreed was a suitable distance before she ventured another remark. Ross, she was certain, would maintain a stony silence for the rest of the voyage if she allowed him to.

'What will you do when you return home?'

For a moment she thought he was not going to answer her. Then, two steps later, he said, 'Learn to be a country landowner.' He sounded less than enthusiastic, although the note of utter indifference to his own fate that had so worried her before was missing. It had been replaced with distaste, which she had to suppose was better.

'Is it a big estate?' It could be nothing very impressive, not if he had come into his inheritance four months ago and had not bought so much as a new shirt.

Ross shrugged. 'Big enough for someone who doesn't know the front end of a pig from a stook of corn.'

Pigs and corn sounded considerably less intimidating than town life and society, but then she had been brought up in the country. No doubt for a soldier it must seem both dull and difficult. Oh, well, a small estate would give him plenty of leisure for recreation. He would hunt and fish, like all country gentlemen, find himself a wife—one who could manage without smiles or affection—and father a brood of dark, scowling children.

'What?' Ross enquired, catching sight of the amused twist of her lips. 'You know the difference, do you?'

'Certainly I do.' Meg made for the hatch cover again, their walk at an end. 'The stook of corn has more ears than the pig.'

She was brought up short by a crack of laughter. 'Now what is it?' Ross enquired as she turned, hardly able to believe her ears.

'You laughed.'

'You made a joke,' he countered, once more poker-faced.

Perhaps, if he could remember how to laugh, she need not worry about Major Ross Brandon when they parted company in Falmouth.

Chapter Six

❦

Ross leaned on the port rail of the *Falmouth Rose* and stared at Pendennis Castle in the early morning haze. At the shoreline the gun emplacements and Henry VIII's old battery were all still manned, all still flying the Union flag. It would be a while before the commander of the castle felt confident enough that the peace would hold and he could pull back his men.

He was trying to find some sense of his feelings about this homecoming, but the sight of familiar shores from an unfamiliar angle was not much help. They had sailed into the Carrick Roads at dawn on the fifth day after leaving Bordeaux and he had been up to see it, to watch the steep, gorse-covered slopes of St Anthony Head slip past before the captain dropped anchor to wait for a pilot and the harbourmaster's gig to come out to clear them to enter harbour.

It had not been any nostalgia that had driven him on deck, but the now-familiar discomfort of waking up next to Meg's warm, slumbering body. She appeared to have no trouble sleeping in the same bunk, once she had recovered from her awkwardness over that embrace. That kiss. He wanted her and yet he wanted her gone. *So you can wallow in your own misery again,* he sneered at himself.

'Coffee, Major?' It was Johnny, bright as a button, grinning his gap-toothed smile.

'Aye. Then take coffee and some hot water down to Mrs Brandon. Here,' he added as the lad turned away, 'I'll pay you now.' He counted out the three pence a day he had promised, then added a shilling on impulse.

'Cor! A whole borde! Thank you, Major!' Johnny thrust the mug into his hands and was away, not risking Ross changing his mind over the munificent tip.

Ross was still brooding when the anchor was raised and sail set again.

'Home!' Meg said beside him. She came to lean her elbows on the rail, her mug clasped between her hands. There was a cool breeze, without the heat of the sun in it yet. 'Are you glad to see Falmouth?'

'I've never seen it from the sea before.' Ross avoided a direct answer. 'When I left England I sailed from Portsmouth.' Without any intention to confide he found the words spilling out of him. 'I was terrified, but I was damned if I was going to show it. You should have seen me.' He closed his eyes for a moment, trying to conjure up the boy he had been. 'A lanky seventeen year old with his hair in his eyes, feet I still had to grow into and filled with the terrible triumph of thwarting my father and all his plans for me.' And guilt. But he was not going to talk about the guilt that rode him still.

'So how did you get a commission? And you must have been so upset at leaving your mother, at least.'

'I had no commission, not then. But I was in the Rifle

Brigade, a private, and that was all that mattered to me, even though I was as wet behind the ears as they come. It wasn't until we were well out to sea and I'd finished casting my accounts up over the side that it occurred to me that my mother would worry.' God, but he'd been thoughtless—or perhaps, just a typical boy—but he'd salved his conscience with the thought that he'd written to his godfather and told him what he was doing.

Of course, it did dawn on him after a few weeks that he had landed Sir George Pierce with the unenviable task of dealing with his parents. 'My godfather got my letter, broke the news.' And, mercifully at the time, kept it from him just how anguished his mother had been. It had not been until she died and her last letter had reached him that he realised what he had done to her peace of mind and her health. It was his first lesson that he could kill at a distance of several hundred miles without needing any weapon, as well as face to face with his finger on the trigger.

'And when I was eighteen, when he discovered that I hadn't managed to get killed or flogged, my godfather bought me a commission.' Stick to the facts. His mind skidded away from the dark, deep hole of his conscience. Away from Giles. 'Since then I've made my own way, spent my money on my own advancement.'

'I should imagine that merit had something to do with it as well,' Meg observed. 'I have asked Johnny to bring us food out here; I didn't think you would want to be down below, not now.'

She still thought he had been driven out here by the pangs of homesickness, Ross realised as the cabin boy put a tray on the hatch cover and the smell of fried pork wound its way through the air. He slapped some rashers between slices of bread and went back to the rail, leaving Meg to make a more decorous picnic. That way he did not have to talk. Meg's simple, direct questions had extracted more from him than he had confided in anyone else, ever, but the urge to recount his past history had fled as fast as it had come upon him.

Sailors were beginning to bring baggage up on deck, deploying the nets that would swing it ashore. Ross drew Meg out of the way of the men who came to the sides to lower sail and throw ropes as the harbour wall loomed larger.

'I hope the *signora* has a firm hold on young José,' Meg said, and he realised she was eyeing the narrowing strip of water between the ship and the dock apprehensively. 'That was so brave of you.' She gave a little shudder. 'The tide was ripping out so fast—'

'I have seen enough death, too much to leave a child to drown,' Ross said starkly. But the memory still troubled Meg, he could tell. How much courage had it taken to climb down that ladder into the swirling water and hang on to an unconscious stranger for the time it took to get him out? A stab of remorse told him that afterwards he had been unthinking and probably unkind. His own exhaustion, pain and depression were no excuse; if it had been one of his men he would have spoken to him, shown he understood what guts it had taken, made sure he was all right.

Too late now to go back. 'What will you do when we land?' he asked abruptly. 'Where will you stay?'

'I will find a decent inn while I find out about stage-coach routes, plan my journey.'

'It is quite some distance. You have adequate funds?'

'Oh, yes.' She held up her reticule. 'Doctor Ferguson insisted on paying me. It isn't much, but enough.' She opened the bag and reached inside. 'See…' The blood left her cheeks and she began to rummage. 'It has gone! The roll of notes!'

'Are you certain? Did you not notice before?'

'Yes, I am certain.' Meg stared at the bag, upended on a barrel, its contents spread out. 'The coins are heavy, I never noticed the difference. And I have had no cause to open it since I came on board. I have not needed money.' She pressed her hand to her lips, visibly fighting for composure. 'I dropped it with all my things when José fell in the water. Someone must have taken the notes then.'

'Let me.' Ross reached for his wallet.

'No. Thank you, but, no. I have no idea when I could pay it back.'

'For heaven's sake, Meg! A gift—I probably owe you my life.'

She shook her head and he could see his persistence was upsetting her. 'I will find some work for a week or so. I will find an employment office, register my name with them. Someone will want practical help, I am certain.'

'As what?' Ross turned his back on the dockside and studied Meg properly for the first time that day. She was wearing a gown he had not seen before, one she must have been saving for the occasion. Her hair was neatly braided under her plain straw bonnet and she looked both subdued and compliant, not at all like the managing, competent, arousing woman who had been saving his leg and wrecking his sleep. 'A governess?'

'Goodness, no!' There was the spark of the Meg he was used to. 'My own education was sadly lacking in everything except sewing, accounts and Bible studies. I speak Spanish and Portuguese—and much of that not repeatable in polite society—and very poor French. I could assist a housekeeper or perhaps be a nurse-companion to an invalid or elderly person.'

Mrs Fogarty, the housekeeper at the Court—he could not think the word *home* in connection to the place where he had grown up—was a sour-faced, bitter woman. His younger brother, Giles, had been her favourite and she had always disapproved of Ross, for some reason he had never been able to understand. Perhaps it was simply because she didn't like most boys and he had been a fairly wild example and not an attractive, handsome specimen like his brother. Looking back, Ross could not count the times she had sent tales of his various misdeeds to his father, but she had earned him a goodly number of thrashings. After Giles's accident her antipathy had changed to outright hostility, and that he could understand.

Her name had still been on the list of staff the lawyers had sent him. She must be in her early sixties now and probably looking forward to seeing him with about as much pleasure as he felt at the prospect of the reunion. It would be like having a dark spirit lurking in the corner, knowing Agnes Fogarty still controlled the household.

'You do not look like any housekeeper I have ever met,' he told Meg as the mooring lines were heaved over the side and the ship nudged up to the quayside.

'No?' She managed a half-smile and Ross felt something twist inside him.

He did not return the smile. 'No. You look too young,' he said flatly. She would be all right, surely? She was practical and hardworking and sensible and she did not want his help. 'They have let the gangplank down. Come, I will help you find your luggage.' He limped away before she could reply, or tell him to slow down. At least he would not be fussed over any more, he told himself, crooking a finger to a reliable-looking porter with a barrow as his feet hit solid land.

'That bag there,' he said, pointing. 'You will go with this

lady, wait while she makes some visits and then be sure she gets safely to a respectable inn. Do you understand?' He passed the man a coin as he spoke. 'Make sure you find her something suitable.'

'Aye, sir.' The man tugged his forelock, pitching Ross back years to his childhood with just two words in the soft Cornish burr.

'Thank you, Major. That is most thoughtful of you.' Meg spoke formally, as though they had not spent nights together in the same bed, as though she had not flown into his arms for comfort, lifted her lips for his kisses. 'I trust your leg heals well and you find your way home safely.' She turned to the porter and then swung back, her face animated with concern. 'Do take care of that wound. And please—give yourself time to adjust. It will all be well, you will see.'

And then she was gone before he could answer her, walking away over the cobbles, talking as she went with the porter, who was nodding and steering his barrow towards the steep street to the town.

Ross stood and stared at her slender back, the brave set of her shoulders as she walked off into the unknown. Courage and humour when surely she had as much to dread from this landfall as he had. More, for he knew what he was going to. She was adrift in her own country with only a few guineas to her name.

'Porter, sir?'

'Yes.' He looked at the man. 'Take my luggage to the Red Lion Hotel.' When he had left, that had been the most exclusive inn in the town. 'I'll follow you.' He glanced back and saw that Meg had vanished. As though she had never been there. Off to a new life as a drudge to some invalid or to a post as a housekeeper before she set off, not knowing what awaited her when she got to what had once been her home. 'No, wait.' The man stopped, resigned to the whims of the gentry. 'Wait one moment.'

'This one along here's where my sister got her post as a cook,' the porter said, trundling his barrow along in the roadway while Meg walked on the flagged pavement. 'She said it was a fine, smart place. Made her nervous to go in, because they only serve the real gentry there. No shop assistants or maids of all work.'

'Thank you. I'll try it first, then.' Meg stopped outside the office and studied the shiny dark-green front door with its brass knocker. The plate read, Empson's Employment Bureau. She struggled for calm composure, despite her anger and panic over the stolen money. *Just a few weeks,* she promised herself. *I won't need so very much, I can earn enough for the stage.* 'It looks very—'

'Genteel, that's what our Kate said,' the man confided. 'She got a smart lawyer to cook for. An Honourable, she says he is. And *they* don't grow on trees.'

'No, indeed,' Meg agreed gravely, turned the handle and went into a square room with a row of upright chairs along one wall and a desk set across the far corner. An odd assortment of people waited in silence on the chairs. The man sitting behind the desk raised his head from a ledger and placed eyeglasses on his nose as she crossed the boards, conscious of every squeak of her shoes on the surface. *Genteel. How on earth am I going to learn to look genteel? I must not look too desperate, however I feel.*

A wiry young man with highly polished shoes glanced up at her from the book he was reading, then politely looked away, but the plump woman with a vast bonnet stared openly and the neat woman in black next to her watched her from the corner of her eye.

Valet, cook, governess, Meg guessed.

'Yes?'

'Good morning. I am seeking a position as an assistant to a housekeeper or as a nurse-companion.' Meg placed herself before the desk. A sign on it read Eustace Empson, Proprietor.

'I see.' Mr Empson opened a ledger, picked up a pen, dipped it in the standish, peered at the page, then sharply up at her. 'Name? Experience?'

Meg set herself to make the very best of her somewhat chequered past, editing the details heavily. '…and I am told I read aloud to invalids most effectively,' she finished. 'Oh, yes, and I speak Portuguese and Spanish fluently.' Behind her the doorbell tinkled.

'Hah! Not a lot of call for Portuguese housekeepers in Falmouth,' Empson said sourly. He scribbled on a form, handed it to Meg and gestured at the chairs. 'Wait your turn there. Mrs Empson may have some nurse-companion positions. You have your references, I trust?'

'Of course,' Meg lied, inwardly cursing. She had never thought of that. References? Where was she to get those from? 'At my lodgings.'

'Did you say Portuguese-speaking housekeeper?' a deep voice enquired.

Meg dropped the note and her reticule and scrabbled for them on the floor. *It cannot be*… But it was. Her gaze, ascending from her crouched position, travelled up scuffed boots, salt and smoke-stained uniform trousers to a broad chest and a very familiar, very forbidding face.

'Indeed, sir.' From Empson's voice he was a trifle uncertain as to the status of this latest arrival. Ross Brandon sounded like an officer and a gentleman; he hardly looked like one as he loomed over the desk with her crouched at his feet. 'A Mrs—' he glanced at his ledger

'—Halgate who has just registered is so qualified. You seek such a person?'

'Yes,' Ross said, standing in the middle of the immaculate, prim office like a prize fighter in a vestry.

'Er...I see.' Mr Empson, in the absence of any further explanation, patently did not see. 'I believe you are not registered with us as seeking staff, Mr, er—?'

'Lord Brandon,' Ross said and Meg stood up so abruptly that she banged her elbow on the edge of the desk. *Lord* Brandon? 'Very well, I will register if that is required. Brandon, Trevarras Court. Do you need anything else?'

'No, my lord. Indeed not.' Mr Empson was on his feet, washing his hands together in an ecstasy of delight at having secured a titled client. 'May I offer my condolences on your recent loss? A great man, hereabouts, your late father.'

'Thank you,' Ross said, his voice frigid enough to stop Empson's gushing dead. 'And the housekeeper in question is where, exactly?' He gazed past Meg, who stood rubbing her elbow and trying not to gape.

'Here, my lord. Mrs Halgate stands before you, my lord.'

The black eyes travelled up and down as though assessing her plain gown and modest bonnet. As though he had never seen her before. A perfect example of an arrogant lord, the clever man. Or perhaps it was not pretence. Perhaps this really *was* Ross. 'Very well. She will do.'

'We have not yet seen Mrs Halgate's references, my lord,' Mr Empson blurted, prudence finally overcoming his desire to offer his noble client immediate gratification of his needs. 'We cannot guarantee... The reputation of the agency requires—'

'If she turns out to be inadequate or dishonest, or her Portuguese grammar is faulty, I will return her to you.'

Ross sounded profoundly uninterested in Empson's worries. 'Mrs Halgate? We may discuss terms later.'

'I believe you also require a valet, my lord.' Ross, Empson and Meg all stared at the wiry young man who had got to his feet and was addressing Ross.

'I do?'

The young man blinked in the face of Ross's full, intimidating, attention, but stood his ground. *Brave man,* Meg thought. 'If your lordship has a valet at present, may I be so bold as to observe that he is not doing his job.'

'And you can do better?'

'Most certainly, my lord.'

'Your name?'

'Perrott, my lord.'

'Perrott was with the late Mr Worthington,' Empson hurried to intervene. 'A local gentleman of the dandy persuasion, if I might be so bold. A follower of Mr Brummell in his own way.'

'And you think you can make a dandy of me, do you, Perrott?' Not a line of Ross's face indicated the slightest amusement at the prospect.

'I would venture, my lord, that you would suit the severity of style advocated by Mr Brummell. That or uniform.'

'I'll take them both.' Ross might have been referring to two new pairs of gloves. 'They can come with me now to the Red Lion Hotel. We will travel to the Court this afternoon. Good day to you, Empson.'

Meg stared at the young valet, who looked back with a decided twinkle in his eye. What on earth was Ross about? He knew she needed employment: proper, paid employment. He might indeed require a valet, but his home, the name of which she had only half-heard, must be fully staffed already, surely? She was *not* going to take his charity.

And *Lord* Brandon? Why had he not told her that?

'After you, Mrs Halgate,' the valet said. 'We must not keep his lordship waiting.'

Lord Brandon—would she ever get used to it?—was indeed waiting for them, radiating the impatience he seemed able to convey despite his outward calm. He clicked his fingers at her porter and set off with his small entourage straggling behind him.

And he was walking far too fast, his limp getting worse as he ignored the need for caution, or, presumably, the pain.

'My lord!'

He stopped, turned. 'Yes, Mrs Halgate?'

'Would you be so kind as to proceed more slowly, my lord? I have wrenched my ankle on these cobbles.' Meg managed a pained smile.

Ross narrowed his eyes at her, then turned and walked on at a more moderate pace.

'He's going to be a challenge to dress,' Perrott observed out of the corner of his mouth. 'I don't suppose I can persuade him to stay with the uniform. He'll be selling out, I have no doubt.' He walked on, studying Ross with frank professional interest. 'At least I won't have to pad anything.'

No, Ross certainly did not suffer from spindly calves, narrow shoulders or a pigeon chest. 'You'll need to talk him into a lot of shopping,' Meg murmured back. 'He hasn't a decent shirt to his name.'

It did not take the expression on the young valet's face to make her realise her error. 'You know him already?'

'I came over on the same ship from Bordeaux,' Meg confessed. 'I have nursing experience and I dressed his leg when he first boarded—that is a nasty bullet wound.'

'I see,' was all Perrott said. Meg hoped profoundly that

he did not, and that he would keep his mouth shut about whatever speculations he had formed.

'I had no idea he had a title,' she added, hoping that made the acquaintance seem even more remote.

'His father was the third Baron Brandon,' Perrott told her as they picked their way around a spilled basket of herring. 'A big man with a nasty temper, very hot.'

'Well, his son is very cold,' Meg said. 'From what I have seen,' she added cautiously. 'There was an incident on board and he dealt with it ruthlessly and with all the heat of an ice house.'

Perrott gave a snort of amusement, then sobered. 'He doesn't seem too worried about the existing staff. His old lordship must have had a valet and there's definitely a housekeeper in residence. What is he going to do with them?'

'Oh. I hadn't thought of that.' Drat him—now she felt guilty as well as confused. Ross was proving nothing if not autocratic; he did not appear to have given the question of the existing servants any thought at all. Surely he would not just arrive and turn them out?

He came to a halt in front of a long, low whitewashed building with a statue of a red lion projecting out over the street. 'Where are your possessions, Perrott?'

'At my lodgings, my lord, not ten minutes away.'

'Then fetch them. We leave at one.'

Meg followed Ross inside, her porter at her heels, to find him already ordering a private parlour and a noon meal. The landlord quite obviously realised who he was, from the obsequious *my lords* that peppered every sentence.

'Toadeater,' Ross snarled before the parlour door had quite closed on them. 'Well, Mrs Halgate? And why are you looking at me as though I've grown another head?'

'Because I am so confused, you may as well have done!

You really are the most outrageous, arrogant man, Ross Brandon.' Meg put down her reticule and stood right in front of him. 'I say goodbye to *Major* Brandon and the next moment *Lord* Brandon is taking over my life. Has it not occurred to you that there will already be a valet and a housekeeper and that she will not be best pleased to have some unknown assistant wished on her? You have no idea if I will be halfway competent to run whatever sort of establishment you are dragging me off to, and neither do I, come to that. I told you I would not accept money—'

'I did not drag you.'

'Well, I could hardly stand there in the middle of the employment exchange and say, "This is so sudden, my lord. One moment we are sleeping in the same bed and the next you are employing me", now could I? I expect I will be back there tomorrow looking for a proper position, so I needed to leave with some dignity. Why make me go through this farce when you know I need to earn some money quickly? And why,' she added, recalling another grievance, 'did you not tell me you are a baron?'

'Because I do not want to be a damned baron,' he snapped back. 'And because I want you.'

There was no chance to step back and no hope, once Ross's hands had banded on her upper arms, of pulling free. She was lifted up on her toes as he bent his head and then he was kissing her as though to bend her to his will by sheer force of his sexuality. His tongue was possessing her mouth, his hips were thrust against hers, leaving her in absolutely no doubt that he was more than ready to simply toss her on to the couch and take her, and the deep growl that vibrated through her spoke of nothing but a savage need that he was barely containing.

Chapter Seven

Ross showed no sign of needing to draw breath. Hanging in his grasp, Meg was afraid, outraged and shockingly aroused. Somehow she got her hands up, clenched her fingers into the cloth and buttons of his uniform jacket and clung on while he ravaged her mouth. He wanted no tender give and take, that was the only thing that was clear to her reeling brain as he freed her arms, clasped her buttocks and lifted her against the rock-hard ridge that was so exciting her.

Yes, yes, yes, the words chanted in her head as the taste and smell and heat of him overwhelmed every other sensation, every coherent thought.

There were coloured lights against the darkness of her closed lids, a strange buzzing in her ears. Air. She needed air or she would faint. Meg pulled back her head just enough to breathe and with the air came reality.

This could only lead to one thing. The clamouring voices in her blood still shrieked *yes,* but she fought them, got her mouth free, dragged down more air and managed to say, 'No.' It was a whisper, hardly audible above the thud of her pulse. How could she trust her instincts after last time, after James? How could she risk entangling her life with another man when her future was so precarious?

Ross did not seem to hear her, but buried his face in the curve of her neck, his big hands sliding round to cup the weight of her breasts. The touch felt like naked skin on skin. 'No,' Meg said again, on a sob, and hit him, hard, on the ear.

Any other man would have reeled. Ross merely lifted his head and looked down at her. 'No?' He must have seen the conviction in her face, for he opened his hands and stepped back. 'Meg, I am not playing with you. Won't you be my mistress?'

'*No!* Of course not. What are you thinking of? What am *I* thinking of?' she added distractedly. 'I am not your mistress, I do not want to be your mistress.' Meg hit him on the chest with her clenched fist, a thump for every sentence as though she could make herself believe her own protestations. Ross was silent, accepting her blows without trying to parry them. 'You stalked me from the quayside, caught me in a position where I could not refuse to come with you. You know I need money—'

'No.' He spoke at last, frowning as her final, half-hearted blow faltered and she stood there, one hand on his chest, her breath coming in sobs. 'It was not like that. I realised, suddenly, that I could offer you a position, one where you would be safe.'

'Hah!' Meg snatched back her hand. 'Safe?' She was not safe from her own desires, let alone Ross's.

'It wasn't until just now, when I realised just how bad this felt… Oh, Meg. I don't want this title, I don't want this life. I don't want to be here. You are the only thing I know

I do want, just at this moment. The only point of reference I've got.'

'Then why are you here?' she demanded. 'Why come back if it makes you feel like this?'

There was a long silence while Ross seemed to be asking himself the same question. 'Duty,' he said at length. 'Duty. There have been Brandons at the Court for three hundred years. The land is mine and my responsibility. The people are my responsibility. The damned title is my responsibility. My brother's dead; I cannot even tell myself I can leave it to the better man any longer.'

The bitterness shook her out of her own anger and confusion. *The better man.* Had he really thought that about his own brother? 'And you reach for me like another man might have reached for the brandy bottle or the laudanum,' she said, thinking aloud.

'No, I am not seeking oblivion.' Ross's dark eyes rested on her face. 'I want you, not a drug. Did I hurt you, Meg?' He reached out and ran his right forefinger with surprising gentleness across her swollen mouth.

'No,' she lied. 'I was kissing you back.' She moved away, went to sit at the table near the window. It was easier to manage when she was beyond the possibility of touching him, beyond the temptation of these new feelings surging through her. Why had she never felt like this with James, even though she had believed herself in love at first?

This was wanton, however, utterly wanton, and she would not put herself back in a man's power again. She needed to be free, her own mistress, not his. She needed to be independent, to find her sisters, to start again. She needed to fight this romantic yearning to trust him and surrender to him or she would be as much at a man's mercy as she had been with James. 'I must go back to the agency.

Do you think your lawyer would write me a reference? I realised when I got there that I do not have any.'

'No, because I will not ask him.' Ross came and sat opposite her. 'You will not be my mistress, Meg? You kissed me back just now, you admit it. You do not seem repelled by me as I thought you must be.'

'Repelled?' She stared at the harsh face. 'Never that—I hope I have more sense than to be blinded by superficial beauty. You know I have responded to you as I should not have done.' His mouth twisted in something that might have been a sardonic smile. 'But, no, I will not be your mistress.'

'Then be my housekeeper. You may change your mind.' Meg opened her mouth in denial, but he overrode her. 'I will not touch you unless you ask me to.'

Meg felt her face flame. He knew she was attracted to him, she had just admitted it, but even if she had not, he must have realised. But he could not have realised how new and frightening the overwhelming reaction to his caresses was. Surely it was wrong to feel like this without love? It was certainly dangerous, for the only thing it could lead to was a broken heart and along the way she would have been distracted from her quest, weakened in her need to be self-sufficient and independent. She no longer felt strong enough to risk everything for love, not when it was hopeless.

Meg fell back on common sense. 'You already have a housekeeper at your home, surely.'

'The Court is not my home, it is the place where I must live,' he said bleakly. 'And the housekeeper in residence will leave, today, with a good pension. With you, or without you, I won't have that sour-faced harridan in the house. My mother was intimidated by her, I imagine my father hardly cared, provided the place was run efficiently, but I'll not have her brooding like a black spider below stairs.'

'And your father's valet?'

Meg kept talking, anything rather than face the dilemma before her. Could she live in the same house, even for a few weeks, knowing what it was to be in Ross's arms? She would feel that hard, angry mouth on hers every time she looked at him. But if it were a means to an end, if it would give her the financial security to search for her sisters, then perhaps it would be worth the longing and the struggle to keep her feelings to herself.

'He is an elderly man. I will pension him off too. If he wants one of the estate cottages, then he's welcome to one.'

'I cannot stay for long, you know that. I must find Bella and Lina.' She picked up her reticule. 'I should go back to the agency, explain that we decided mutually that I would not suit.'

'I can give you a secure place and a salary that would allow you to employ a Bow Street Runner to send after your sisters.' Ross propped one foot on the fender of the empty grate and laid his arm along the mantelshelf, not looking at her. 'He could start at once, travel faster than a lone woman, follow them if they have moved away. You are out of touch with England. You need help to search.'

Meg put down her reticule again and stared at his bleak profile. Bella, Lina… And she could send a man at once, if Ross would advance her salary. When the Runner found them she could go to them just as soon as she had paid Ross back, or they could come to her. But it would mean staying with Ross, close to all that temptation and attraction, even if it was only for a month or two.

'Thirty pounds, all found,' Ross said, still without looking at her.

It was an excellent wage for a housekeeper, and they

both knew it. With that wage she could easily afford to send a superior investigator to track down her sisters, one she could rely upon to search diligently and to preserve confidentiality. Ross had chosen a figure that would tempt her, not named the going rate for the position. But she would work for the money, earn it. It was not like taking a gift.

'I accept the position. As your housekeeper, nothing else. And only for as long as it takes to find them.' Then a thought struck her. 'Can you afford it?'

Ross did look at her then, his face showing a hauteur that convinced her that he was, indeed, a baron. 'Yes,' he said baldly.

'Pensions for two long-serving, senior members of staff. An overpaid housekeeper, a new valet. Your wardrobe to replenish…'

'I shall expect you to economise: tallow candles, pease pudding on a regular basis, darn the sheets, set the gardener to dig up the rose beds for vegetables.'

'Very well.' How serious he was she could not tell. But economy was something she knew about, she had had enough practice. At the vicarage waste and excess were mortal sins. And when she was married she found that James had not calculated the cost of keeping a wife on a lieutenant's pay. It did not occur to him to give up his old bachelor lifestyle of gambling, drinking and keeping a string of horses. Nothing could be cut, James insisted—he was sure his clever Meg would contrive. And contrive she had.

'How large is the Court?' She tried to think ahead.

'The old house is very small—' Ross broke off as the waiter came in with food, Perrott on his heels.

Well, that was a relief. Meg moved away from the table to let the man set out dishes while Ross took the valet aside, presumably to agree terms. It was foolish of her to have imagined that just because there was a title the family must own some vast mansion. He was not an earl or a marquis. A small house might even explain Ross's decision to run away from home—living at close quarters with a father he was at odds with would be intolerable for any spirited seventeen-year-old lad.

'We will eat and then leave immediately. I have hired a chaise; we can get the luggage on behind.'

'My lord…' Perrott waited until Meg and Ross had both sat down before taking his own seat. 'Might we not stop at the linen drapers on our way through the town? I think—'

'No.' The young valet shut his mouth with a snap. Ross waved a hand at the platters. 'Eat. You are not dragging me round shops, Perrott. You and Mrs Halgate can make lists to your hearts' content, but not if it requires my active participation.'

Effectively snubbed, Perrott retreated into the silent consumption of a large lunch. Meg pecked at her food, her pulse still uneven, her thoughts tumbling. Could that big, abrupt man who was silently demolishing a chicken-and-ham pie with the air of someone half-starved for a week be the same person who had just kissed her with near-violent desperation? And was he the same man who had inflicted such inventive and whimsically shocking punishment on the two men who had tried to assault her?

And why, when she should be fleeing from him, had she accepted a temporary position as his housekeeper when she knew he was simply waiting for her to weaken and come to his bed?

For the money and the chance to rebuild her family it promised, of course. But also, she feared, because she wanted him more than prudence or sense. Wanted him although he had spoken no words of love—words she knew would be lies. Meg made herself eat some ham and told herself it was the money and she was a romantic girl no longer.

'If you have finished shredding that unfortunate slice of ham, Mrs Halgate, we can be on our way.'

'My lord.' Meg put down her cutlery and made herself smile. Had the wretched man *no* sensibility at all? He must realise how she felt after what had happened between them in this parlour, surely? Then she saw his eyes and realised that he was focused on something long ago. His haste to get to the Court was like the urgency of some men to get into battle when at least the waiting would be over and they could finally face their nightmares. Even when they knew the nightmares would come true.

'Let us go and supervise the luggage being loaded, Per...Mr Perrott.' She must remember that they were both upper servants now and he was entitled to his title from her. How many other indoor servants would there be? A cook, a housemaid, a scullery maid and a footman or two, she supposed. A butler of course. Not so very bad, provided the cook and the butler were congenial, for they would be her equals in this strange new world.

The journey was pleasant, the scenery, after Spain and the Pyrenees, lush, green and achingly English. The hedges were filled with flowers, the fields with fat cattle. After a few miles they crossed the River Fal by ferry. The horses were apparently used to this alarming experience and walked steadily on to the low deck for the crossing, and Meg was fascinated by the steep wooded banks tumbling down to the wide river, the mysterious way it wound its course out of sight. Then there was rolling country, small fields, high hedge banks and occasional glimpses of sea. The names seemed alien, as though they were in another country. But it was beautiful, even through the eyes of someone fighting against nerves.

Bella would be perfect as a housekeeper—practical, calm and with a natural authority that overcame every kitchen squabble or difficult tradesman. But Meg had learned her own housekeeping in circumstances far distant from an English country house. Her expertise was limited to life in a tent, an abandoned building or the occasional luxury of a billet in whichever town they found themselves in. She would just have to pretend she was Arabella and bluff it out for as long as she was there. It would not be long enough to do any damage, she reflected. Or at least, not damage to Ross's household. She was not so certain about the price it would exact from her.

Lord Brandon, as she must be certain to think of him, for she could not risk the slightest slip before the other staff, had seated her beside him, facing forwards. She could not see his face without turning to stare, but as the pair slowed she felt the tension coming off his still frame like heat from a fire.

'This is beautiful country,' she ventured.

Ross turned his head to look at her as though surprised to find she was there. 'Yes. It is beautiful. After Spain I had forgotten how green Cornwall is.'

The chaise swung round a corner between two lodge houses and she glimpsed a man tugging his forelock as he held the gate. Then they were trotting briskly through parkland.

A park? Meg glanced at Ross's face. It was set, dark and utterly forbidding. The carriage turned again, slowed, stopped. Stopped in front of a long façade of textured grey stone, punctuated by three storeys of windows and a balustrade shielding a basement area. Stopped before a sweeping flight of steps up to a vast front door flanked by potted bay trees. Stopped in front of an imposing house that could not be called *small* by even the grandest aristocrat.

It was, without a shadow of exaggeration, a mansion. 'You said it was small,' Meg blurted out, saw Perrott's expression and added, 'My lord.'

'I said the old house—which is a wing at the back—is small,' Ross said as a footman flung open the door and let down the steps. 'We were interrupted before I could finish, if you recall.'

'Sir...' the footman began. Meg saw his face as he looked fully at Ross. *He must resemble his father,* she thought as the man's expression changed. 'My lord!' He turned and gestured urgently to the second man who had followed him across the wide sweep of carriage drive. 'His lordship is here!' The other man turned on his heel and ran back to the house.

'My lord, we had no idea when to expect you, but your rooms are prepared.' Ross got down and stood looking round him as Meg and Perrott followed. For a moment he thought he saw rapid movement, the coltish grace of a fair young man running to greet him, then the ghost was gone. Giles was gone.

Act, he told himself. He had shown a calm face before battle, even when his stomach was turning to water and his legs wanted to turn right round and run away. If you were not afraid, you were a fool. The knack was never to let anyone know and never to give way to the urge to do anything but your duty. And this, beyond argument, was his duty.

Behind him he could almost feel Meg's seething indignation at the way he had deceived her, but she was keeping silent, thank God. As Ross took the first stride towards the steps the double doors were flung open and servants began to troop out, women to the left, men to the right, one on each tread, lining the route he must take. At the top stood Mrs Fogarty, opposite her Heneage, the butler.

Ross stopped at the foot of the steps, freezing the lowermost maids in the act of curtsying. 'Heneage, take the staff back inside. I will speak to them later. Mrs Fogarty, a word with you in the study at once, if you please.'

'My lord.' The butler bowed, collected the attention of his puzzled subordinates with a glance and stepped inside with the procession of black skirts and dark blue livery at his heels. Heneage was as impassive as he remembered, Ross thought as he walked through the Great Hall without a glance to left or right and into his father's study.

The housekeeper was waiting for him, hands folded, lips tight, her heavy bunch of keys by her side. As Ross entered she looked up, pointedly, to the portrait that hung over the fireplace. His father. It was like looking into a mirror. He repressed the shudder, kept his face neutral.

'Mrs Fogarty. I will not beat about the bush. You have, I believe, connections in Truro?'

'My sister, Master Ross.'

So, she was not going to allow him his title. It broke no bones. 'It will be no surprise to you that I have made my own arrangements for the post of housekeeper. I will write to my bankers in Truro to pay the first instalment of a pension to you immediately. It will be commensurate with the length of service you have given this family and will reflect the lack of notice.' He handed her the packet he had put together at the Red Lion. 'This contains the address of my bankers, a letter of introduction and twenty pounds to cover your expenses until the pension is paid.'

Ross paused, waiting for some response, but she maintained her silence, her face disdainful. 'The chaise will remain to take you on to Truro. I expect you to return the keys to me and to depart within the hour.'

'You do not want me to hand them to your mistress, then?' The housekeeper's lip curled.

'If you cannot keep a civil tongue in your head, you will wait in the chaise and I will have your things packed and brought out to you,' he retorted.

'I anticipated this.' She swept to the door in a rustle of bombazine and flung it open. Heneage was standing outside with Meg and Perrott. 'My bags are packed,' Mrs Fogarty said, her bitter voice clear and carrying. 'You think I would stay under the same roof as a man who murdered his own brother? A pity the French did not do for you—the wrong man died and that's a fact.'

She passed the group outside without a glance. Ross followed her out into the hall. Was he as white as he felt? he wondered. 'Heneage, would you be so good as to fetch Usborne?'

The butler was so impassive, and it was so many years since he had last seen him, that Ross could not decide whether he was outraged by the housekeeper's parting shot or entirely in agreement with it.

'Mr Usborne had a heart stroke three weeks ago, my lord. He is living with his sister-in-law in Falmouth. Mr Tonge, the solicitor, thought you would wish his medical expenses to be taken care of.'

'Certainly. I am sorry to hear he is unwell. I will speak to Mr Tonge about his pension. Perrott, here, is my valet; show him to my rooms and have the luggage sent up, if you please.'

With a sidelong glance at Meg, the butler nodded to Perrott. 'This way, Mr Perrott.'

'And, Heneage, see the staff are assembled in the hall in an hour—I wish to introduce them to Mrs Halgate, the new housekeeper.' Ross waited until the two men had vanished through the green baize door under the stairs. 'Mrs Halgate, the study.'

As he expected, Meg went straight to the point the moment the door was closed. 'That woman accused you of murdering your brother.' Her shock was clear, and so was a trace of fear she could not suppress.

Ross looked at the desk with its tooled leather top, worn where his father's and grandfather's hands had rested, the carved chair, designed for a family of big men, the reading lamp and the standish with its rack of pens. How many times had he stood on the wrong side of that desk, hating the man in the chair? Deliberately he walked round, sat down and folded his hands on the leather. It was smooth against his skin. Suddenly he wished he could still speak to his father, man to man, try to understand him, try to make him understand the man his rebellious son had grown into.

'Will you not sit down, Meg?' He was going to have to speak of Giles, to explain. Lay bare the raw guilt that haunted him, haunted this house.

'No. Thank you.' She paced away from him, then back. There was anxiety in her eyes; he could almost feel her efforts not to judge, to hear his side of the story. Most people, looking at him, would not have hesitated to believe the worst. 'What did she mean?'

'That I am responsible for my brother's death. I shot him.'

He waited, braced for the revulsion to show in her voice, on her face, but she just stared at him, distressed and questioning.

'But he died six or so years after you joined the army, you said. Surely you were in the Peninsula then?'

'I shot him when we were boys. The bullet entered Giles's chest and could not be removed. It left him weak, prone to every disease and infection that were around. Eventually it killed him.'

'Oh. Oh, no.' Meg did sit down then, looking at him with painful earnestness. Her hands were shaking and she clasped them tightly together. 'Did you mean to shoot him?'

Chapter Eight

'Did I intend to shoot my brother? No,' Ross said. 'It was my own damn carelessness, my lack of responsibility for him, but it was an accident. It was hushed up—two boys hunting, one of those things.'

'How did it happen?'

'All I wanted to do was to join the army, to shoot. I was good at one thing only, but in my father's eye the ability to shoot well was simply one of the attributes of a gentleman, not a way of earning your living. I told you I had two fine tutors: the head keeper and a wicked old poacher. By the age of fourteen I could hit anything, still or moving. Giles was the model son, the obedient, intelligent, hard-working, sweet-tempered son. Unfortunately I was the elder, the heir. Obedience could not be beaten into me, although God knows, my father and tutors tried, but my father could, and did, refuse to let me join the army when I was seventeen as I wanted.

'All he wanted, of course, was Giles to be the heir.'

'But you loved your brother,' Meg said. 'I can hear it

when you say his name. You weren't jealous or resentful of him, were you?'

'No. You could only love Giles.' He made himself look then, look up to where he knew it would be, hanging opposite his father's desk. He had loved his brother and he hadn't even been able to take care of him when he was doing the one thing he was good at. 'See for yourself.'

Meg went to stand in front of the portrait, hands behind her back, like a child in a picture gallery. Ross found himself looking at her, not at his brother's face, watching the graceful line of neck and shoulder, the weight of hair at her nape, the inquisitive tilt of her head.

'What an extraordinarily good-looking young man,' she said at last. 'He has kind eyes. And, of course, people are inclined to equate beauty with goodness.'

'Oh, yes,' Ross agreed without resentment, looking up at last. His mother's pointed chin and high cheek-bones, her green eyes and sensitive mouth allied to his father's height and jet black hair had resulted in a youth who looked, so the impressionable ladies of the district used to say, like a prince from a fairy tale. And the delicacy of his health left him pale, slender, even more beautiful. 'He had our mother's looks. I, as you can see, have my father's. Just for once, the looks did not lie. He was everything he seems to be.' *And I killed him because I was headstrong and heedless and always had to score a point against authority. Because I would not do my duty. Because I did not love him enough to deny him.*

Meg turned and studied Lord Brandon's image. 'Black eyes, slanted brows, a stubborn jaw and a mouth that does not know how to say "I Yield",' she observed. 'You must have made a handsome pair, you and your brother.'

'Raven and dove.' The comparison had been made often enough. *Devil and angel.*

'What happened?'

'I was almost seventeen, Giles was two years younger. One day when I cut lessons with our tutor to go rook shooting he followed me, wanted to come too, hung on my sleeve, teased me to let him come. For an adventure. I said yes, just that once. I was the elder, I should have been responsible. I should have said no, looked after him.' But of course, the opportunity to kick over the traces, to be defiant, was far more alluring than any thought of what his duty to his young brother might be.

'I was used to stalking, used to the woods. He was not. I had my gun raised, my finger on the trigger and he tripped on some brambles, crashed into me. The gun got jammed between us and went off.'

'You must have been terrified.' Meg watched him with those wide, candid blue-grey eyes that seemed to see so deep inside him. 'But you got him back, of course. And he would tell everyone it was an accident.'

'Of course.' A good officer gets his men back. But he doesn't shoot them himself in the first place. *All that blood. And Giles, white and terrified and hurting, saying over and over,* accident, accident. *Blood trickling from the corner of his mouth, the panic. What should I do? Move him? Leave him?*

'Never, since that day, have I felt so helpless, so useless. I got Giles back somehow, carried him for half a mile in my arms, knowing I was hurting him, seeing the bleeding I could not stop, hearing the breath sobbing in his lungs. But Giles never protested, never cried out, because he trusted me.' And that was perhaps the worst pain of all.

'So you ran away to join the army.' He could not tell whether there was condemnation or understanding in Meg's voice, only that she was struggling to keep it steady.

'I left as soon as I knew he was not going to die. It was

only later, from my godfather's letters, that I realised how sick it had left him. And then it did kill him. I killed him.'

'No!' she protested. 'No, it was an accident. How could you blame yourself?' He just looked at her and saw the understanding dawn. 'You felt the responsibility, that you had failed him. Yes, I can see if I had hurt Lina so badly accidentally I would feel that too, however irrational it was.' She hesitated. 'The accident did not put you off shooting?'

'No.' Meg's lack of condemnation, her understanding, shook him. She seemed to think he was not to blame. That was comforting—if he allowed himself to believe it. 'I think now, looking back, that I wanted to do something useful with the skill. I had shot my brother—I could kill my country's enemies.' As many as possible, as coldly and as efficiently as possible. Even if it made him a machine for killing he had to make that mistake right somehow. 'And I had failed in my duty to him—that made me want to be a better officer.'

'And now it is time to stop killing and to begin growing things,' Meg said so softly he was not sure he had heard her correctly. 'Thank you for telling me.'

Ross found himself surprised, almost shocked. He had expected revulsion, horror, condemnation, and instead he had received understanding and thoughtful sympathy. Something hot burned shamefully at the back of his eyes and he made an abrupt gesture, rejecting her kindness. Meg did not really understand, that was all. It was impossible that she could see into his motives and his conscience and absolve him.

She looked, for a moment, as though she would speak, then her lips tightened, perhaps in response to his rejection. 'And now, kindly explain why you let me think this place was no larger than a country squire's house?'

'Because you would never have come otherwise.'

'And just how many servants are there? How many rooms?' The questions were obviously rhetorical, for she swept on, 'And how on earth do you expect me to manage it all, even for a few weeks?'

He was saved from answering as the door opened without warning. Mrs Fogarty stalked in, tossed the bunch of keys on to the desk and smiled pure acid at Meg. Ross admired the way Meg's chin came up. Yes, she was a lady to her fingertips.

'You be careful, young woman. This one's his father's son, whatever else he is. The temper of the devil and his pride too. And no woman's safe either, not with the Brandon men. A good thing this one ran away before any babes got laid at his door, which doesn't mean there weren't any to lay. You think you're the one and only? They all think that.'

Ross got to his feet. 'Get out.' He found he was so angry he could hardly speak. She thought that after his father's whoring he would treat women the same way?

The door shut behind the housekeeper. He stormed out from behind the desk, too angry to sit still, and was brought up short by Meg's expression as he passed. He stopped, bent over her chair, one hand on each of the arms pinning her in place, and stared into her face, searching for the disgust and the condemnation that she must surely be hiding.

'Don't go looking askance at every twelve-year-old brat around here,' he said. 'They won't be mine and my father did his whoring in Truro.'

'How awful for your mother,' Meg said. She looked back at him steadily, nothing but compassion in her eyes. 'And not pleasant for you and your brother, either. I cannot imagine what it must be like... That is one good thing about having a father who is a vicar, and a puritanical one at that.'

Ross straightened up and limped over to stare out of the window. The rose garden had been neglected, he noticed with the part of his mind that was not fighting bad memories. His mother would have been upset about that. What the devil were the gardeners about?

'He had enough sense of decency not to foul his own doorstep, except once with the daughter of Billy Gillan, the poacher who taught me how to shoot. How does a girl like that say no, when the family is in a tied cottage? He could pretend it wasn't rape, of course. When he left her with child Billy marched up to the front door to tell my father what he thought of him, so the family got thrown out of their cottage with its scrap of land anyway. Billy's poaching was all that fed them. I tried to pay him for shooting lessons, but he wouldn't take it, so I gave the money to Lily direct; at least it helped her bring up my baby half-brother.'

'Where did you get it from?'

'I stole it from my father, of course. I never took so much at any one time that he'd notice. He'd come home, his pockets full of winnings from the card tables and stuff it into this big lacquer box without counting it. It is the only useful skill I seem to have inherited, the ability to play to win. The money was a bagatelle to him, life and death to Lily and her family.' Ross felt all over again the hot pleasure that had coursed through him when he succeeded in picking the lock on his father's strong-box for the first time, the pleasure of sliding out the shiny coins. It was as good as sex.

'And Billy taught me about girls too. Told me never to take anyone who wasn't willing and how to make sure I didn't leave any mongrel pups behind. A bit agricultural in his metaphors, is old Billy, but a good teacher for all that.'

'He is still alive then?'

The thought had never occurred to him that Billy could be dead. 'Must be. He's the indestructible sort,' Ross said with a confidence he did not feel. A cold trickle of fear ran down his spine. How old had Billy been when he left? He'd go down tonight once he had introduced Meg to the staff and done all the things the returning fourth Baron Brandon was supposed to do on the day he came home.

The clock struck. 'Time to review the troops,' Meg said, as she got to her feet, a little pale around the mouth. *Nerves, or the realisation of just whom she was working for?*

'Here.' Ross handed her the housekeeper's keys on their chain and she took them gingerly. 'Your badge of office,' he said and something changed in her expression. Her lips firmed, the lashes came down over those clear eyes, but she only nodded.

Mr Heneage had arrayed the staff in the Great Hall as he had on the steps, women to one side, men to the other, in ascending order of priority. Meg saw Perrott standing beside the butler: valets, like ladies' maids, took the status of their employer in the servants' hall. He looked as pale as she felt. Ross walked to the foot of the stairs, drawing her with him by a touch on the arm.

'Good afternoon.' He stood on the first step, towering over her. 'Some of you will remember me, others will be new since I left. You will find that I do things differently from my father, but I am sure you will adapt.' From their faces they had no trouble interpreting that: *Accept my ways, or you may leave.*

'There are some immediate changes,' Ross continued.

'Usborne, as you know, is unwell and is retiring. Perrott is my valet. And Mrs Fogarty has also retired. Mrs Halgate is our housekeeper from today and I expect her to receive your unwavering support in managing the Court. Mrs Halgate is used to managing Portuguese households,' he added smoothly. 'There will doubtless be some differences. Heneage, will you introduce the staff?'

Meg fixed a tight smile on her lips and fell into place one careful step behind Ross.

Portuguese households, indeed! Army tents, rather. Wretched man. He has got a sense of humour, I do not care how well he tries to hide it, and a wicked one it is too.

Here, for one hideous moment in the study she had thought Ross was confessing to murder. She had been prepared to believe that of him. Guilt lashed through her; she should have known better. He was brave and stoical and kind, under his scowl, and he did not deserve her mistrust. Meg could only hope and pray she had kept her feelings from showing; he needed to heal, to forgive himself, not deal with even more condemnation.

All she could do for the moment was to carry out her new duties as best she could and make his home comfortable for him. The keys swung heavy from her belt as she walked up the line of maids, trying to fix names in her head, but all she could manage was to hope the face and the position were clear. Three scullery maids, two kitchen maids, two laundry maids, the laundress, the four downstairs maids, the four upstairs maids and Mrs Harris, the cook. Then over to the men. Boot boy, page, three underfootmen, three footmen, Perrott and Heneage. And all the outdoor staff still to come.

She and Mrs Harris, Heneage and Perrott comprised the upper servants and she could not hope to manage this large house without their willing co-operation. Meg smiled at the cook and received a guarded smile in return.

'Where is my estate manager?' she heard Ross ask the butler who murmured a response. 'At the Home Farm? Then send someone out for him; I want to speak with him as soon as possible. That will be all. Carry on Heneage, Mrs Halgate.'

Carry on, Sergeant-Major, Meg thought with a twitch of her lips. Time to exert some authority. 'I shall need a maid.' She studied the array of eight young women.

'I was Mrs Fogarty's maid, Mrs Halgate.' The girl was thin, anxious, with a sharp nose and pale, darting eyes. 'I did my best, ma'am.'

'I am sure you did.' Meg dredged into her memory and came up with a name. 'And I am sure you deserve a change from those duties, Annie.' The girl smiled, obviously relieved. Mrs Fogarty could not have been an easy mistress.

'Now, Damaris. I am sure you would do admirably.' The quiet redhead who had been trying to fade into invisibility behind a plump neighbour jumped. 'Will you show me to my rooms, Damaris? And the rest of you, carry on as usual. Come to me if you are uncertain about anything.' *Please don't!*

Her one shabby bag was standing outside the door when the maid led her downstairs. 'All the rest got lost in France,' Meg explained, glossing over battles and baggage trains. 'I must go shopping as soon as possible.'

It felt strange stepping into another woman's rooms, especially one that she so disliked. The housekeeper had a good-sized parlour, easily capable of entertaining the other upper servants in, and a smaller bedroom, both with windows overlooking a paved yard with a herb garden at its centre. It was all very comfortable, somewhat dark and almost entirely lacking in personality. Meg supposed Mrs

Fogarty had removed every item that gave the space any individuality.

'We can unpack later,' she decided. 'First, I want you to show me round before dinner. I need to learn my way about this house.'

In the event they got no further than a tour of below-stairs, ending up in the kitchen where Mrs Harris produced tea and a running stream of one-sided conversation while presiding over preparations for dinner.

'The spitting image of his father, God rest his soul,' Cook pronounced.

'That isn't likely to be *God's* concern, the old so-and-so will have headed in the other direction.' The gardener grinned at his own parting shot as he left a trug full of vegetables on the kitchen table.

'And how did he come to employ you, Mrs Halgate?' Cook asked. 'He's not been back in England any time to advertise, that's for certain sure.'

'Mr Empson's agency. He came in to find a housekeeper and heard me explaining my Portuguese experience. After his long service in the Peninsula I suppose he thought I might suit.' Best not to explain that it was temporary as well, she decided.

'Portugal! Now there's a thing,' Cook marvelled. 'Was it very different to here?'

'You could not possibly imagine,' Meg said with some feeling.

One of the underfootmen appeared: George, Peter or John—she had still not fixed all their names in her mind. 'His lordship's compliments, Mrs Halgate, and he says that he understands from the agency that you read aloud very well.'

'Er...yes?'

'And would you join him in the library after dinner and read to him.'

'Please tell his lordship that I would be glad to.'

Meg waited until the footman had removed himself. She felt instinctively that it was important to get the female staff on her side, and to prevent the slightest suspicion of any impropriety. 'My goodness! I told Mr Empson about reading aloud in case he could find me a place with an invalid, I never dreamed his lordship would require me to read to him. I do not like to refuse, although it seems a trifle unconventional.'

'You keep the library door open, Mrs Halgate,' said Cook with a knowing look. 'You won't come to any harm with the door open.'

'That is very sound advice, Mrs Harris,' Meg agreed fervently. It would protect her as much from herself as from Ross, she rather feared.

With no guests and no lady of the house the maidservants, and Meg, had a relatively easy time of it after dinner. There was his lordship's bed for one of the upstairs maids to turn down, curtains to be drawn, hot water to be taken up later, but that was all. Meg apologised to Mrs Harris and Heneage that she could not entertain them to tea in her parlour and went up to the library.

The heavy oak door was shut. Meg stood regarding the panels, one hand raised to knock. *Think like a servant. That's what you are now. An upper servant. His servant from the moment you took those keys. No more confidences, no more intimacies. He is your master now.* She shivered, despite the warmth of the spring evening air, and knocked.

'Come!'

'Good evening, my lord.' Meg bobbed a curtsy and

came into the library, leaving the door wide open behind her. It was a dark, oppressive room with bookshelves that ran from floor to ceiling, lined with leather-bound volumes. A big globe stood in the window bay and deep leather chairs with small tables at their side were set about the space. The pictures all seemed to be etchings of classical sites and the thick carpet smothered the sound of her footsteps.

Despite the temperature of the air and the richness of the materials it felt emotionally cool. The whole house did, she realised. Or all the rooms she had seen so far above stairs. Cool, clean, orderly, sterile.

'Good evening.' Ross laid down the book in his hand and frowned at her. 'Close the door and come and sit down, Meg.' She shook her head at him as one of the footmen went past in the hall. 'Mrs Halgate, then.'

'I think it best if I leave the door, my lord.' Meg sat down in the chair opposite his. 'You asked me to read aloud, I believe.'

'Yes.' The frown deepened at her defiance, but he passed her a familiar book. '*Gulliver's Travels.* I have reached chapter two,' he added with a pointed look at the open door, 'if you will continue from there.'

Meg took it, avoiding touching his hand as she did so. 'Certainly. But before I do, there are some things I must ask.' She tried to frame all the questions that were tumbling through her head in a way that was concise and would not irritate him with detail.

'I need to know whether you want everything left exactly as it is or whether I may move things around, make changes. I need to know if there are any changes you wish to have made—any redecoration, for example. I am not certain what I can achieve in a few weeks, but I will do my best.'

'A few weeks?' He regarded her quizzically and she stared back, defiant. 'No. Nothing.' He looked around, apparently indifferent to his environment. 'Do what you like, spend what you like.'

'You told me to economise,' she pointed out, her heart sinking at the apathy that had come back into his tone. He did not care. Or perhaps he cared too much and was erecting barriers against memory and familiarity in this house that had once been such an unhappy home.

'I was being sarcastic. Check with me before you actually demolish and rebuild anything, otherwise I really have no interest.'

'Very well.' Somehow she must make him take an interest, make him care, or one day there would be nothing of the man left, just a cold, dead shell, quite safe from pain and pleasure alike. Meg opened the book and found her place. 'Chapter two,' she began.

Chapter Nine

It was eleven o'clock before Meg retired to bed. She had read two chapters to Ross, then removed herself, conscious of his heavy-lidded gaze on her as she went through the door. Neither of them had forgotten that kiss, it seemed, nor his promise to wait until she came to him as his mistress. Those memories seemed to be in the room with them like a third person. She could not delude herself he had not meant the words.

Mrs Harris was in the kitchen, pouring tea for Perrott and for Heneage who was comfortable at the table in a loose frock coat over his striped waistcoat and knee breeches. Meg accepted a cup gratefully. The warm, fragrant kitchen shared with the two middle-aged people at their ease and the amiable young valet felt like coming out of an emotional storm into tranquillity.

Damaris had changed the bed linen and brought her hot water and she had asked for her morning tea at six. But despite the luxury of a bedroom that did not rock under her feet and that had room to move about and the promise of a bed that was all hers to rest in, Meg found that she was not sleepy. Tired, most certainly, but her mind was running in circles like a dog in a spit-wheel.

She put the bunch of keys on the dresser, opened the window a little and sat by it with a notebook and a candle. Perhaps making lists would help her stop thinking about Ross as a man and not as her employer.

Clothes. Urgent! Falmouth shops, she wrote at the top. Or perhaps Penryn, which had seemed to have shops suitable for ladies rather than the needs of sailors. She must ask Ross for an advance on her salary if she was to wear something other than a sun-faded cotton gown. She would also ask him for the direction of his solicitor who would probably be the best person to ask about an enquiry agent. *Solicitor,* she added. Then she must hurry back to the house and explore from top to bottom and get to know the staff and the routine. *House.* Then there was the question of housekeeping. *Mon—*

Outside something moved across the courtyard entrance where it opened out into the gardens. She had the impression of a big man, moving in the moonlight without lantern or candle. Ross?

Meg sat for a moment after he vanished, wondering why she felt so uneasy. Why should he not walk around at night? They were his grounds, after all. She had not explored yet, but she realised they were virtually on the coast and that this side of the house must look out towards the sea.

She could not settle to her orderly list-making again. Meg got up, threw her shawl around her shoulders, took the key for the back door off her ring and went out into the darkened passage. At least being on the ground floor meant it did not take her long to get outside. She locked the door behind herself and ran across the courtyard, her skirts brushing the herbs in the central bed and sending a cloud of fragrance into the still air.

She found herself at the side of the house on a sweep of terrace that gave directly on to a sloping lawn. And, yes, now she was in the open, there was the sound of the sea and a breeze bringing the smell of it. In the distance the lights of a fishing village twinkled.

The tall figure in its fawn-coloured greatcoat was still in sight, limping. Yes, it was Ross. Was he all right? The pain and guilt in his voice when he had told her about his brother came back to her. Should he be alone? As she watched, he crouched down and vanished, all but his head, and she realised there was a ha-ha separating lawn and fields, an invisible wall to keep the cattle in their place.

Meg picked up her skirts and ran, her light shoes making no sound on the scythed grass, the moonlight showing her the dark line that marked the drop. It was easy enough to scramble down, provided she had no care for her old gown or the nettles at the bottom of the wall. Sucking her stinging hand, Meg walked on more cautiously now. The grass was rougher and the evidence that the cattle had been there was difficult to make out until one almost trod in it.

Ahead was the edge of a wood, a rarity on this wind-swept peninsula. In the moonlight the trees looked strange and gaunt, shaped by the wind and twisted by winter gales. Ross entered it and disappeared into the darkness. When Meg reached the place she found a narrow path descending quite steeply into a gully. Telling herself that English woodlands held none of the terrors of Spanish ones—wolves, bears and French snipers—Meg hurried on, wondering how far ahead Ross was. He made no noise at all, despite his size and his wounded leg, whereas she was all too aware of twigs snapping under her feet.

The path led her down to a stream, over a plank bridge,

over a fence, up and into a wilder, denser patch of trees. The path became narrow and steeper—any moment now she would be out on to the low cliff top, surely?

Just when Meg decided she must have lost him, that her vague uneasiness was foolish and that any prudent woman would turn round and go back to her bed, she saw a light through the trees and realised there must be a cottage ahead.

Taking great care where she trod, Meg crept forwards and found herself on the edge of a small clearing with a tumbledown dwelling in the centre that resembled nothing so much as some large woodland creature's nest. Its owner was outside, and must have been sitting by the fire that blazed halfway between the cottage and the edge of the wood. But he was on his feet now, turned to face Ross who had stopped, perhaps four feet from him, as though uncertain of his welcome. Meg could see clearly in the firelight that he was a small man, whiplash thin with a brown, wrinkled face and grey hair that straggled from under a battered felt hat.

He must be Ross's poacher, she guessed, as the two stood there, silent.

Then the old man spoke, his accent so broad that Meg had to strain to understand him. 'You've been gone a powerful long time, boy.'

'Aye, Billy. I'm sorry.'

'Don't be. It's made a fine man of you.' And the poacher stepped forwards and pulled Ross's head down to kiss him on both cheeks.

The prodigal son, Meg thought, tears blurring her vision for a moment, then Ross straightened up and she saw his face and realised that he could smile, could be happy, and that there was still one person on this earth that he loved.

That's all right, then. She swallowed hard, then turned to creep away as the baron hunkered down beside the poacher and began to talk. While that old man lived, Ross had someone to live for. But there had to be more to root him here and take the darkness out of his soul.

Ross buried his face in his hands, then raked his fingers through his hair, muttering obscenities in Spanish under his breath. Two solid hours of studying the estate books that had been deposited on his desk by Tremayne, his steward, had done nothing but make his head spin and the man's stolid explanations were not much help.

Livestock prices, feed prices, manuring schedules, stone-walling repairs—it might as well be in Russian. One thing was sure—he was never going to get a grip on this by staring at books.

'There is really no need for you to trouble yourself with it, my lord,' the steward ventured. When Ross began to curse he had wormed his way back into the deep wing chair like a rabbit into its burrow. 'Your man of business audits the books every quarter day and your late father did, if I may be so bold, give me his complete confidence.'

'I am certain you are most capable, Tremayne.' Ross shut the ledger and leaned back. He had ordered the desk moved so he was looking out over the rose garden and set the gardeners to bring it back into order. 'And that my father's confidence in you was well placed. But I have been an officer; I need to know what is going on under my command. Understand it. And I am not going to do that from ledgers. Tomorrow I'll ride out with you and I'll do so every day until I know this estate and its business at least as well as I knew my regiment and our strategy and tactics.'

There was a tap at the door, then a stranger was standing there. Ross stared and discovered it was Meg clad in a dark blue gown of plain cut but with a rich sheen. Her hands, crossed at her waist, were highlighted by crisp white cuffs, a white scarf was pinned precisely around her shoulders and on her head was an endearingly prim white cap. She had asked him for money first thing that morning and permission to take the carriage into Penryn—it seemed she was a rapid and effective shopper.

'My lord. Excuse me for interrupting, but the tea tray has been set out in the Chinese Salon.'

Ross looked at the clock. Three o'clock—he had been in here precisely two hours. His self-appointed nurse obviously thought it time he exercised his leg. 'We have not yet finished our business, Mrs Halgate.'

'I have put out two cups, my lord,' she countered, meeting his glare with an expression of bland incomprehension. She was attempting to manipulate him in some way, he was sure of it.

But Tremayne looked in need of tea, if not something stronger. Ross decided to humour them both, although why she had decided on the Chinese Salon, the most cluttered and uncomfortable room in the entire house, he had no idea. His great-grandfather had secured some lovely Chinese wallpaper and his wife had proceeded to ruin the effect by packing the room with every piece of Oriental ornament she could lay her hands on. He was going to be like a bull in a china shop in there.

Ross flung open the door and stopped dead. The jade-green curtains had been drawn back further than he had ever seen them and the salon was flooded with light. All the bronzes had gone and with them virtually all the tiny tables that had been covered in a jumble of porcelain. The exquisite wallpaper with its flowing patterns of birds and flowers and insects filled the room with colour and beauty and the only ornaments were a collection of white-

and-green jade bowls. From the chimney breast the full-length portrait of his mother surveyed the scene in elegant approval.

'My God,' Ross murmured, walking in. 'What have you done with it all?' He found himself relaxing just standing there.

'It is in the large dining room. I thought I had better see if you approved before I had it packed away. The portrait seemed to fit so well here.' She hesitated, sending him a glance that seemed to assess his temper and the distance to the door. 'But we can put it back on the stairs if you prefer.'

'Leave it. Have all the rest sent up to the attics; there's enough room up there to billet a regiment and I might want to hold a dinner party for fifty next week.' There was that flickering glance again. Meg had not decided whether that was humour, sarcasm or if he truly was threatening to begin large-scale entertaining at the Court.

'I suggest you postpone that until your leg is somewhat more healed, my lord. Standing around being pleasant to so many guests would be quite exhausting,' she said, perfectly straight-faced, and Ross realised that she knew he had been teasing and was answering him in kind. He was not used to being teased by a woman. It was curiously pleasant to feel that other mind touching his, picking up the threads of his thoughts for a second and then passing them back again, twisted into another shape. Giles had done that, he recalled, and he had missed that.

But this was also arousing, he realised, watching Meg as she poured the tea and moved a dish of small cakes into the centre of the tea table with fussy precision. *She is nervous because she wants to please me.* It was somehow rather touching, and he found that he was interested in how her mind worked, why she was acting as she was. It was something he seemed to have lost a long time ago, this caring about someone else's feelings, not just how they performed what he required of them.

'Please ring if you require more hot water, my lord,' she said, and was gone, leaving Ross frowning after her. For some reason he had thought she might stay for tea. But of course, Meg was his housekeeper now. Only his housekeeper.

'Settling in all right, Mrs Halgate?' Perrott looked up from brushing the breeches spread on the flat table and smiled at Meg.

'After three and a half days?' Meg paused in the doorway, shopping list in hand, and thought about it. She supposed that she was already developing a routine. 'Yes, I am, and very comfortably.'

Certainly, from the practical point of view she could hardly hope for more pleasant employment. She breakfasted in her rooms, then walked around the house inspecting the maids' work and issuing orders for the day. Then she would discuss housekeeping matters with Mrs Harris and Heneage and make lists. A housekeeper's life appeared to revolve around lists: things to do, things to buy, things to mend, things to make.

'And you, Mr Perrott?'

The valet grimaced. 'If his lordship would be more predictable, life would be easier. And a smile wouldn't come amiss, not that he isn't pleasant enough. Please, thank you, makes his mind up and sticks to it. But as for persuading him in the direction of a tailor—I despair. And he's hardly the size for ready-made. I've had to get out some of his late lordship's clothes.'

'I appear to have the easier task in making changes,' Meg admitted. The chilly, overstuffed formality of the house did not suit Ross and could hardly help him come to terms with his new life. He had given her *carte blanche* to make changes, and after his positive response to the Chinese salon she was determined to carry on. After luncheon in her room she would direct the maids in attacking whichever room was next on her list: the Chinese Salon the first day, the Great Hall the second. She was wary of making anything too pretty, too feminine. Ross's house needed to be a fit setting for a very masculine man, but she could see no need for it to be depressing.

By dint of borrowing two footmen she had removed the moth-eaten animal heads from the hall walls and had the displays of antique weapons polished until they shone. Some dark tapestries depicting the gloomier episodes in the Old Testament came down and a set of vivid, if rather bloodthirsty, hunting scenes were hung in their place. Bowls of ferns and red roses set the finishing touch and the old oak furniture seemed to glow in response. If Ross noticed, he said nothing, but she would not be downhearted. She was resolved to tackle his study next.

'Will he be entertaining soon, do you know?' Perrott shook out the breeches and folded them over his arm.

'He has said nothing to me.' There had been that remark about dinner parties for fifty, but presumably that was him teasing her.

Some visitors would make more work, but might lift Ross's spirits, she supposed. For herself she was content with her quiet evenings. After dinner in the servants' hall she read *Gulliver's Travels* to Ross for an hour, then took tea in the kitchen before retiring to bed to read to distract herself from her worries about all the things that she did not know she should be doing and the things that she had probably done wrong.

She had found a battered copy of *The New Town and*

Country Housekeepers' Guide on the shelves and was working her way through a daunting agenda of matters that had never occurred to her to think about before, like taking ink stains out of mahogany.

There were moments when she felt something like a stab of fear at how easy it was to slip into the fiction that she really was a housekeeper, that she would be working here, not for weeks, but for years. When she was seeing Ross at a distance it was tempting to simply enjoy being near him, to probe the bittersweet ache of desire as one might a sore tooth. But when she had to act the housekeeper to his face, take his orders, behave as a servant, she could not deceive herself that this was anything but a painful charade. He did not want her as a housekeeper, she did not want him as an employer, in any capacity.

She was here for one thing only, she reminded herself: to earn enough to find Bella and Lina. Ross had promised to do something about an enquiry agent for her, and she tried to be patient about that, so now at night she drew the curtains tight across her window and read until she was too tired to lie drowsily, wishing for a big warm man to take up three-quarters of her chaste bed. If Ross went out at night poaching in his own coverts, she did not know.

On the morning of her fifth day at the Court Meg made a discovery in the shadowy recesses of a long corridor on the second floor. It was the portrait of a young man, a youth, and at first she did not recognise him, for he was smiling, the humour and the life simply shining out of his dark eyes.

Ross? Meg stared at it. 'Damaris, come and help me lift this down and carry it into the light.'

'Lifts your spirits just looking at that smile, doesn't it, Mrs Halgate?' They propped it on a window seat with the sun full on it. 'Who do you think it is?' She flicked her feather duster at the heavy frame.

To Meg the subject was quite plain—it was Ross at perhaps sixteen, long limbed, rangy, his hair over his eyes, his nose and chin too dominant in his young face. *Where has all that joy gone?* she wondered. Had his brother's accident killed every trace of it?

'It is his lordship.' What it would it feel like to have those eyes smiling at her? 'Come along, Damaris, we are going to take this downstairs.'

'Hell's teeth.'

The maids had finished their work in the study and departed, leaving Meg to hang the last of the charming amateur watercolours of the estate that she had found in the attic. At the sound of the voice behind her she jumped, bit her tongue and swung round, aware of a certain degree of apprehension. She was moving into Ross's own rooms now and she was not at all sure how tolerant of interference he would prove to be in practice, whatever he said about change.

It was sunny enough to make energetic polishing warm work and Meg had pushed up the full-length windows on the west side of the study. Ross had entered simply by stepping over the sill from the terrace. He stood there, hands on hips, rifle slung over one shoulder, looking round.

The inner set of curtains had been removed from the windows to let in as much light as possible; the dark etchings had gone, replaced by the watercolours; a big vase of greenery stood on the hearthstone and old roses, dark red and crumpled like velvet, stood between reading lamp and standish on the desk.

It was the first time since the day she had arrived here, Meg realised, that she had been completely alone with Ross without the formal pretext of her reading to him and it felt as though all the air had been sucked out of the room, leaving her breathless and light-headed. 'You no longer look like a soldier,' she said without thinking.

'No?' He frowned at her, but she found she was unsure whether it was displeasure or puzzlement.

'No. You look like a country gentleman.'

'That is what I am pretending to be.'

'I do not think you are pretending,' she said, making herself be bold. 'This is your roots, where you belong. The things that went wrong when you were a young man, the things that made you unhappy, those do not change the fact that this is your destiny.'

'Hmm.' His mouth twisted into a sneer that was as much for himself as for her, she suspected. 'My destiny to be unhappy? Thank you, Meg.'

'You can be happy if you let yourself be. I was happy, most of the time, with James—there is always something to be happy about.'

As soon as the words left her mouth she realised how betraying they were. And so did he—she could see the questions in his eyes as she averted her head. After a moment, when she feared he would ask something she was not prepared to answer, he turned away and continued to scan the room.

Meg had left his brother's portrait in place and Ross stopped, staring at it for a long time. 'I wish I had been here when he died,' he said eventually. 'I wish I had been able to say goodbye. Did he think I had deserted him, I wonder?'

It seemed to be a rhetorical question, Meg thought, relieved that she did not have to answer that painful doubt. Now she waited with bated breath while Ross turned slowly to face the wall where his father's portrait had hung. 'What have you done with it?' he asked at length.

'I hung it where yours was.' It had been gratifying to consign that arrogant face to the shadows of an obscure corridor. 'I will bring it back if you wish, naturally, my lord.' *Remember your place, before you both forget it.*

'Don't "my lord" me while we are alone, Meg.' He was still staring at his own portrait. 'Was I ever that young?'

'Perhaps you still are, somewhere inside,' she ventured, coming to stand beside him.

'Ever the optimist, Meg?' He turned and looked down at her and she smiled, shaking her head, trying not to show how his closeness affected her. He had been riding and he smelt of fresh air and green things and horse and leather. The strain had gone from around his eyes and she had to fight the urge to go up on tiptoe and kiss the tender spot at his temple where the blue veins showed under the skin and the soft hair feathered over the tanned skin.

To touch him would be to be overwhelmed by her feelings, the sensual longings that simply thinking about him evoked. And she must not give way to them—there was no future for a scandalously bigamous camp-follower and a baron except for a financial arrangement that took her independence and allowed Ross to have what he wanted without ever engaging his emotions. She wanted more from him than his lovemaking, and that, once she became his mistress, was all she would ever have.

'You have a knack for making a house seem like a home,' he said, just as the tension became unbearable.

'I hope I am not making it feminine.' His praise glowed warm inside her. Meg knew she should move away from him, but stayed anyway. Ross was so solid, so still. James had always fidgeted, always wanted to be moving, talking, finding something new. She had never felt entirely secure with her husband, yet for all her fears about Ross he was like a rock to cling to. 'You must tell me if anything is not to your taste. But, of course, there will soon be all of your things around to give it your personality.'

'I don't think I have *things*, Meg. You know soldiers— we live out of a pack. One trunk if we're lucky.'

'Oh, yes.' She looked at the desk with its tidy piles of ledgers and papers. It looked joyless, somehow. A task to be done, a duty carried out. 'You will find things. A shell from the beach, a favourite little carving your fingers stray to when you are thinking, a book of poetry you browse through when you heart is heavy.'

'Have you *things*?' he asked, moving closer.

'No. I lost them all with the baggage train at Toulouse.' The tears welled up and she blinked them away hard. Ross made a wordless sound deep in his throat and she shook her head, defying him to weaken her further with sympathy. 'Foolish things. A needle case Bella had worked, a tiny peg doll of Lina's. A pressed leaf from a willow tree across the lane from the vicarage. A book of verse of my mother's.'

'Nothing of James's? You do not wear a wedding ring.'

'I pawned it.' It had been easy, when it came to it, to barter that symbol of the marriage that had never been. She had to move away from this; it was too personal, it hurt too much. 'Have you been riding around the estate again?'

'Yes.' He moved to prop the rifle up by the window and came back to her side, apparently accepting her reluctance to confide. 'What seemed to a boy to be simple countryside filled with streams and cliffs and coves and trees to climb now consists of nothing but problems and decisions. Do we put this field down to hay? Should that barn be replaced? Are the cattle thriving? What do I do about the fact that my father left the tenants' cottages to rot?'

'Why, repair them, of course. Or build new ones.'

'There—more decisions to make.' And then he smiled at her properly for the first time.

Meg felt her legs go weak with the realisation that this was the man inside, the real man, who was smiling at her. Not the one who was hurt, brooding, angry. She had desired that man, cared about him, worried for him. But this one…this one was different, this was the youth in the portrait grown to manhood. *This* man she felt something else for, something she had no word for, but which dizzied her mind.

All that power and strength and intelligence—and now charm. It was so unfair when all her hard-earned caution and common sense seemed to be at war with the old, romantic Meg who was stirring within her, telling her the world was well lost for… For what? Something must have shown in her eyes, for his own darkened, became questioning. Ross lifted one hand almost to her cheek, but he did not touch; he had given his word, after all, Meg thought, shaken, as she looked into the depths of that gaze.

'How is your leg?' She turned abruptly and the mood, and his smile, shattered. 'Are you riding too much? What does your doctor say?'

Doctor Greenaway had called the day before. He was invited into the study for half an hour and had then left. Ross had not chosen to confide the doctor's opinion to her.

'That it is healing well and that I must have had a good surgeon. He rebandaged it, before you ask,' he added, forestalling her question. 'And I refused to be bled. I left far too much blood in France to want to shed any more just yet.'

'And the riding? I will wager you did not ask him about that.'

'Then you would lose. In moderation, leaving it to

my own good sense.' His mouth quirked. 'Was that a snort, Meg?'

'Ladies,' she said repressively, 'do not snort.'

'Oh, Meg,' He was very close now. So close. All she had to do was put out her hand. She wanted to touch him, to believe that she meant something more than a commercial exchange of sexual favours to him, that her foolish heart was not utterly misguided. 'I promised, Meg, but I haven't changed,' he murmured. 'I still—'

'Harrumph.' Heneage clearing his throat was magisterial. Meg just managed not to move away guiltily as the butler came into the room. She had not heard him knock, but then, upper servants in great houses did not knock, she had read once. Something else to look up in her reference book. 'Lady Pennare, Miss Pennare and Miss Elizabeth Pennare have called. Not knowing whether you are at home to visitors, my lord, I took the liberty of seating them in the Chinese Salon.'

'Tell them I'm out.'

'My lord, your neighbours will all call soon, and keep calling until they find you at home. Would it not be better to deal with them sooner rather than later?' Meg withstood the full force of angry dark eyes. One of them had to be practical and sensible; she was so tired of it being her. 'I will go and offer them refreshments while you change.'

'Why the devil should I change?' he demanded. 'They invited themselves, they can take me as they find me.'

'They have called at a perfectly reasonable hour for social calls. And you smell of horse,' Meg said frankly. She was aware that the butler had become glassy-eyed. Presumably no one ever spoke to his late lordship like that. Not and remained employed for very long.

'Mrs Halgate, you are depressingly commonsensical.'

'I strive to be, my lord. I hope I know what is right,' she added, holding his gaze and saw he knew she had answered his unfinished sentence.

Chapter Ten

'Good afternoon, my lady. Miss Pennare, Miss Elizabeth. I am Mrs Halgate, the housekeeper. Lord Brandon will be down directly. May I bring you refreshments? Tea, perhaps?'

Meg stood respectfully just inside the door and withstood the concerted scrutiny of three pairs of very blue eyes. The Pennare womenfolk were individually attractive; all together they were a vision of blonde curls, periwinkle eyes and exquisite dressmaking. She tried not to feel plain, brown and freckled and could only be thankful for the good quality of her gown and the starched perfection of her cap.

'Tea, thank you, Mrs Halgate.' Lady Pennare nodded graciously. 'Where is Mrs Fogarty?'

'She has retired, Lady Pennare. And moved to Truro, I understand.'

'I see.'

Meg hoped profoundly that she did not. 'I will bring your tea, ladies.'

As she crossed the hall Ross came down the stairs looking respectable in a corbeau-blue tail coat and cream pantaloons with Hessian boots. When he reached the bottom step she saw the fit was hardly tailor-made.

'Well?' he enquired, one brow lifting in sardonic acknowledgement of her scrutiny.

'That coat does not fit very well.' The pantaloons fitted rather too well.

'Young Perrott is beside himself. If his lordship had listened to his advice, his lordship would not be receiving ladies in his father's clothing. He flatters himself that the shine on the boots—which pinch like the devil, incidentally—does him justice, but he begs his lordship to visit the best tailor Truro can offer at the earliest opportunity.' The imitation of Perrott's reproachful voice was wickedly accurate, made funnier by Ross's completely straight face. Meg struggled for some composure.

'I am fetching a tea tray.'

'What are they like?' Ross eyed the door to the Chinese Salon as though expecting it to conceal French artillery, not three attractive women.

'Very pretty,' Meg said primly and left him to make his entrance.

By the time Meg returned with a footman and the tea things Ross was feeling decidedly harassed. Lady Pennare, an elegant matron in her early forties, quite obviously expected him to admire her daughters who were, he had to admit, a credit to their mama. They were pretty, beautifully turned out and well mannered. Unfortunately he could detect not the slightest hint of personality in either of them.

Miss Pennare, just eighteen, and Miss Elizabeth, seventeen, had not had a London Season this year, their mother confided, owing to the uncertain health of their paternal grandmother. 'But they will enjoy their London débuts next year, if they have not already contracted eligible alliances,' she added.

So you expect the old lady to depart well before then, Ross thought cynically. Lady Pennare surveyed the room with approval, leaving Ross with the decided impression that she had valued every item in it, including himself. Her daughters made determined conversation.

'Will you be holding a party soon, Lord Brandon?' Miss Pennare asked.

'I had not thought to,' he said as Meg began to pass cups of tea, a simple figure in plain blue amidst the feminine furbelows. It seemed to him that of the four women in the room, she was the only one whose true nature shone through.

'Oh.' Miss Elizabeth pouted. 'But we had heard that there is a *huge* reception room here. It seems such a pity to waste it. It might even be big enough for a ball,' she added, widening her blue eyes at him.

She will flutter her lashes in a moment, Ross thought. *There, I knew it. Little peahen.* 'I do not dance, Miss Elizabeth.' It was a lie, he danced perfectly competently, as most officers could. From informal dances to full-scale balls, Wellington had encouraged the social life of the English forces in the Peninsula.

'Your wound. Of course,' she said soulfully, gazing at him with admiration in her remarkable eyes.

Ross blinked, suddenly aware of a danger he had not even considered. Far from being a tiresome social call, this was a hunting expedition. He was a titled bachelor and therefore fair game for every matchmaking mama and single young lady in the district.

'I never dance,' he repeated, injecting as much chill as he could into the statement. Her smile turned into a pout at the tone and whatever she saw in his face and she put down her tea cup with a little clatter. He was not the handsome and charming young man she had hoped to find, of course. She hadn't the nerve that Meg did, he reflected. Meg had never flinched, however frightened she was of him. Except for that terrified reaction when she had woken to find herself in bed with him looming over her, he reminded himself, crossing his legs.

'Then we ladies must try that much harder to introduce you into our social circle, Lord Brandon.' Lady Pennare was made of sterner stuff than her younger daughter. 'An eligible gentleman must expect invitations to every event, you know,' she added in rallying tones.

Half an hour later, after one cup of tea and one tiny lemon-drop biscuit each, they fluttered out.

'Hell and damnation,' Ross exploded as the carriage rolled away down the drive. 'That's the first of the flood, I suppose. I am obviously naïve, but I was not braced for matchmaking mamas.' He was the baron now, he should marry, father an heir. He had not even thought about that before. Now it was staring him in the face, his fundamental duty to his name.

'What did you expect, my lord?' Meg had come back to supervise the clearing of the tea things and now stood, hands neatly clasped at her waist, her lips twitching with what he strongly suspected was an almost irresistible desire to laugh at him. 'You are an eligible bachelor, therefore you must be in want of a wife.'

Ross reached out a hand and palmed the door closed with a thud that sent the smaller pieces of jade shaking on their stands. Her smile vanished. 'What I am in want of,' he said harshly, 'is you in my bed. As you can no doubt see,' he added with deliberate crudeness, almost as he might have picked up one of the jade bowls and thrown it into the hearth to assuage his temper.

He was aching with arousal and it had not been the pretty feminine tricks of the three Pennare ladies that had caused that. It had been Meg's closeness in the study and then the startling contrast between her reality and the other women's artificiality. And those young women and their like were the ones it would be suitable for him to court and to marry.

Meg gave a little gasp. 'You gave me your word…' she began.

'I promised not to touch you. I said nothing about attempting to persuade you.' Ross stalked over to the window to put the width of the room between them and caught his still-bandaged leg on the sharp corner of one of the little tables that had been brought in for the tea things.

He couldn't bite back the grunt of pain as he grabbed one of the long window curtains to steady himself. The wound had been healing well and he had been able to walk and ride with less and less pain each day, but it was not ready to stand a sharp corner of solid mahogany being driven into its centre. Ross swore viciously under his breath, taken aback by the wave of nausea that hit his stomach. Then there was a flurry of skirts and Meg was on her knees in front of him, her hands gentle on his leg.

'Oh, no! Has it opened it up?' Her head in that ridiculous cap was so close that its frills brushed his groin, with predictable results. One small warm hand was resting on the inside of his thigh while the other touched the bandage through the thin barrier of his knitted pantaloons. 'There's no blood,' she said, her voice anxious.

'Meg,' he managed through the effects of a vivid fantasy of her kneeling in front of him like this, her hands on him—and both of them naked. 'If you do not want me to touch you, I suggest you take your hands off my leg. Now.'

She sat back on her heels and looked up at him, then the flood of colour rushed up to her hairline as she found herself so close to an erection that the clinging jersey did nothing to veil. 'Oh!' She scrambled to her feet and retreated behind one of the sofas. 'If you need a woman that badly, I suggest you take yourself off to Truro—I am sure there are any number of establishments that cater for a gentleman's every need.'

'But I do not want a whore, Meg. I want you,' he said softly. 'I want you to be my mistress.'

'No.' Her fingers were white as they gripped the back of the sofa. Was she stopping herself running from him, or to him? 'No, you cannot have me.'

'Then I will just have to burn,' he said, his voice harsh as he realised that was the choice. It was Meg or nothing. 'And the fire is very hot, Meg. So very hot.'

'Once, I gave my virtue because I was in love,' she said, fiercely. 'And then I gave my reputation in return for protection. But I am not going to give my freedom in return for money.'

'I have not offered you any yet,' Ross snapped back. This was probably not how a gentleman negotiated with a prospective mistress. He should have thought what he could offer her, laid that out, discussed provisions to be made after the *affaire* was over. No doubt that was how it was done.

But he had realised what he wanted in a blinding flash and asked for it. The women in his life before had come and gone easily with an exchange of coin, or sometimes of food. Or perhaps a pretty shawl or a trinket.

Meg was a lady—or had been. He could not offer her

coin in her hand like a whore and he had no idea what she might accept as a business arrangement.

'Tell me what would you like,' he said more moderately. Her eyes were like flint as she glared at him. 'A house, of course. Penryn is a charming town, you would like that. Your own servants. A carriage, a dress allowance, those too, naturally. I would set up a bank account for you…'

Her eyes were shooting daggers now and she looked too angry to answer him. Up to now he had always seemed to understand women well enough; now he appeared to have strayed into shallow waters and had no idea how to read the chart. 'Meg, you have been in my arms, you have kissed me. Don't tell me that you did not want me then. What has changed? I am offering you security, comfort. I cannot be *that* repellent to you.'

'Oh, you arrogant man,' she hissed. 'Just because I kiss you that does not mean I want to be your mistress, your… plaything! You think I want to be tucked away like a gem in a jewel box for you to take out and toy with when it suits you? I am earning my living, honestly, with a fair exchange of money for labour and loyalty and you want—well, you want what you lust after. Never mind what I want.'

'What do you want?' he asked, genuinely baffled.

Meg took an agitated step away from the shelter of the sofa. 'Don't men realise that it is not the lying together that is important to women—however good that is—it is all the other things. Friendship, companionship, trust, give and take between two people…'

'Love?' he finished for her, the word sounding like a jeer. 'You are quite the romantic.' She flushed, as though the word was an insult. 'If that is what you want, Meg, then I am sorry, but I cannot give you that, whatever it is.'

'I never said *love*,' she shot back. 'Do you think I am going to hold out until you lie and use that word, whisper sweet nothings and then yield?' Her expression said quite plainly that she could hardly imagine him doing any such thing as whispering soft words of love. 'Do I seem so foolish, so empty headed? If you only employed me because you thought you could talk me into your bed, then you had better have your money back now and I will leave,' Meg said, haughty as a duchess. 'I am afraid you will have to accept two gowns, a pelisse, a bonnet and a quantity of underthings in lieu of part of it, but I have not worn all of them.' She stalked to the door.

'What,' Ross demanded, 'am I going to do with a pile of female underwear?'

They glared at each other, then the corner of her mouth twitched. 'I am afraid I could not possibly speculate,' Meg said, sweeping out into the hall.

Damn the woman! He might not be in love with her, but he was deep in lust and whatever it was he felt for her was rapidly becoming an obsession. An uncomfortable one.

'My lord?' Heneage was standing in the door, regarding him with some caution. Ross supposed he was frowning again.

'Yes?'

'Tregarne is here and asking to speak to you, if it is convenient, my lord.'

'Very well, I'll see him in the study.' What did he want? Ross wondered. He had intended visiting the head keeper in the next day or so.

'My lord.' The man who had taught him to load and clean his weapon and how to shoot safely and accurately seemed hardly unchanged until Ross saw the light full on his face and realised he must now be in his sixties.

'Tregarne! You see, your tuition has got me home again safely.' *And God knows how many men dead.* Ross shook his hand and gestured towards the chair opposite his own beside the fireplace. 'How are you? And Mrs Tregarne and the boys?'

'All well, my lord.' The weatherbeaten face cracked into one of its rare smiles. 'James has joined the navy and Davy's one of the underkeepers now. But you took a bullet in the leg, so they tell me. That's not good news.'

'It's a lot better now and the limp is going. I was coming to see you tomorrow; I thought we could go and bag some pigeons and a rabbit or two for the kitchen.'

'That would be just like old times, my lord, if I might say so.' The keeper grinned. 'But my, you've filled out some from the gangly lad you used to be. Grown into your feet, just like my lurcher pups do.'

The keeper hesitated. 'There was something I needed to talk to you about though, my lord. You recall that old rogue Billy Gillan? He's still alive and tough as hobnail boots— and he's still taking our pheasants, the wicked devil. And smuggling from down in the cove, if the rumours I hear are right. Now, I want to set a trap and catch him at it. He was too wary while your father was with us, God rest his soul, but Billy won't have your measure yet—he'll be careless, I'm hoping. We'll catch him red-handed, haul him up in front of you—'

'I'm not sworn as a magistrate, Tregarne,' Ross interjected.

'No, of course, you won't be.' The keeper's face fell. 'You will soon enough, won't you? But we don't have to wait—Sir John Vernon at Hall Place, he'll have the old rogue behind bars, soon as look at him.'

It would kill Billy. And it was a miracle he'd escaped capture before now. But Ross wasn't going to let him fall foul of Tregarne if he could help it. If he could only think of a way to keep the wily poacher on the right side of the law—but that was like looking for ways to stop cats chasing mice.

He could tell Tregarne to ignore whatever Billy was up to—but that would be openly condoning smuggling as well as undermining Tregarne's authority with his underkeepers.

'Leave him be for a few days,' he temporised. 'I'll see about getting sworn—I don't want to export my own troubles over to Sir John to deal with.'

'Aye, I can see that.' Tregarne nodded agreement. 'You'll call in tomorrow then, my lord? There's a field of young beet with the tops being shredded by those darned pigeons. I could fancy a pie.'

Ross found the conversation had calmed both his anger, and his desire. There was Billy to worry about, but he'd think of something. As Ross crossed the hall on his way to the library he met Meg, just emerging from the door to the back stairs.

'Mrs Halgate.' Ross felt an unfamiliar sensation in his cheek muscles. He wanted to smile at her, although he was not at all sure why, infuriating woman.

'My lord.' She sounded just a touch wary.

'I have come to the conclusion that I have no use for two gowns, a pelisse and some female undergarments. I suggest you keep them.' Meg opened her mouth as though to speak, then closed it, her eyes intent on him. 'Because you are not going anywhere just yet, are you, Meg Halgate?' And then he did smile as he turned and took the stairs two at a time.

'Ow!' He reached the turn of the stairs and the half-landing, out of Meg's sight, before the stab of pain in his leg brought him up short. Ross hopped a couple of steps and sat down at the foot of the next flight to wince and stretch his leg. That had been a damn fool thing to do, but the sudden attack of high spirits had made him act like a twelve-year-old. Which was ridiculous. The estate and all its problems had not vanished; there was Billy, just as much of a rogue as he'd always been, and now adding smuggling to the tally of his offences, at least one household full of simpering blonde damsels in pursuit of his title—and Meg.

Meg, with whom he had erred so badly she was talking about leaving him. Meg, who he was aching for and who he had to have. Somehow, if he could just fathom what she wanted. Meg. Ross leaned back against the stairs, closed his eyes and contemplated the things that were so desirable about Meg Halgate.

There were her blue-grey eyes and those long dark lashes. There were her curves. There was the way that one corner of her mouth dimpled slightly more than the other when she smiled and that tiny mole at the corner of her right eye. And the way she stood up to him and the wicked flashes of humour and the strange sensation that he was waking up from a long, nightmare-racked sleep and she had him by the hand and was teaching him to see and feel again.

'My lord?' said a voice from above him.

Ross tilted back his head, opened his eyes and saw Damaris, Meg's red-headed maid, looking down at him.

'Are you all right, my lord? I thought you must have fallen, but then I saw you were smiling. I can go round to the back stairs, only—'

'No, that's fine, Damaris.' Ross got to his feet and stood aside to let her pass. 'I was just thinking.' And dreaming.

Chapter Eleven

'Mrs Halgate, ma'am?'

Meg blinked and found she was standing in the hall with a foolish smile on her face. *He smiled! He smiled and he made a joke.* Damaris was standing in front of her, looking worried. As well she might with the housekeeper behaving in such a hen-witted way.

'Yes, Damaris? What is wrong?'

'It's his lordship,' the maid hissed with a glance over her shoulder. 'I found him sitting on the stairs, just at the landing, with his eyes closed and a big grin on his face. And when I asked him if he was all right, he said he was thinking. Seems an odd place for a gentleman to be thinking. Don't they have studies for that?'

'I believe that thought can strike a gentleman anywhere. Unlike we poor females who must do our work first and then think, if we have the leisure. Come along, Damaris, I've sure we have a lot to be doing.' *Only just at this moment, I cannot for the life of me remember what it is.*

Damaris was looking doubtful. 'We've done everything

on the list for today, Mrs Halgate. Unless you was wishful to be making a start on the linen cupboard?'

The Housekeeper's Guide was most insistent about the importance of maintaining an up-to-date register of the contents of the linen cupboard, with every item and its condition noted, and Mrs Fogarty's linen list had a date of almost twelve months ago.

'No, we will save that treat for tomorrow.' She needed to read the relevant sections in the *Guide* first. Linen cupboards sounded straightforward, but there was sure to be some vital detail she must not miss.

'I am going for a walk, Damaris. You may have the rest of the afternoon off.'

There, that's another smile, she thought as she made her way to her rooms for a shawl and to change her shoes. At this rate the entire household would be beaming.

But what was making Ross smile? Meg walked round the side of the house and found a footpath leading in the direction of the sea. He had not enjoyed the visit from Lady Pennare and her daughters, so that could not be the cause. Then they had had that ridiculous row over her becoming his mistress. Men did not like being refused, especially about sex. James had never had any patience with her when she had let any reluctance show and he had positively sulked when she had her courses.

The path reached an old gate, just right for leaning on and thinking. Why refuse Ross when it made her feel this strange inside? She wanted him. It would be so good in his arms, she knew that. He might be big and fierce but he could be gentle. And he would know what he was doing. A smile tugged at her lips at the thought of Ross knowing what he was doing.

But it would be a financial transaction and that left her heart cold. What had Shakespeare said? 'The expense of spirit in a waste of shame is lust in action…' and Ross meant more to her than that. Quite what, though, she was not certain. She had not felt like this with James and she had believed herself in love with him. But Ross, so much tougher and harder than James, made her shiver with both tenderness and desire, longing and lust. She would not surrender to him—but might she go to him, as an equal? Would that be worth the broken heart that would surely follow?

Too much thinking—she needed to walk. With a shake of her head Meg pushed the gate open and found herself in a lane, deep between grassy banks higher than her head, their slopes studded with wild flowers. She had noticed the flowers as they had driven here, but they had passed in a blur. Now she could stop and enjoy them individually. Bluebells in indigo profusion, primroses, the vivid magenta heads of ragged robin and sheets of wild garlic with nodding white heads.

Shuttlecock-heads of hart's tongue fern were unfurling themselves and the soft leaves of foxgloves promised towering spikes still to come.

Enchanted, she strolled down the lane, stooping to examine trails of scarlet pimpernels and the blue bird's-eye periwinkle and reaching up to pluck a spray of wild cherry blossom to tuck behind her ear.

When the lane petered out suddenly into sand she was right on a beach, a sandy half-moon between two arms of low brown cliff. The sea was breaking in tiny waves, smoothing the sand like well-ironed linen, and bisecting the half-moon was a tiny stream. It must be the stream that ran near Billy's cottage.

There was no one in sight, no reason not to give in to temptation, take off her shoes, roll down her stockings and paddle in the frothy edge of the water. Under her bare feet the sand was cool and grainy; the water when she ventured in a few inches made her gasp—despite the sunshine the sea was icy. Once she had learned to swim in still, fresh water, the deep calm of the millpond with the sun on her back. A long time ago.

But this was curiously both soothing and stimulating at the same time. She lifted her skirts to her knees and ran a little, splashing, then retreated up the beach as a bigger wave came in.

How Bella and Lina would love this! The three of them, free, happy, running over the sand and laughing in the sunlight. *I'll find you soon,* she promised silently. *We will be together.*

Toes numb, she walked back to her rock and sat with her feet on a smooth boulder to dry so she could brush off the sand. Seabirds swooped and shrieked, a fishing boat sailed past, the sun shone and Meg sank into the puzzle of Ross's smile.

It was not that she did not wish him to smile, it was wonderful that he had, but she felt uneasily that it was to do with her and that, in some mysterious, masculine way, he had not been discouraged by her refusal to be his mistress.

Which was worrying, because she so much wanted to say *yes* that she was shocking herself. The old, romantic, yearning, loving Meg, whom she thought had been buried in disappointment and the need for sheer common sense in order to survive, was still there.

Was the only thing that was stopping her yielding to him the fact that he was offering her money, the position of a mistress? That he wanted to buy her, which would ensure for him that all the inconvenience of emotion and feeling could be set aside? Did that freeze the spontaneous impulse to follow her instincts and go to him? If he had set out simply to seduce her for one night of passion, she might have succumbed. Because, however much Ross looked like the Grim Reaper most of the time, there were those moments when every nerve in her body seemed quiveringly aware of him and the inevitable unhappy ending of all this no longer seemed to matter.

'You be that new housekeeper up at the Court?' The strong Cornish burr was right by her ear.

It was Ross's old poacher. He must be able to move like a ghost. How long had he been there? And her with bare feet, bare head and a bunch of cherry blossom behind her ear. 'Yes. I am Mrs Halgate. I've never been at the seaside before,' she added, as though to excuse her eccentric behaviour. 'It is beautiful.'

He watched her with unusual amber eyes that seemed startlingly youthful in his wrinkled face. She should get up and walk away, she knew, but something about him fascinated her. 'You be as pretty as he told I.'

'Who? Ross? I mean, Lord Brandon?'

'Aah,' he said, a complicated noise with more vowels in it than she could count. He sat down on a rock facing her. 'You looking after that boy properly?' A black-and-white dog, long haired with a plumy tail, crept up, belly to the sand, and curled round at his feet.

'Boy? He is hardly that. You are Billy, are you not? I'm afraid I don't know your last name.' Dreadful old reprobate he might be, but this was the man Ross seemed to regard almost as a grandfather. If she wanted to understand Ross, perhaps he could help her.

'Billy'll do. He talk about me, then?'

'Lord Brandon spoke fondly of you. He told me that you taught him how to shoot and how to treat girls.'

The old man gave a crack of laughter that had the dog looking up. 'Well, he shoots damn fine, I just hope he listened about girls.' He got at least one *u* into the word, but Meg was beginning to understand the accent now.

'I really would not know.'

'Aah.'

'I am his housekeeper,' Meg said repressively. 'Lord Brandon—'

'Don't be calling him that, that's his father, God rot him. Ross ain't his father.'

'Well, it is his title now, and he has to manage this estate and find himself a wife and settle down. And be happy.'

'Why not marry him yourself then, maid?' Infuriating old man. Meg glared at him. He had hardly any teeth and the few she could see were brown with tobacco. She suspected he hadn't washed in a year and probably, if the sea breezes were not blowing from her to him, smelt like a ferret, and he had no business whatsoever talking to her like this. But Ross loved him. And he obviously loved Ross. Ross needed love. She couldn't bring herself to snub Billy.

'That would be impossible. He is a baron. I—' *I am forbidden from marrying any decent man because of what I have done.*

'You're a widow, and an officer's widow too, he says. A lady. Respectable.'

'Not respectable enough.' Impossible that she ever could be. She should be sinking with shame at such a frank conversation, but talking to this old man was more like confiding in a wild animal or an ancient tree than confessing to a person.

'Boy's a fool,' the poacher said. At least, that was what Meg guessed he said. 'I'll sort him out for you.'

'No!'

The dog sat up and barked. Old Billy blinked at her,

slowly, like a very thoughtful lizard. 'Don't you want him then, maid?'

'I… Certainly not.'

'Hah! Never thought Ross'd be such a gommuck. Good day to you, maid.'

'G-good day,' Meg stammered. The old man picked up his stick and walked away up the beach to where the scrubby woodland ended. He whistled, sharply. The dog sprang up, swiped a hot tongue over Meg's bare feet and when she looked back to the wood both man and dog had vanished as mysteriously as they had appeared.

She brushed the sand off her feet, put on her stockings, laced her shoes and made her way back up the lane, uncertain whether she was amused or alarmed by that encounter. Would he take Ross to task and lecture him on marriage? What if Ross thought she had put the idea into Billy's head and not the other way around?

The thought of marrying Ross had never entered her mind—her conscience was quite clear about that. She had married once, thinking herself in love, and that had not been what her romantic soul had thought it might be. She was older and wiser now, knew that no man was all hero, all saint, however handsome his face and sunny his smiles. And Ross was not handsome and he rationed his smiles like a miser. Was she—could she be?—in love with him?

'Have you been out a-gypsying?'

Meg stopped short. Without realising it she had reached the edge of the terrace and there was Ross, his shoulder propped against one of the lichen-encrusted urns that edged it, towering over her as she stood on the grass below him. Her insides did the complicated flip-flop that the unexpected sight of him always produced.

'I have been down to the beach.'

'And returned without your bonnet, with flowers in

your hair and, I will bet a guinea, you have sand between your toes.'

'I am afraid I have.' He straightened up and kept pace with her as she walked along to the shallow flight of steps in the centre of the terrace. 'But I have never been beside the sea before, so I could not resist paddling.' She put up a hand to remove the cherry blossom before she utterly undermined what authority she had with the staff by walking in with it in her wind-blown hair.

Ross leaned down and plucked it out before she could reach it, his fingertips ruffling into the fine hairs at her temple and sending a shiver down her spine. 'Did you meet any smugglers?' He stuck the stem into his buttonhole and waited for her to climb the three steps to his side.

'Why, are there any? I saw a fishing boat, that was all.'

'My head keeper tells me we have smugglers in the bay. There are caves if you know where to look and the tide is right—not big ones, but enough to stow a few barrels of brandy in.'

'Oh.' Smugglers had a romantic reputation, but no doubt in reality they were just as unglamorous and unpleasant as highwaymen. 'Did your father turn a blind eye to it?'

'He must have done.' Ross set his shoulder against another urn and looked out towards the sea. 'The brandy I've been drinking is the good French stuff, and the barrels it is coming out of have no marks on them.'

'And do you condone it too?'

'They did a lot of damage when we were at war. It was a prime route for intelligence to reach the French. That danger has gone now, but I must take a stand before they start intimidating people on the estate. And when I'm sworn as a magistrate I will have to take an active interest, and not just on my own land.'

My own land. An admission at last that it was his. The

relief at hearing the unconscious note of possession in his voice made her suddenly light-hearted. 'Ross, what is a gommuck?'

'A fool, a clumsy fellow. A clodpole. Why, where did you hear that?'

'Oh, just a country person I passed.' Would Billy tell Ross he had spoken to her? Was it best to admit she had seen him, or not? Then the moment to mention it was passed. Ross laid a hand on her forearm as she turned to go in and her breath caught.

'I have heard from Kimber, my solicitor. He has a young man he recommends as a confidential enquiry agent and he is sending him up to speak with you on Monday. His name is Patrick Jago, the second son of the squire of a parish a few miles north of here. He has carried out some commissions for Kimber and he speaks well of him.'

'Thank you, it was thoughtful of you to arrange it. It is such a relief to be taking action at last.' His hand was warm on her arm and she did not want to move. Or think. But she must. 'You will make an accounting of Mr Kimber's time and deduct it from my wages, of course.'

'Why? In case I should extract payment for it in some other way later?' His brow lifted in that devilish way he had when he was on his dignity.

'No.' Meg moved away so his hand fell from her arm. 'In case you should suppose that I presume upon my position.'

'That, Meg, is nonsense. But I am sorry, I touched you, forgive me.'

'Oh, for goodness' sake,' Meg snapped, suddenly losing her temper with the slow dance they were performing around each other. 'This is ridiculous. I do not suppose for a moment that because you put a hand on my arm to detain me that it is some kind of demand. I am perfectly capable of telling you if you do something that upsets or offends me.'

'So, you give me back my promise not to touch you?'

His mouth, that sensual, sinful mouth that so shook her willpower when it curved into a smile, was not curving now. 'Yes, I do.'

Then she lifted her gaze and met his eyes and caught her breath, for *they* were smiling, and something hot and wicked and mischievous was dancing in the black depths. Without speaking he put his hands on her shoulders and drew her to him as he stepped back under the shelter of the first-floor balcony and she went, without a murmur, her feet stumbling a little on the uneven flags. Ross leaned back against the wall and gathered her into his arms and she found herself held against his chest with no strength in her, either of will or body, to push him away.

His mouth found hers, hot and demanding, yet without force. Her lips moulded to his, opened to the pressure of his tongue, softened as he licked inside, finding the intimate, sensitive places, the places that made her melt into longing. Her hands slid up his chest, coming to rest over the beat of his heart, reading his arousal and his gentleness with her fingertips, sensing the tightly reined passion beneath.

When Ross lifted his head she went up on her toes and kissed the corner of his mouth before sinking down to rest her head where her hands had been, strangely soothed and at peace. This was so right, this was where she should be. She sighed, content, willing the moment to last.

'Why do you give me what you will not let me buy?' His voice was husky against her hair.

'Because I can give you a gift freely and remain myself,' she said into the soft, warm linen of his shirt, explaining it to herself as much as to him. *Because that kiss was two*

*people attracted to each other, not a man with money
buying a woman.*

'I see. And you gift me one kiss?'

'Just one, and no promises.' Meg managed to step back.
It seemed she could smile quite successfully. 'I will see you
after dinner; we should finish *Gulliver's Travels* tonight.'

Ross's mouth twisted. 'No. No tonight. Not again,
in fact. I do not think I can sit in the library alone with
you, even if the door is open, and concentrate on Lemuel
Gulliver's troubles. I must think on my own.'

'Then I am sorry.' Her spirits plunged at the realisation
that this was going so very wrong. 'I should not be here,
in this house. I do not want to tease you, to seem to flirt,
to make you suffer. I was right when I said I must go—it
is selfish to stay when we feel…' Meg turned, knowing
only that she must walk away from him, now, this minute.
Down towards the lane she saw a flash of black and white,
the wave of a plumy tail, then the dog was gone. And with
it its master? Had Billy been standing there watching that
foolish, impulsive kiss?

'No, Meg, don't go. Don't leave, not yet. Between us
we will learn to control this—whatever it is. And if you
must—I confess, the last thing I want is to stop kissing
you.'

She turned back from the view, to find him just where
she had left him. 'I don't want… I do not want to make
you more unhappy.'

'Unhappy?' The shadow swept over his face as though
the sun had gone behind a cloud. 'Is that how I seem to
you?' He shook his head in an abrupt rejection when she
nodded. 'No. I do not think I am unhappy. For a while I
was in despair, deep enough in to make death not something to be courted, but a fate that I would not avoid if it
found me.

'Now? I am frustrated by wanting you, but you make me see this place differently. I am...challenged by all the things I must learn and the things your questions make me confront. I am terrified of Lady Pennare, her daughters and all the matchmaking mamas for twenty miles around and I wake at three in the morning wondering when I will come round from the nightmare and discover I am not here at all, but somewhere I understand and can control. Is that unhappiness? I do not think so. It is certainly no longer despair, even if it is not contentment.'

He frowned, but the old, deep darkness was not there. This was thought, a man deep in a puzzle. 'But perhaps challenge is a way of knowing you are alive. You have brought me something, a way of looking at this house, this estate. The reminder that I owe it more than duty.'

'I am glad of that at least. I was frightened for you.'

'And that is why you kissed me just now?'

'Oh, no.' She shook her head, unable to explain to him without revealing the fear that she was falling in love with him. He had rejected the notion of love, had sneered at it—she could not bear the thought that he might guess how her heart was betraying her. 'Do you have any mischievous spirits in Cornwall? Elves, perhaps?'

'We have piskeys. Why, have you met one?'

'I think perhaps I did just now. Down on the beach. Yes, a piskey up to mischief. That would account for it.'

Chapter Twelve

Ross might confess to waking in the small hours to brood on his new life, but Meg was having trouble even getting to sleep in the first place. That kiss, the tenderness she had felt in both of them as his lips brushed over hers, haunted her. He was recovering, becoming again the man she suspected he had always been. He had never lost his courage, his endurance, his basic decency, but the young man's sense of humour, his capacity for joy, *that* had been knocked out of him by guilt and hardship, the loss of the life he loved and the pain of his wound.

It was fragile still. Meg gave up on sleep and sat up in bed. That darkness needed little excuse to swoop and fill up his soul. Had she ever felt that bleak? She had been miserable at home at the Vicarage, but there had always been her dreams to give her hope. It had been hard when she had realised that James had feet of clay and that she would always be the stronger of the two of them, but she had learned to make the best of things. His death had been a grief and the time after his will had been opened still had her shivering at the memory of his betrayal and what it had made her.

But she had never despaired. She locked her arms around her bent legs and rested her chin on her knees. If Death had come looking for her, she would have kicked and screamed and punched him on the nose rather than give in.

And Ross had not given in either, although he might think he had. Meg bit her lip. He thought he had given up and he felt diminished by that? But he had fought to live after he had been wounded or he would never have had the will to stop them cutting off his leg. He had been at the end of his strength in the river and yet somehow he had clung to that ladder and to life.

He was finding his way out of the darkness. Was she really being any help to him, or was her refusal to be his mistress making it worse? There were ways he could deal with physical frustration, Meg told herself firmly. She must not talk herself into going to him by pretending it would be an act of charity. If she did, then it would be because she loved him and she could share that, know him fully for the little time they could have together before the realities of their respective positions, his duty, his need for a wife, her search for her sisters, took them apart for ever.

But that did not stop the yearning to be held, the need for tenderness, for the thrill of another's body in tune with yours, that rare, soaring ecstasy that she believed, deep in her romantic soul, she would find one day when everything was right, and the man was the right one, and both of you were utterly transported.

That had been what that kiss was about, for both of them: a yearning, a reaching out for joy. 'Go to sleep,' Meg said out loud, turning to punch her hot pillow before she lay down again. 'Go to sleep and dream about Bella and Lina.'

* * *

Sunday. How long was it since she had been in a proper church, sat through a service, listened to a sermon? It must have been the day before she ran away from home and the sermon had been Papa at his dourest. Following the army there had been drum-head services every Sunday, prayers by graves scratched in the dusty earth, baptisms with water dipped in a bucket from the nearest stream, weddings in the sight of God, but not a clergyman.

Now she had to dress in her best, braid her hair tightly under her bonnet, process with the other servants behind Ross down to the church in the next valley. They said it was very beautiful. She had been avoiding it as though it had been a plague pit.

It was beautiful, almost exotic, once you removed your gaze from the back of Ross's neatly barbered head under the tall hat Perrott had magicked up from somewhere. The church was down in the bottom of a steep combe, its toes almost in the water, Heneage said. It was like plunging into a jungle; she almost expected parrots instead of the jackdaws who wheeled and chattered overhead, squabbling with the gulls.

Trees dripped with moss, ferns grew waist high, grey headstones stood and leaned on every flat place as the path wound down to the grey granite tower. Beside the steps a brook chuckled and tumbled its way to the sea.

The beauty seduced, calmed, but even so, her hand was rigid on the butler's arm as they went into the little church, the servants from the Court after them, filling the back pews.

The choir shuffled into place, small boys uncannily well behaved under the eye of the older choristers. A plump woman bustled up to the organ, which had been wheezing for the past ten minutes while another small boy pumped at the bellows. She played a chord and the congregation winced, but with the air of long familiarity and acceptance. The vicar emerged from the vestry, tripped on the edge of his cassock and took his place.

'Dearly beloved, we are gathered here today… What?' The tallest chorister was hissing from the stalls. 'Oh. Yes, not a wedding, of course. Dearly beloved brethren, the Scripture moveth us, in sundry places…'

'He's a good man, but given to muddles, is Mr Hawkins,' Heneage murmured in her ear. 'Much loved, hereabouts. And Miss Hawkins, his sister, for all that she murders that organ.'

The sermon, once Mr Hawkins had found his papers in the vestry and then dropped them as he climbed into the pulpit, was all about lost sheep and the joy of their finding. It was to give thanks for the safe return of one of the fishing boats, thought lost a week since, that had limped into harbour the day before. But it was also about Ross, Meg sensed, as the vicar's mild blue gaze swept over his congregation, pausing for a moment on the front pew.

Meg swallowed the lump in her throat. This was what a vicar should be, she thought, looking at the happily weeping fishermen's wives in one pew, Ross's bowed head, the earnest, scrubbed faces of the choir.

When she came out into the sunshine Mr Hawkins was waiting, shaking hands with his flock as they dispersed. He kept hold of her hand. 'Welcome to our parish,' he said, smiling kindly at her. 'You need some peace, my dear. You will find it here. My lord, have you shown Mrs Halgate our holy spring yet?'

'No.' Ross, hat in hand, was being fussed over by Miss Hawkins. 'Do you mind a longer walk back, Mrs Halgate?'

'Not at all.' His arm in the fine broadcloth, another

of Perrott's victories, was steady under her hand. Behind
them the chattering congregation took the path up out of
the valley.

'Did that help?'

'The church?' So, he had realised how difficult it had
been, how much she had dreaded the memories. 'Yes, it
did. Mr Hawkins is a good man. That sermon was for you
as much as for the fishermen, was it not? He is glad you
are home.'

Ross did not question her use of the word. 'I thought I
was past praying for.' But he smiled.

'Where is your brother's grave?' she asked and his arm
became rigid under her palm. 'I should like to see it.'

'I—' He stopped and Meg saw he had gone pale.

'It must have been a comfort, to see it in this beautiful
place,' she persisted gently.

'I have not been. His killer should not stand at his grave-
side.'

'It was an accident. He knew it was an accident. You
know that, you know in your heart that you did all you
could, that there is nothing to forgive. Giles would want
you to go.' She stood her ground when he would have
walked on, trembling a little at her own presumption. 'Is
it in the church or here?' You could hardly describe this
mossy, flower-studded slope as a graveyard.

'There.' His face like granite, Ross jerked his head
towards a little terrace on the slope above them, away
from the main path down. 'My grandparents' graves are
there. Giles always liked the view from up there. Go and
see, if you like.'

'I would, very much. But with you.'

'I have no wish to. It will do him no good.'

'Not for him, although he would have wished it, surely.

But for yourself,' Meg persisted, not moving towards the steep little path.

She felt the tremor that went through the big body so close to hers, then he turned and strode up the mossy steps, leaving her behind. Meg followed and found him standing, hat in hand, beside the group of three stones, two lichen-covered, leaning a little, the other crisp still, despite the humid air. As she watched from the edge of the little clearing Ross knelt, dropping his hat, and ran his hand over the mound as though caressing a body beneath a green velvet coverlet. He was speaking, she could hear the murmur of his voice, although not the words.

When he fell silent Meg turned and went back down and along the path they had been following at the edge of the creek. If he needed her, he would find her.

She heard it before she saw it. Water bubbled out of the ground in a rough circle of grass and wild flowers, ran over pebbles, vanished again and emerged in the creek a few feet away. Metal glinted from its bed and someone had tied a child's bonnet to a branch. There had been ancient magic here long before the Christian saints had come to Cornwall. A blackcap started to sing in the thorn bushes, heartbreakingly lovely.

Tears were sticky on her cheeks and she dipped her hands in the water and washed her face, then waited until she heard his step on the path behind her. He stopped beside her, but she did not look up, giving him the privacy she suspected he needed.

'Thank you,' Ross said. 'I had expected pain and grief and I found peace there.'

'That was what Giles would have wanted you to find,' she suggested.

'Yes,' he agreed. 'You did not know him, yet you understood far better than I.'

Ross stripped off a glove, bent and scooped water into his palm, offered it. It was cold in her mouth and his hand, as her lips touched it to drink, was warm. He drank after her, their eyes meeting over his cupped hand, then he shook it, droplets flying in the sunlight.

'A steep climb now,' was all he said and by the time they had climbed to the road they were speaking of practical, safe subjects, but the feeling of tranquillity went with them.

Young Mr Jago seemed to be all that Mr Kimber had promised. He sat down on the other side of the table in Meg's sitting room, looking bright, intelligent and sensible. He was also attractive to look at, with steady hazel eyes, a strong, cheerful face and thick blond hair. Living with six foot six of brooding dark masculinity was not enough, it seemed, to prevent an appreciation of good looks in other men.

'I understand from Mr Kimber that you wish to trace the whereabouts of your two sisters with whom you have lost contact.' Meg passed him a cup of tea and sipped her own while she ordered her thoughts.

'Yes. I have not seen them since July 1808 when I left home. We were all living in the vicarage of Martinsdene in the north of Suffolk with our father, the Reverend John Shelley. My elder sister, Arabella, is twenty-five now and my younger sister, Celina, twenty-three. I have written down a description of them.' She pushed the paper across the table and Patrick Jago read it through before tucking it into his notebook.

'They may still be at home, in which case I wish you to give a letter to whichever of them you can contact without my father discovering it and await their reply. If they are not there, then I wish you to trace them for me.'

'May I use your name when I am making enquiries?'

'No. Absolutely not. My father is a strict man of strong temper. A domestic tyrant, to be quite frank. I would not wish to put the parishioners in such a position that they had to hide anything from him. We are estranged.' It was more painful than she had expected to have to admit that to a stranger, but she had to be honest or he would never understand all the nuances of the situation and might miss some clue because of it. 'I eloped and I have never received any response to letters since.'

Jago nodded and jotted a note. His manner was more like a doctor's than anything else, Meg thought with a sudden flash of insight. He put down the notebook. 'You will wish to know my terms. I would charge you my return stagecoach fare and my lodgings in whatever decent inn there is available that will lend credence to my cover story—when I work out what that is. Plus incidental expenses such as postage or bribes.'

'And your fee?' In any other circumstances it would be amusing to hear this very proper young man discussing bribery; now she just accepted it as a necessary, if sordid, tactic.

'Two guineas per week.'

If she stayed in Ross's employ for a few months then she could afford that, for surely Jago would know within a few days whether Bella and Lina were still at the Vicarage. If they were not…but she would not let herself think about that, not yet.

'Very well. But if you cannot locate them within three weeks, please let me know.'

'Of course. I will report every few days, but if they have left the village we will need to discuss how to proceed.'

Meg pushed the letter she had written for her sisters across the table to him, her fingers lingering on it, reluctant to let it go into the hands of a stranger. It held all her hopes and fears, all her dreams of the three of them together again. She could find a little cottage somewhere. They could all find work and they would be together, safe.

Her hand would not lift to release it. Jago's long, competent fingers settled over hers. 'Too many hopes and fears riding between those pages?' She looked up, blinking away tears, to find his eyes warm and understanding.

'So foolish,' she murmured, obscurely comforted by him.

There was a peremptory knock on the door and it opened on the sound. 'Mrs Halgate, there is another invasion of blasted ladies. Will you kindly—?'

Ross stopped just on the threshold. For a moment Meg had no idea what he was staring at, then she realised that her hand was still under Jago's and pulled it free.

'There, that is the letter, as I said. I think you have everything now.' She got to her feet. 'Thank you. I must go and see to the arriving guests, if you will excuse me, Mr Jago.'

'Of course. I will see myself out. My lord.' The young man inclined his head.

'I will see you out.' Ross's mouth was a thin line. 'This way.' He gestured towards the servants' entrance.

'You are too kind.'

'Not at all.'

They were so polite that Meg almost missed it, the current of frigid anger in Ross's voice, the wary note in Jago's. *Oh, my lord. He thinks we were flirting and he is being possessive.* She emerged into the hall to find one party of mother, two daughters and a sulky-looking son, and another of husband and wife with a single daughter, exchanging greetings and filling the space with chatter. Heneage was looking decidedly put out. This was no time to get into a fluster about Ross's assumptions or what they meant.

'Mrs Halgate, I was just explaining to Sir Richard and Lady Fenwick and Mrs Pengilly that I was not certain whether his lordship was at home this afternoon.'

'Oh, yes, he is, Mr Heneage.' She curtsied. 'Good afternoon. I am Mrs Halgate, the housekeeper. Would you care to come through to the salon and I will have refreshments brought? His lordship will not be long.'

She shepherded them towards the Chinese Salon, then ran downstairs again. If Ross was in a foul mood the last thing she needed was him stalking into the salon and alienating his neighbours. And she was determined that he was not going to shirk his obligations to hospitality, matchmaking mothers or not.

'Tea for eight in the Chinese Salon, please, Mrs Harris.' Meg popped her head round the kitchen door. 'Have you seen his lordship?'

'Heading towards the stables not a minute ago.'

'Thank you. I'll see if I can catch him.' She opened the back door and walked straight into Ross.

'Catch who?' He fended her off with both hands to her shoulders.

'You. You know you have guests.' She turned on her heel and made for the stairs.

'I saw them from the window and told Heneage I was not at home this afternoon.' The tread of his boots behind her sounded ominously heavy.

'Well, I told them that you were, I'm afraid. There are some gentlemen this time.' There was no response from behind her. It was like being followed by a very large dog, she could almost hear him growling. 'I have ordered tea to be brought up.'

'Excellent. Then you may stay and pour and inform me

afterwards which of the young ladies I must pay court to.'
Ross strode past her and into the salon, leaving Meg to
stare at the door panels while she waited for the tea trays
to come up.

Pay court? Had Ross decided that he must marry and
settle down? That was a good thing, it had to be. He needed
a family around him, an heir to bring up. But why was he
talking about marriage now? Perhaps Ross had decided,
after that strangely tender kiss on the terrace, that he must
put aside thoughts of mistresses and lovers. But why was
he looking so grim again?

And why was she feeling so empty all of a sudden? Meg
caught a glimpse of herself in the mirror. It was not only
Ross who was looking unhappy—she looked stricken. Her
hand was pressed to her breast as though it could comfort
the empty ache inside and something suspiciously like tears
were burning at the back of her eyes.

Whatever it was, the relationship that would have been
so unwise, so temptingly sinful, was over before it had
begun. She should be thankful that her strength had held
out long enough for Ross to come to his senses and before
she allowed her own feelings to show too plainly.

The green baize door opened to a chink of china and
the laboured breathing of Peter the footman managing the
heavy tea urn. Meg blinked hard and led the way into the
Chinese Salon. Inside was a babble of voices. She could
hear Sir Richard talking to Ross about a mutual problem
with fences, so she imagined the Fenwicks must be neighbours.

Lady Fenwick took the proffered cup with a vague
smile at Meg before nudging her daughter surreptitiously.
'Anne!'

'Sorry, Mama,' she whispered, both of them oblivious
to the fact that the by-play was obvious to Meg. The girl

turned wide, grey eyes away from the young man who was wedged uncomfortably between his two sisters and fixed them on Ross's face.

Meg moved over to offer tea to the Pengilly family. From Mrs Pengilly's deep violet gown with black trimmings and the wide hair ring that she wore next to her wedding band, Meg deduced she must be a widow. Her stolid daughters, neither of them blessed with the blonde good looks of the Pennare girls, or the sweet demeanour of Miss Fenwick, accepted their tea cups without a word and turned their attention to the silver cake stand.

Ross made no attempt to engage any of the young ladies in conversation and completely ignored the sulky youth, instead drawing both the married ladies into the discussion of the rebuilding of the nearby church tower.

Mr Pengilly got up and slouched over to the window next to where Meg waited behind the tea things, ready to refresh cups or pass biscuits. Seventeen, with aspirations to dandyism, she decided after a fleeting glance at his towering collar-points and the exaggerated cut of his lapels. He shifted restlessly, walking close behind her. One hand settled firmly over her right buttock, the fingers closing to squeeze.

Meg bit back the instinctive gasp of outrage and stepped back, her heel making contact with his toes before she put all her weight on that foot. With a muffled oath he jerked away and everyone turned to look at them.

Meg put all the concern she could into her voice despite her cheeks burning with indignation and embarrassment. 'Mr Pengilly, I do apologise! Did I step on your toes? I had no idea you were so close.'

'You—' He was furious, as flushed as she must be, then Meg saw him catch Ross's eye and he subsided. 'The slightest touch. It was nothing.' He flung himself into a chair on the far side of the room and turned what he doubt-less thought was a brooding Byronic profile to them all.

The two parties left together after rather more than the normal half-hour, which probably meant it was a success, of sorts. Ross came back and shut the door with an emphasis that sent the curtains flapping in the sudden draught before she could reach the bell to ring for the tea things to be cleared.

'I'm surprised those were the first gentlemen to call,' she remarked, her attention on the unstable arrangements of biscuits.

'I'm meeting them as I'm riding round with Tremayne,' Ross said curtly. 'What the devil was that puppy Pengilly about?'

'He put his hand on my...behind me. So I trod on his toes.'

'And was Jago flirting with you?' Ross picked up a biscuit as he passed the table and ate it whole in one snap. 'He was holding your hand.'

Those biscuits were looking extremely attractive to a woman who wanted to sink her teeth into something—or up-end the plate over Ross Brandon's raven-black head.

'He is a nice young man who realised that I was upset when I was giving him a letter for my sisters and he held my hand for a moment to comfort me,' she said calmly, as though addressing a short-tempered hound.

'What was there to be upset about?' He frowned at her. 'He will find them for you, I am sure.'

'You insensitive gommuck!' Oh, yes, that was a very fine word. Suddenly very weary of controlling her feelings, soothing his, Meg shoved Ross hard in the middle of his chest. He rocked back on his heels, but did not shift his position. 'I haven't heard from them in years, I do not know if they are well and happy—or even alive! I want to just rush up there, not send a stranger.

'I love my sisters. How would you feel if you came back to England after all those years abroad and had no idea what had happened to Giles? Am I not allowed to feel any anxiety or to cling for a moment to someone who shows me a sympathetic, smiling face?'

'I am sorry,' Ross said, his teeth still gritted. 'I saw him with his hands on you and something… I should know you better. It was not rational,' he added doubtfully.

'He is a nice person, he makes me feel secure. I have confidence that he will help me.' His hands were heavy, trapping her shoulders in a grip that had only to tighten to crush her bones. 'What is the matter with you?'

'He touched you. They both did. It made me angry and now I have alarmed you.' He stroked his fingertips down her flushed cheek. 'I am sorry, Meg.'

'I can take care of myself.'

'Can you? Have you any idea what you want?' Her heart was slamming against her ribs and she had no idea whether the vibration running through her was her own body or his, trembling.

'Yes, I want you. We both know that. But it is not… not…' Meg wrestled for the words to explain her confused feelings. 'I will not sell myself to you, Ross Brandon.' *Tell me you love me,* she thought hopelessly. *I know you will break my heart, but love me…*

Denying him seemed the hardest thing she had ever had to do, harder than facing the shocked and scandalised faces of the ladies of the regiment after James had disappeared, harder than pretending she was another man's lover only weeks after being labelled a sinful adulteress, harder by far than it had been at the time to elope, heedless and innocent in the July dawn, leaving her sisters behind her. But she just did not think she had the strength to cope with the inevitable pain.

'Then give yourself.' She was in his arms, carried against his broad chest as he strode towards the sofa, before she could catch her breath. 'Take me,' Ross said as he went down on to the broad satin seat with her tumbled in his embrace.

Chapter Thirteen

His mouth was hard and demanding and utterly ruthless on hers. It asked no questions, for he knew what he was doing, where he was going and he was no more prepared to discuss it with her, Meg thought as she tried to find the strength and the will to fight him, than he would have discussed his orders with his men.

On the terrace she had gone willingly into his arms and now he was not going to give her the opportunity to explain or argue or reason with him. *I want you,* she had said just now and he was taking her at her word.

Ross's weight was on her, his hands were at her breast, then at her waist, then, as lawn and cotton slid over her skin, on her thigh with her skirts rumpling up under the pressure of his fingers. And his mouth never left hers, capturing her gasps, her moans, her protests that were as much at her own response as at his onslaught on her.

She was losing herself in him, in his heat and in the scent of him, his strength, his masculinity. The reasons why she should say no to him were slipping away from her like mist under the first rays of the sun and all that was left was the delicious, aching torment of wanting and touching and being touched.

Ross's hand found the soft mound at the junction of her thighs, cupped it, wringing a moan from her lips that had him raising his head to look down into her face. His eyes were black, intense, deep with arousal and emotion, and everything female in her responded to that look.

'Ross…'

'Mine,' he said hoarsely, burying his face in the angle of her neck, his teeth rasping over the quivering flesh, nipping at the tendons with a delicacy that his strength belied. 'You are mine. I will not have other men touching you.'

The possessiveness shocked Meg's eyes open. She stared over Ross's disordered hair at the table still laid out with the tea things, at a display of jade bowls. They were in the Salon, on the sofa, in broad daylight and her entire body was flooded with feelings so overwhelming, so thrilling, that they were almost painful. This was the truth of what she felt for him, of what he made her feel. This was not for a tumble on the sofa, this was something else entirely, something precious and wonderful and utterly terrifying.

'No. Ross, stop! Someone could come in at any moment, we are in the Salon, for goodness' sake—'

'Then come up to my bed.' He raised his head and fixed her with a look that spoke of raw sensuality and need. 'You are mine and you know it.'

'I am not yours.' *Not yet, not like this.* Meg realised that his fingers were still laced into the intimate, damp tangle of curls, still sending quivering darts of lust through her belly and down the inside of her thighs. 'Stop it, take your hand off me… Let me go!' She wanted him so much it was an almost physical pain as he left her, thrust himself off the sofa and stood staring down at her, baffled desire and anger etched on his face.

'Come to my bed, Meg,' he repeated.

'No. You think I am yours and I tell you I am not. I am no man's.' She dragged her skirts down, almost panting with reaction, the words all wrong because of the one she dared not use to him, her agitation emerging as anger when all she wanted was to sob out her feelings in his arms. 'You are so strong—'

'You think I would force you? Was I forcing you just now?'

'No! I mean your personality is so strong. You command, you demand, you expect obedience. You expect to get what you want. And I must stand up to you or I will go down like wheat before the scythe and I will hate myself for it. And I will hate you,' she flung at him as she got to her feet and went to the looking glass, her fingers desperate amongst pins and lace to order her hair and set her cap back on her head.

'You own this house, this land, your title. But you do not own me.' The long hair pins hurt her skull as she jammed them back. A good pain, a deserved one. 'My father owned me, my husband owned me—now nobody does. You pay my wages,' she told him in the mirror, his face a stark reflection over her right shoulder, 'and for that you get my services as a housekeeper.' *I love you and I need you to love me too, or my heart will break and I am too weak to bear it.* And she was too weak to say the words and face his rejection, the truth that he wanted her body and that was all.

'You would deny yourself?' he said softly, moving up until he stood directly behind her, speaking to her reflection as she had to his. 'Just to keep me in my place?'

'No, that is not why.' Meg whirled to face him, refusing to move aside when he stood his ground, however much her knees were trembling. She could not say what she felt and the frustration was making the words tumble out heedlessly as she snatched at excuses. '*Mine*, you said. I am not one of your fields or coppices for you to put a fence round and nail a *No Trespassing* sign to.'

'You are saying I am jealous?' Ross laughed, a short, mirthless sound.

'I am saying you are territorial and possessive, my lord. You are beginning to fill your father's shoes very well.'

That was unforgivable, she knew it as soon as the words left her mouth. Ross had confided in her about his relations with his father, had given her a glimpse of what the late Lord Brandon had been and how he had scarred the boy whose dark eyes stared at her from the man's face. Now she had told him he was turning into that person.

Perhaps his deep reluctance at coming back was not only sadness at what he had lost or the guilt that had tormented him over Giles's death, but fear of becoming the man his father was. The thoughts flashed through her mind even as his expression began to change, to close against her, every emotion masked behind the harsh bleak face she had recoiled from at first sight on the dockside.

'I…I am sorry, Ross.' *What have I done? No…undone. All the peace that his meditation by Giles's grave had given him dissolved into anger.*

He held up a hand for her silence. 'No. Don't say anything.'

Somehow Ross got himself out of the Chinese Salon before he started to shake. The pain in his wounded leg was a nauseating ache. He must have knocked it when… when he had lost his mind, picked up his housekeeper and began ravishing her on the sofa in an unlocked room in broad daylight.

He had to get out of the house before he either went back in there, dragged her upstairs and finished what he had begun or—

'My lord!'

'Heneage, are you unwell?' Ross put out a hand to steady the butler who had walked round the corner without seeing him and was now white to the lips. How old was the man? Was his heart affected?

'I am quite well, my lord. Forgive me—it is just that I did not hear you and you looked, for a moment, so like his late lordship when he was displeased that I was quite taken aback.'

Ross stood there in his own hall, all the surging frustration and anger and misery of his childhood building up in him like a fermenting wine bottle that was ready to blow. He had schooled himself never to show those feelings, never to give his father the satisfaction of seeing how effective his disapproval, his punishments, his scowling anger were at withering his son's heart. He had fought back with insolence and disobedience and that, in part, was why Giles's accident happened.

'I am sorry I gave you a shock, Heneage. You are not seeing ghosts.' *But I am.* 'I am going out. My apologies to Mrs Harris, but I will not be in for dinner.'

'Very good, my lord.' The butler was recovering his colour. 'Shall I send round to the stables for your horse, my lord?'

'No, I'll saddle up myself.' Ross paused with one foot on the bottom stair on his way to pull on a pair of breeches and topboots. The thought of waiting patiently for even ten minutes was intolerable. He had to get out of the house, away from Meg. Away, if that were possible, from himself.

His father had never stinted himself on his stables. Ross strode across the cobbled yard, waving aside the groom who was sweeping out the central gutter. He had been riding out daily on one of his father's cover hacks, a well-bred but sturdy animal that stood placidly while Ross grappled with the intricacies of crop rotation, but would take the hedge banks in its stride if necessary. And it was a sensible animal to ride for someone who had a healing wound in his leg. Despite what Meg thought, he was capable of some common sense as far as that was concerned, he reflected sourly, reaching for the bridle that hung by the door.

A black head appeared over the door of the next box, ears pricked, eye rolling warily. His father's last acquisition, Culrose, the head groom, had told him.

'Fabulous blood line and it cost him a pretty penny, my lord. But it's the very devil to ride. Threw your father, first time out, and he never rode him again. I exercise it on the end of a leading rein—I don't fancy having my neck broke, and that's a fact.'

At the time Ross had simply made a mental note to sell the animal. Now he put back the bridle and went to look at it. As he let himself into the box he saw it was no gelding, but an intact stallion. 'Stop that.' He grabbed its forelock as it snaked out its neck to bite him and hung on as it countered by trying to rear. 'Do you want to get out of here and gallop, or not?'

The horse showed the whites of its eyes, but stood still, obviously realising that he was not to be intimidated. With one hand still fast in its forelock, Ross shouted, 'Get me the tack!' and found, when he looked over his shoulder, a collection of grooms and stable lads all watching the half-door with wary anticipation. He hoped they would have the guts to come in and haul him out if the creature kicked him down.

'My lord.' One lad heaved the saddle up on to the door and hung the bridle over the pommel.

Ross managed, one handed, to get the bit in its mouth, then the bridle over its head. The horse stood with remarkable, and suspicious, meekness when he released its mane and began to fasten buckles.

'What's its name?'

'Trevarras Dragon, my lord.'

Appropriate. Ross could imagine it breathing fire. As he hefted the saddle on to its back he felt the muscles twitch under the glossy coat. Did it have the intelligence to work out it could do him a lot more damage once he got up on its back? Probably.

'Open the door and stand clear.' As Dragon charged for the opening Ross swung up into the saddle, ducked under the frame and jammed his feet into the swinging stirrups before the horse realised what had happened. It erupted into the open, the men and boys scattering, then stopped dead, legs braced, ears back. Ross could almost hear it thinking how it was going to kill him. He shortened the reins, closed his legs and dug his heels in as the stallion went sideways across the yard, bucking, then dragged its head round to the gateway and slackened the reins.

As he hoped, the chance to run won over the desire to unseat and trample its rider. Dragon gathered his haunches under him and took off, all seventeen hands of black-coated muscle thundering down the carriage drive like one of Congreve's rockets. *And just about as predictable,* Ross thought, concentrating on staying on until the stallion tired itself.

His leg hurt like the devil, his arms were aching and his mood had lifted miraculously. It was not just

Dragon who had wanted violent physical exercise. Ross laughed as his hat flew off, squinted against the sun and galloped on.

It took all of twenty minutes before Dragon allowed himself to be pulled up to a canter, by which time they had jumped too many banks and hedges to count and devoured the length of the gorse-covered commonland.

'Give up?' Ross enquired. One ear swivelled back, then, to his surprise, the big horse responded to the rein, dropped down to a trot and finally a walk. 'You see? If you are reasonable, I let you run,' he continued as they came to the edge of the common and turned into the lane.

Dragon snorted, but it was the peal of feminine laughter that startled Ross. A tall woman in a plain gown with an apron, her blonde hair piled up on her head and a basket at her feet, was leaning back on the gate opposite. She must have been resting and admiring the view, Ross guessed, and had turned at the sound of hooves.

And then a cloud moved across the sun and took the dazzle out of his eyes and thirteen years dropped away. 'Lily!' He swung down out of the saddle and went to her, catching her around the waist and kissing her, right on her wide, generous mouth. 'My God, but it is good to see you! Billy told me you were down on the Lizard.'

'I only went to help my cousin with a birthing.' She put out her hands to hold him away so she could look at him and Ross saw the lines of laughter and sadness around her eyes, the silver hairs in the gold, and realised she must be in her mid-thirties now. 'Look at you now, all grown up.'

They stood grinning at each other and Ross felt the darkness lift further. Lily was another of the good memories from his youth. Three years older, she had been the sister he had never had. When he had discovered that his father had forced himself on her, leaving her with his child, a killing rage had washed through him. Even as he smiled at her now the lash of that remembered anger, hot and acid, touched him.

'I've someone for you to meet. William!' she called. 'He's grown a bit since you last saw him.' A gangling lad appeared from round the bend of the lane, a bundle of driftwood slung over his shoulder.

'My God.' The boy was the spitting image of himself at fifteen—black hair, height, build, the formidable Brandon jaw and nose still to be grown into. 'Does he know?' he asked Lily urgently. 'Does he know who he is, who I am?'

'Yes…' she nodded as his father's discarded bastard broke into a run '…he knows.'

'Mam.' The boy stared at Ross with Billy's amber eyes. He was not all Brandon then.

'Say good day to his lordship, William. Where's your manners?'

'Good day, my lord.' He reached for his forelock to tug it.

Ross put out his hand and caught his wrist. 'Don't do that. And not "my lord". I am your brother, Ross.'

Lily gasped. 'You can't mean to acknowledge him?'

'I don't need to.' Ross let go of William's wrist and tipped up the boy's chin. 'Look at that jaw.' He ruffled the boy's hair. 'But, yes, he is my brother and I will make no bones about it. You call me Ross, William. "Sir", perhaps, when we don't want to shock the servants.'

'Yes, my…sir. Ross.' The Cornish burr was rich in the boy's voice, warm under the more refined accent Ross suspected Lily had schooled him to use. She'd been his mother's maid until his father's eye had lighted on her. 'You're fifteen now?'

'Yes.' The amber eyes were wide, full of intelligence and wary speculation.

'He's starting on the fishing boats next month,' Lily said. Ross could hear the pride and the fear in her voice. Pride that her lad was growing up, working and earning. Fear because the churchyards of St Just and St Anthony were full of the graves of fishermen from this treacherous coast.

'Do you want to be a fisherman, William?'

No, those eyes said. 'It's a steady job.' The boy shrugged. 'The money's not bad.'

'What do you want to do—if you could do anything, any work?'

'Be a lawyer.' The answer shot back, even as William ducked to avoid his mother's exasperated cuff round the ear.

'Fool of a boy.'

'Why? Can you read and write, William?'

'I can, sir. Ross, I mean. I love reading—books, newspapers. Whatever I can get my hands on.' He grinned, revealing a missing front tooth. 'And lawyers make sure people get their rights,' he added pugnaciously.

'Oh, be quiet do, Will!' Lily shook her head at Ross. 'He reads all the newspapers he can find—he's turning out to be one of these radicals, that's what I fear. He'll end up with some mob, breaking windows.'

'Not if he is training to be a lawyer.' Ross wondered what had left the boy with such an idealistic view of the legal profession. 'They aren't all knights in shining armour, you know, William.'

'Well, it's pie in the sky anyways.' Lily picked up her basket. 'A man's got to go to university to be a lawyer, I know that.'

'He'll need a tutor, certainly.' Ross turned and found, to

his surprise, Dragon was standing where he had left him. He picked up the reins and began to walk alongside Lily and William. *My brother.* He'd lost Giles, but this one had his whole life in front of him. 'And he can go and work in Kimber's office one day a week. When he's old enough, university. There's more to it than that, but Kimber can tell us what's needed.' He looked down at William who had stopped dead, his mouth open. 'Would you like that?'

The boy stared back, then bit his lip, his expression clouding over. 'Thank you very much, but I have to earn a wage.'

'You are my brother, so you get an allowance. I'll talk to your mother about it. Now, take that firewood home and leave us to sort out the details. Oh, and, William, you may use the library at the Court at any time.'

His brother just looked at him, his throat working, then he muttered, 'Thank you, Ross,' turned and took to his heels.

Ross smiled at Lily, who stood there staring at him.

'He's grateful,' she began. 'But he's…'

'He's a bit overwhelmed. It is all right, Lily. I can remember being that age. What's the matter?'

'It's a dream, it's perfect. But you can't do it, Ross. People will think he's yours.'

'He *is* mine—my brother—and I'll tell anyone that, straight out. My father's habits are well enough known for people to believe it if I acknowledge him. I was coming to see you when you got back, Lily, to see what I could do to help. There's a cottage on the estate you might like and there will be an allowance for you, as well as for William.' She tried to protest, but he closed his hand over hers and squeezed. 'Let me help, Lily. Let me try to make it right.'

She squeezed his fingers in return. 'Thank you. Yes,

I'll accept, for William, and be thankful. You've grown into a fine man, Ross.'

'I'm a soldier, Lily, a killer who has got to learn to be a landowner. I'm so far out of my depth I think half the time I'm drowning.' The relief of having someone who knew him so well, someone he could pour it all out to, was shattering. And with Lily there were none of the feelings that almost overwhelmed him when he was with Meg. Feelings that were more than lust and longing and which he could not understand.

But even to Lily he could not speak of the death and the blood and the feeling that all he had seen and done made him unfit for decent people, for the life duty told him he must lead. Or for the wife he knew he should take.

'You'll learn,' Lily said comfortably as they strolled down the lane. 'Just don't be your father, that's all anyone round these parts would ask of you.'

The sense of happiness vanished abruptly. 'I look like him. I scared Heneage half to death this afternoon—he thought he'd seen a ghost, poor old devil. But it was just me scowling.' Meg's words, the words he had pushed away into a corner of his mind so he did not have to look at them, came back. *Territorial, possessive...your father's shoes.*

'Did he rape you, Lily?' he asked abruptly. 'Did he force you, or was it that he threatened ruin and dispossession for the whole family so you had to give in to him?'

'He had no need to use force,' Lily said. 'Just threats. He owned me, he said. He was the lord, I was his to do with as he wanted or we could all get out and starve. *Mine,* he said.'

Ross felt physically sick. *You are mine and you know it,* he had flung at Meg. *Mine,* he had said as he crushed her body under his, his mouth on her neck. She was right, he was turning into his father.

'I must go.' He mounted Dragon and sat looking down at her tired, open, loving face. 'Come and see me tomorrow, Lily, if you can, and we'll decide which cottage you'd like—there are three empty. Bring William and we can talk some more.'

'Thank you, Ross.' She put her hand on the rein. 'My father is so happy you are home.'

He forced a smile and dug his heels into Dragon's flanks, urging him into a canter as soon as they were clear of Lily. He had not trusted himself to reply. Home? Perhaps he was coming to feel like that about it at last. The torrent of information about the farms, the estate, the fishing boats that he owned, that was all beginning to make sense now. He had a brother to discover and old friends to talk to.

And Meg was chasing the ghost of his father out of the house, room by room, making it warm and light and alive again, fit for a young wife to inhabit, fit for a family.

'Oh, God. Meg.' Ross reined in, provoking a display of temper and resistance from the stallion that had him cursing and sweating by the time the animal accepted that he had to walk again. What the devil was he going to do about Meg?

Chapter Fourteen

'Mrs Halgate.' Meg jumped, water splashing from the flower arrangement she was positioning on to the polished mahogany of the table in the small dining room. She mopped at it, then made herself turn.

'My lord.' She could speak, thank goodness—for a moment she had thought her heart had lodged in her throat.

Ross filled the intimate space. He stood, booted feet apart, face expressionless. 'Please confer with Mrs Harris and tell me when would be a convenient evening to have a dinner party. There will be a full moon next week, which will make travelling easier for guests.'

The request was so abrupt and unexpected Meg thought she must have misheard. 'A dinner party?' He nodded.

'For how many?'

'The large dining room will seat twenty-four.' Ross moved past her to straighten his neckcloth in the mirror.

'Twenty-four? Forgive me, but are you on receiving terms with twenty-three people yet? My lord,' she added, laying one hand over her stomach. It was suddenly queasy.

She had been dreading his return, fretting about where he had gone, rehearsing over and over what she might say in the wake of that heat, that passion and anger. And now this, the cold, hard man, was back and she could see no way to speak the words.

'Yes, that many. You forget, I have been riding out every day. I make social calls as well as endure lectures on foot rot in sheep and the value of seaweed as a manure, but I saw no reason to report them all to you. We may not be able to accommodate every young lady in the neighbourhood at the first dinner, but I can certainly start the inspection process.'

'You wish to inspect the young ladies?' Did he mean what she thought he meant?

'Certainly. I am sure, as a vicar's daughter, you can put me right, but it was St Paul who said "It is better to marry than to burn," was it not? And it is certainly my duty to marry.'

His attention appeared to be fixed entirely on his neck-cloth. *He isn't even watching to see what effect his words have on me.* Meg gripped the back of the nearest chair. 'Paul's first epistle to the Corinthians, chapter seven, verse nine.'

Two could play at pretending this did not matter, that this frigidly polite exchange was not in fact a blazing row. But of course, Ross did not feel sick, his nerves were not dancing so close to the surface that his skin hurt, he was not feeling confused and humiliated. Only frustrated and angry with her, no doubt. 'You have nothing suitable to wear.'

'Perrott has been nagging to some effect, so I visited the tailor again two days ago. It will all arrive by the end of the week. The bootmaker, too—I will not, I am glad to say, have to wear my father's actual shoes.'

'Excellent.' He was throwing her own words about his

father back at her and she was not going to pick him up on it. 'I will go and consult with Cook immediately.' Mrs Harris would know what to produce for a wife-hunting dinner party. Something to demonstrate taste and wealth to appeal to the parents and something festive enough to charm the young ladies.

She dropped an immaculate curtsy to Ross's unresponsive back and left. Her control lasted exactly as long as it took to get herself out of the dining room and down the stairs to the privacy of her own room where her churning stomach finally revolted.

The strength of her reaction was alarming. Was it just the aftermath of frustrated passion, the tension crackling between them, or the news that he was looking for a wife? Meg wrung the washcloth between her hands and buried her face in the cold dampness, hoping to shock herself into clear thinking.

Of course it was right that Ross should be looking for a wife. It was exactly what she had wished for him. A wife and a family was what he needed to root himself to this place. His own heir would give him the purpose to care for this beautiful estate, this old house. And a wife would give him the love he needed, the affection his life had been lacking for so long.

Am I so utterly miserable because I am falling in love with him? Meg dried her face, frowned at the wan image in her mirror.

Perhaps she was simply unsettled because she had heard nothing from Patrick Jago. When she knew where Bella and Lina were she could plan her own life. That must be it—Ross was finding his place in his own world, she was simply uneasy because she had not. She could not let her old, romantic self sweep her away into another misjudgement as great as her feelings for James had been. Whatever it was, she could not skulk here, she needed to talk to Cook.

'Why, whatever's the matter, Mrs Halgate?' Mrs Harris's reaction put paid to any illusion that she could put a brave face on this. Cook put down her rolling pin and stared, her forearms floury to the elbows. 'You look quite put about.'

'I *am* quite put about.' At least she had a genuine excuse for her troubled face. 'His lordship intends to throw a dinner party for twenty-four next week and wants to know when would be a convenient time for it. And the large dining room is not turned out yet, let alone the fact that I haven't checked the formal table linen. It could be covered in iron mould.' Or eaten by moths or whatever happened to linen.

'Lord love us. What sort of dinner party? We haven't had one of those here for, what, eighteen months? Still, Heneage will be pleased—he says it's a crying shame, him and the lads polishing all the silver every week and no one to show it off to.'

'Lord Brandon is inviting families with unmarried daughters.'

Mrs Harris's eyebrows shot up. 'So that's the way of it.'

'Exactly. We will be setting out to impress, don't you think? I will have a look at the large dining room now and see what we can do with it. And I suppose we had better turn out the long drawing room overlooking the gardens; the Chinese Salon is too small for twenty-four.' There, she was doing this quite successfully, sounding positive and energetic. The butler came in with the postbag in his hand. 'Mr Heneage, his lordship wants a dinner party for twenty-four next week.'

'Does he now? Best say Thursday, don't you think, Mrs Harris? The moon will be at its best and that will give us plenty of time to prepare.'

* * *

On the Tuesday before the dinner party Meg was in the kitchen when Heneage came in with the mail bag. He tipped the post out on to the far end of the table from the bread-making and began to sort it. 'Miriam, you make me a nice cup of tea, there's a good girl.'

The kitchenmaid lugged the kettle off to the pump as Heneage sorted. 'All for his lordship except these, which all look like bills.' He handed a small pile to Meg, then found another at the bottom. 'Here's one for you by name—come quite a way by the look of it.'

Meg took it then stared at the blob of blue sealing wax. It would be from Jago; no one else would send her a personal letter. She picked it up. 'Excuse me.'

There was a seat on the terrace, just beyond the point where Ross had kissed her. Meg found herself there, still clutching the unopened letter. A sharp pain made her realise that she had caught her lower lip between her teeth. She broke the seal and spread out the single sheet.

The Royal George, Martinsdene, May 8th
Dear Mrs Halgate,

As you can see, I have made excellent time and last night reached this inn where I am putting up, convenient to the vicarage. I am representing myself as a student of old church architecture and hope by that means to introduce myself to your father.

However, I must tell you at once that neither of your sisters has been seen in the village for some time.

The words blurred but she made herself read on.

I sought information about the vicar from the landlord under the pretext of wishing to better intro-

duce myself and secure permission to study all parts
of the church. According to him, Miss Celina Shelley
has not been seen since June of last year and Miss
Shelley, not since the end of April.

Where could they have gone? If Ben Wilkins at
the George did not know, then there was some mystery
about it.

After a couple of tankards of his own brew, the
evening being wet and business slack, I had hopes
that he would became inclined to gossip and I did
nothing to discourage him. But he revealed nothing
more and seemed uneasy at having spoken as he did.
I have gained the strong impression that he is wary
of incurring your father's displeasure.

Tomorrow I intend calling at the Vicarage to make
the acquaintance of your father. I shall also exert
every effort to be certain that neither young lady is,
in some way, confined in the house.

I will write again as soon as I have any further
information.

I beg to remain, your obedient servant,
Patrick Jago

The letter fluttered down to her lap. Meg sat and stared
at it. She had thought they would still be there at home,
unhappy, trapped, but safe. Or her best hope had been that
they had found husbands that their father had approved of.
But this—to have vanished with no explanation, not even
substantial rumours of why they had gone—was inex-
plicable.

And how was Jago to find them? A tear fell with a
splash on to his neatly written words, blurring *your obe-*

dient. Then another, then another until Meg was sobbing, sobbing as she had not done since the night they had opened James's will and her already shaky world had utterly fallen apart.

'Meg? Meg, sweetheart, what is it? Bad news?'

Ross. Ross calling me sweetheart. 'I don't know,' Meg managed. 'I don't… I hope not. It is my sisters, they've vanished. Patrick Jago went to look for them for me, but they aren't at home any more and no one knows where they've gone.'

Somehow she got the sobs under control and found a large square of white linen pressed into her hands. She buried her face in it and mumbled, 'It is so long since I've seen them. And none of us was happy at home and now, not knowing… I don't know what to do.'

'Young Jago's got a good head on his shoulders,' Ross said. 'He has only just started—give him time.' He seemed to hesitate. 'Perhaps it is a good thing you were unable to go yourself or you would have been stranded there with hardly any money, and no idea where to go next.'

Meg nodded, wiping her eyes and taking a deep breath. 'Of course, my lord,' she managed to say with careful formality. 'I'm sure you are right and Mr Jago will find them.' She had to believe it.

Then his arm came around her and she was pulled close into warm linen and broadcloth. 'Hush, Meg. Never mind "my lording" me. There is no bad news, hold on to that.'

She should push him away, but his other hand was stroking her hair and he did not appear to mind that she was crying again into his shirtfront. 'You should not,' she managed to say. 'Someone might see us.'

'I am not leaving you to cry, Meg,' Ross said, holding

her tighter. 'You gave me Giles again. You are driving me insane, but for Giles alone the whole of Falmouth can see us, for all I care.'

'The house does you credit, Mrs Halgate.' Perrott joined Meg on the upper landing as she caught her breath in the few minutes left before the first guests arrived. They leaned on the banisters and surveyed the hall below.

'And his lordship does *you* credit,' she countered, her voice low as she studied the dark head and broad shoulders that were all she could see of Ross crossing the hall.

'He does, doesn't he?' The valet surveyed his employer with satisfaction. 'It helps that he's a military gentleman, they usually carry themselves well. And he's fit. Not a spare ounce on him, I'd say, and good musculature,' he continued with professional enthusiasm, apparently not noticing the warmth in Meg's cheeks. 'All that marching makes long muscles, not bulky ones. Makes his inexpressibles fit like a second skin.'

The thought of Ross's thighs in fine knitted silk evening breeches had Meg turning to fuss with the flower arrangement. That half-hour on the terrace when she had cried in his arms and he had comforted her seemed like a dream now. The next day he had appeared to be engrossed writing letters in the intervals between inspecting the cottages on the estate, setting on a veritable army of men to repair them and continuing with his daily rides out with his steward.

His mood had seemed not so much grim as serious, she had thought, watching him pace across the hall between drawing room and library. Meg could only hope that he met a young woman for whom he could feel real affection and attachment.

And then she would have to leave, for she could not

imagine staying at the Court with Ross wed to another woman. But she had kept busy, and outwardly cheerful. Sometimes she had not thought about Ross or her sisters for an hour at a time.

'Any more news of your sisters?' Perrott asked, jerking her away from uncomfortable speculation and back to the main anxiety in her life.

'I have had one more letter from Jago, but he is not getting anywhere. They are definitely not at home and my father informed him that he had no daughters when Jago was making conversation with him when he called.'

'Perhaps they both eloped?'

'There is no gossip—it seems the villagers are keeping silent out of fear of my father's anger.'

'No news is good news, in my opinion. After all, if— forgive me—they had been taken ill or met with an accident at home and died, Jago would find out about that.'

'That is true.' Worrying over something you could not do anything about was not productive, she knew that. Instead, she went over the arrangements for the dinner party for the tenth time that day.

Heneage and Mrs Harris had thrown themselves into preparations for the event with enthusiasm and Meg had been caught up in it, finding to her relief that she now knew enough to fulfil her part.

The large dining room and long drawing room had been turned out, the gloomier paintings removed to the attics and the candelabra lowered for every tinkling crystal drop to be washed. The silver had been polished and the laundry maids attacked the yards of napery with soapwort and starch. Footmen had been set to clean windows on the inside while the gardening staff polished at the outside and Meg had turned the two largest spare bedrooms into boudoirs for the ladies to leave their wraps and to retire to during the course of the evening.

Now, as Heneage threw open the front doors and Ross walked back into the hall, Meg went to check on the maids. She could have watched, seen the guests arrive, but somehow she did not want to, although the maids were all agog and had had to be chased back to their stations. Once, as Lieutenant Halgate's wife, she would have been an eligible guest for a dinner party like this; now she must think herself grateful to be able to attend to the comfort of the ladies.

It was clear, as the footmen led one chattering group after another up to the ladies' retiring rooms, that no one was thinking of being fashionably late. They were all far too eager to see the new Lord Brandon presiding over his dinner table for that, Meg thought, half-amused, half-irritated by the prattle. She should have been attending to the married ladies, but the opportunity to size up the little flock of prospective brides was too much for her curiosity.

Ross had not been so obvious as to invite only those families with daughters, but even so, there were seven unmarried girls to fill the bedchamber with giggles and gossip as they prinked in front of the dressing-table mirror and the long cheval glass.

'He isn't at all handsome,' Elizabeth Pennare remarked as she pinned up one of her elder sister's curls.

'Deliciously brooding, though,' one girl Meg did not recognise countered. 'Like a Byronic hero.'

'And brave,' another added. 'He was a major, after all, and was wounded. I wish he was still wearing his scarlet uniform.'

The Rifle Brigade wears green, you ignorant chit. Meg helped Jenny fold evening cloaks away, her tongue between her teeth.

'And rich,' one of the Pengilly girls remarked. 'Papa says he owns mines and fishing boats and a warehouse in Falmouth.'

One or two of the young women exchanged glances, eyebrows raised, lips pursed, at this vulgar mention of money. But they are all interested, Meg thought. Money, title, looks. *What about the man? What about his character?*

'Well, I think it must be very hard to have to come back after years away in the army and find all your family gone and have to make a fresh start,' one rather mousy girl said. Meg smiled at her sensitivity and her soft voice, wondering who she was.

'Not quite all,' Anne Pengilly remarked, eyes wide with the scandal of it. 'They do say there's a boy who looks remarkably—'

'Come along, girls.' Lady Pennare swept in. 'We must not keep our host waiting.'

They streamed out of the room, chattering and laughing, all except for the quiet one with the soft voice who hung back.

'May I help?' Meg asked. 'I am sorry, I am afraid I did not hear your name. Would you like your mama?'

'Oh, no, thank you. I'm Penelope Hawkins, the vicar's niece,' she said with her shy smile. 'I just… They are a bit overwhelming,' she added breathlessly. 'Like a flock of birds all twittering and pecking. Poor Lord Brandon,' she murmured as she slipped out of the door and followed in their wake.

She would do. Just so long as she isn't frightened of him.

They are all impossible, Ross thought. He scanned the length of the table while paying smiling attention to

Lady Avise Westmoreland, who was regaling him with her opinions on the absolute necessity of visiting London at least four times a year. 'Otherwise, how is one to dress?' she enquired. Ross hoped she was not expecting a serious answer to that.

'Absolutely,' he agreed. 'May I help you to some more of the fricassee?' No, one day—let alone one night—with any of the pretty young things arrayed down the length of his dining table would result in him either strangling his new wife or shooting himself. All except, perhaps, the little brown sparrow halfway down who was, if he remembered correctly, the vicar's niece.

He must have a predilection for the daughters of the church, he thought ruefully, although Miss Hawkins roused no stirring of desire in him. She just looked as though she would be tranquil company and had her fair share of common sense. Which, he was rapidly becoming convinced, Lady Avise singularly lacked.

It seemed an age, but finally he stood on the front steps and saw off the last of his guests, their carriages clattering away down the drive in the moonlight. Ross rolled his shoulders to release some of the tension and took a cigarillo case out of an inner pocket. One of the footmen brought him a candle to light the thin cylinder. He nodded his thanks as he began to stroll along the terrace. 'Tell Perrott not to sit up for me, will you?'

The air was still enough to hear the sea and on an impulse he began to make his way along the path that led towards the lane to the bay. He leaned on the gate, savouring the cigarillo, letting his mind wander as he looked down the moonlit lane.

Then, just at the bend before the lane ran on to the beach, there was a flicker of white. Something, or someone, was down there. Tregarne had accused Billy of smuggling. He had put off confronting the old man about it; now he realised that this was a perfect night for landing casks. If he found evidence, then he must act.

Ross pinched out the cigarillo between fingers and thumb and tossed it aside, pulled the lapels of his coat together across the betraying white of his shirt, climbed the gate and trod silently down the lane to the beach.

Chapter Fifteen

Ross kept to the ridge of grass in the centre of the lane, his evening shoes silent on the soft turf. There was no further movement ahead. At the bend before the beach he stopped, listening, but the sound of the surf was too loud to make out any other sound.

Slowly he eased around the corner, the fragrance of bluebells competing with the smell of the sea as he brushed close to the bank. The beach seemed deserted, the sand bleached white and the foam on the small breakers glinting, but even as he studied it in the moonlight he knew he was not alone.

The old instincts refined by years of hunting the enemy, not rabbits, were sending prickles of awareness down his spine. Ross realised he was smiling, teeth bared, as his blood stirred. God, but he had missed this, the *frisson* of danger, the skill of stalking, the challenge of outwitting the other man. If there was another man out here and it was not just his imagination.

If the other man was Billy Gillan, then it was likely that

he was stalking Ross and could have brought him down five minutes ago, if he was so inclined. But although Billy might enjoy teasing his old pupil, he was no danger. It was not the poacher making every one of his senses alert to peril.

Here, now, he was the man he had been trying to hide under the civilised trappings of a country gentleman. He was the killer again, the man with blood on his hands and death in his heart. He shivered, partly appalled at the bone-deep rightness of what he was feeling, partly sliding easily into the skin of his old self. The difference now was that he was defending his own turf, not fighting his country's enemies.

It was perhaps not the most prudent thing to be searching for an unknown danger unarmed and in evening dress, but it added to the challenge and he was sick of being prudent.

The caves were around the corner. To approach them he would have to leave the cover of the bank and work his way around under the edge of the low cliff, across tumbled rocks and numerous rock pools. He eased off his evening shoes and removed his stockings, his bare feet flexing on the sand as he stripped off all his upper garments. His darkly tanned torso was less likely to show up than the stark white of a shirt he could not completely cover.

Half-naked Ross slid round the corner and headed for the caves. There was a splash, a creak, a sudden flash of light offshore, gone so rapidly that if he had not been alert for just those signs he would have missed them. A boat was rowing in, very cautiously. He crept on a little further to where a jumble of bigger rocks would give him cover.

Someone was humming. Ross flattened himself against the rock as the sound came closer and a figure emerged from the shelter of the rocks.

It was a woman clad only in a shift, her legs visible from the knee down, her arms bare as she walked towards the edge of the sea where the wavelets were breaking in silver foam on the sand. Her dark hair was piled on top of her head and she was humming, it seemed, out of sheer pleasure for she gave a little skip and a low laugh as the first waves touched her toes.

Meg? Here in her shift? Ross straightened up, opened his mouth to shout. If whoever it was in that boat heard him they would turn back, not knowing how many men were waiting for them on the beach. But even as he drew the breath into his lungs Meg ran into the surf to her waist, laughing and gasping with the shock of the cold water. Then she began to swim.

The dark shape of the boat loomed out of the darkness, right on top of her. Meg gave a startled shriek, someone swore and the shutter of a dark lantern opened, revealing six men at the oars and a seventh in the bows holding the lantern. Ross bit back the shout.

'Shutter that damned light.' The growled order carried clear over the water.

'It's a woman—row harder, boys, catch her.' The man in the bows held the light up, illuminating Meg's frantic efforts to swim ashore. She staggered to her feet, still waist deep as Ross reached the water's edge.

'Meg, to me!' She changed direction, floundering towards him as she recognised his voice. 'Run.' Up to his thighs in water he grabbed her, pushed her behind him towards the beach and faced the boat.

One unarmed man against seven with oars, knives and possibly pistols did not seem good odds. Ross showed his teeth; if they touched Meg, he'd kill the lot of them with his bare hands. 'I am Brandon. Get off this beach.'

'Going to stop us, are you?' A big man vaulted over the side into the surf, knife in hand. 'You and your mermaid?'

Ross backed up. There was no point in heroics yet—if he was knifed, Meg would be at their mercy. He had to buy her enough time to run clear. If he could lure the man in close enough to grapple with him…

Then something flew past his ear and hit the big man square on the chest, something else splashed into the water beside him as he roared with rage. Ross looked over his shoulder. Far from running, Meg was on the beach hurling stones at the boat.

He turned and made for her, hearing the creak of oars as the boat was driven towards the beach. 'Get behind me,' he ordered as he reached the sand. He backed up the beach, assessing the situation. There were too many of them, he was in a completely indefensible position and already they were splitting up, flanking him to cut off his retreat to the lane.

At his back Meg was silent, although he could hear her breathing. 'Listen. In a moment they will attack. You run, do you hear me? Tell Heneage to open the gun room, arm the footmen, grooms, tell them to get down here and make as much noise as they can as they come.' If he could provoke them to all go for him, she might have a chance to get away. By the time she returned with any help this unequal battle on the beach would be long over…

'Leave you? I—'

Whatever Meg was going to say was lost in the blast of a shotgun. The men turned as one towards the caves as a figure walked out on to the sand, gun in hand.

'Billy.'

'Aye. Damn fool time to go fossicking about in the water, boy. You lot, get out before I blow someone's thick head off.'

'What about the casks? You promised delivery today.' The big man took a step forwards and the barrels of the shotgun lifted. He stopped.

'You can whistle for them. You don't threaten my boy and his maid and still do business with me. Go on, shift and take your money with you. I've got both barrels loaded if you want them.'

The language and the threats they hurled were predictable, but they backed down, shambling back to the boat. Ross reached out a hand and pulled Meg to him, wet and shivering, but he watched the sea until the rowers were swallowed up by the darkness.

With Meg tight against his side, he looked at Billy. 'Thank you.' There was not a great deal more to say, not in front of Meg. He could strangle the old ruffian for getting involved with smugglers and he could kiss him for saving Meg.

The old man grunted. 'You take that maid back home and her clothes with her. Catch her death, she will, water's that cold.' He stooped and picked up a bundle. 'Here's her clothes. And where's yours, boy? Downright indecent, the pair of you.'

Meg gave a choked laugh. 'He sounds like my father,' she whispered. There was a shake in her voice, Ross could hear it under the bravado, and it was nothing to do with the temperature. He felt like shaking himself, with her near-naked body so close.

'Mine are at the foot of the lane—make a bundle of the lot, would you, Billy?' Ross bent and scooped Meg up in his arms before she could protest. Her chilled wet body against his bare chest made him catch his breath. That was nothing to do with temperature either.

'Ross? What are you doing?' Her voice was breathy now, both her vulnerability and her bravery making him want to kiss her. His heart was pounding from the aftermath of action and the unfulfilled violence that he had been ready to unleash.

'Carrying you home. Can you manage the clothes?' She nodded as Billy dumped the bundle into her arms, her wet hair clinging to Ross's skin. 'I'll come and talk to you tomorrow, you old fool.'

The poacher had the grace to look sheepish. 'Not going anywhere,' he muttered as he melted into the shadows.

'You can't carry me.' Meg was beginning to wriggle. 'Your leg—'

'I'm not limping any more.' It was half-true. If he concentrated and ignored the deep ache that still came back when he was tired, he did not limp. And it gave him a ridiculous pleasure to be able to carry Meg in his arms, although he expected her to start protesting and struggling at any moment. Instead she gave a little sigh and snuggled in to him.

'Are you all right?' Ross asked, suspicious of her sudden docility.

'I am sorry,' Meg said, so softly that he had to bend his head to hear her. 'I should never have gone down to the sea at night.'

'I had no idea you could swim.' Ross slowed and looked up at the house. There was a light in the hall, but he could hardly march in through the front door half-naked with his equally undressed housekeeper in his arms. 'Have you got a back-door key?'

'Yes, in my pocket.' She fell silent, then, as he veered off the path towards the rear of the house, added, 'I learned to swim in the millpond when I was very small, when Mama was still alive. I thought I might be able to remember how and I wanted to…to get away for a while.'

'So did I.'

'Penelope Hawkins might do. The Vicar's niece,' Meg suggested, following his unspoken meaning. 'I liked her. She seems rather sweet.'

Ross grunted. 'I do not want a wife who might do. I wish I did know what I want—other than to make love to you.' She gave a little gasp, but did not struggle in his arms. 'Here we are. Home. Can you stand up a moment and find the key?'

Meg slid out of his arms and handed him the bundle of clothes while she rummaged for the key. 'That's the second time you have said it tonight—did you realise? Home. You have stopped saying *the Court*.'

'So I have.' And he was thinking of it as home now, too. The whole atmosphere of the place had changed since Meg had begun to work her magic on it. The door opened on to a dimly lit passageway and Meg slipped in ahead of him. He must ask her to look at his bedroom next—then he might be able to sleep without feeling he was in his father's bed surrounded by ghosts.

Bedrooms. No, he was not thinking about interior decoration, or ghosts as he reached the door to the housekeeper's rooms, with her standing there, her limbs pale in the gloom, her chemise clinging damply to every curve. Hot, dark desires flooded his body.

'I'll take my clothes.' The after-effects of the incident were making themselves felt now. He could feel the tension in the nape of his neck, the sick feeling in the pit of his stomach. He had been wound up for action and violence and what he had got was a safe anticlimax. *God, am I so addicted to killing that I cannot even be grateful that Meg was spared seeing fighting and bloodshed?*

'Ross?' She looked up at him and the self-loathing gripped him. If he didn't get a grip on the animal inside himself he would just bundle her into that room and take her like the savage he was. Meg was frowning a little, her underlip caught by her teeth, her eyes questioning in the dim light of the passageway lamp.

'Go to bed,' he said. 'Give me my clothes.' He saw her flinch at the brutality of his tone, but he was beyond caring. He just needed to get away from her.

'Here.' Meg thrust the top bundle of clothes into his hands. 'Thank you. We could have been killed, just now, because I was so foolish.' She could feel the doorknob behind her and she turned it, stepping back into the dark of her room without taking her eyes from his face. 'Goodnight.'

'Goodnight.' And he was gone.

He was angry with her, of course, and quite rightly so. Meg put down her damp and sandy clothes and went to find towels and the water jug. She got as far as filling the basin and then sank down on the end of the bed, wrapped her arms around herself and shook.

Ross had stood there, protected her in the certain knowledge that he would be severely beaten, if not killed, as a result. She loved him, she wanted him and he had walked away just now with angry finality. She deserved that.

In the silence she gradually became aware of a soft *tick* she did not recognise. Puzzled, Meg got up and searched for it. There, tangled in her stockings by its chain, was Ross's pocket watch. *Tick, tick*, the smooth gold case with its worn engraving of a coat of arms lay in the palm of her hand. She must give it back to him first thing in the morning. Meg reached out to put it safely on the table, then stopped. It was old, an heirloom. What if he missed it, went out again to search for it? What if the smugglers had returned?

She would go upstairs now, open his door a crack and just hang the watch by the chain over the inner door knob.

Then he could not fail to find it. Meg pulled off her wet shift, scrubbed herself with a towel and put on a night-gown and her wrapper. The house was still as she padded on bare feet out of the servants' quarters and up the stairs towards his room.

There was no light showing around his door. Meg eased the handle round and opened it, just enough to slide her hand in with the watch.

'Blood. God, so much blood. Blood and guts and mud.'

She froze at the sound of Ross's voice, angry and anguished and cracked as though speaking hurt him. For a moment she did not understand, then the deep voice dropped to a confused mutter: he was having a nightmare.

Meg stood there, transfixed, listening. She felt like an eavesdropper and yet she could not close the door and step away. There was so much pain and self-disgust in his voice. He was hurting so badly—how could she leave him? Meg pushed the door open and went in. The click as she shut it did not wake him, nor did the sound of her bare feet brushing over the carpet as she approached the bed.

The moonlight struck through the uncurtained window across the bed where Ross lay, naked in a tangle of sheets, his head turning restlessly on the pillow, his big fists clenched, one of them pounding into the mattress.

'Not dead…can't even manage a decent headshot. He's screaming…like a stuck pig. Die, damn it. Shoot again. Yes, at last. Dead. Another one dead. Come on men, reload, faster, you bastards. They've all got to be killed. Giles, Mother, the French. Killed them all. I've killed them all and they still keep coming.'

Appalled, Meg caught his hand, only to have him pound it painfully down. 'Waves of blood, like the sea. Wade in it. Find Meg or she'll drown in it. I've drowned her in blood like all of them…'

There were tears streaking his cheeks and the sight brought a sob to her throat. 'Ross!' She leaned over the big, tortured body, grabbed his shoulders and shook him. 'Ross, wake up! Ross, listen to me, it is Meg.'

His eyes opened, dark and unfocused. His hands lifted and he surged up into a sitting position, brushing her off like a fly. She crashed into the foot of the bed, rolling over his legs as she went, and he lunged for her.

'Ross!'

'Meg?' The hands that gripped her shoulders relaxed until they were just supporting her. 'God, have I hurt you? What are you doing here?'

'I'm all right. I brought your watch back, I was just going to slip it inside, but you were having a dreadful nightmare, Ross. I tried to wake you.'

He closed his eyes for a moment, then let her go and rolled over to strike a light for the branch of candles by his bed. 'I can just catch the tail of it still in my head,' he said grimly. 'The usual one about blood and death. I am sorry you had to hear that.'

'It sounded so real,' she murmured. 'But then you mentioned Giles and your mother.'

'I killed them, too, one way or another. And then I spent years perfecting being a killer. And now—that is what I am, what I am worth.'

'No!' She knelt up, grabbed him by the shoulders, shook him. 'No. I saw you on that beach. I know what you were planning—you would have sent me away, safe, and stayed to face all of them. You could have been badly hurt and yet you would have fought for me. A killer doesn't think like that.'

'I was enjoying myself, up to the point I knew you were there,' he confessed, as though admitting a crime.

'Of course you were,' Meg retorted. 'Any man of courage would have done. It doesn't make you evil or worthless—it makes you brave and worthy.' His eyes were still bleak. 'You had a tragic accident when you were a boy, you were thoughtless and heedless like all young men—but you cannot punish yourself for that for the rest of your life. Were you a good officer?'

'Yes!' He drew back, affronted. She almost smiled.

'A worthless killer doesn't make a good officer. I've seen the difference, don't forget, every day for years, following the army. Ross, the fact it affects you so only proves that you aren't steeped in evil, that you aren't in the grip of some bloodlust. They will fade, those memories, the dreams will go in time. You didn't dream on the ship or you would have woken me.'

'No, I didn't.' He stared at her, the bleakness fading. 'Perhaps you are my cure.'

Perhaps I might be part of the medicine, Meg thought, watching his face, seeing the nightmare drain away. This was the real Ross Brandon, here in front of her, not the dark, brooding man who had come back to a home he rejected and a duty he loathed. This was the man who had comforted her, even though she had thrown his father's memory in his face; this was the man who was prepared to show her his vulnerability as well as his strength. And she wanted him with every fibre of her being. Years of being prudent, sensible, seemed to melt away and she was Meg the dreamer again, Meg who believed in fairy stories.

How had she ever thought him cold and brutal? There was so much warmth in those dark eyes now, so much gentleness in those big hands. So much potential for happiness.

And there was beauty in those sculpted muscles, in the sheer physicality of the man in front of her. It was time she understood all the joys of lovemaking, a voice inside told her. She leaned forwards and kissed him on the mouth, her lips telling him without words that she needed him.

He responded gently, silently answering, his kiss full of doubt. 'Meg,' he said when he pulled back from her, 'I thought you must be afraid of me. I have given you reason. I want you, but I thought I was too big, too ugly, too much of a brute for you.' He gestured away her protest. 'I thought you could not stay with me for myself, not as my lover, so I had to offer something else, suggest a business proposition as my mistress.' He shook his head. 'I have not been thinking very clearly about anyone but myself, these past few weeks.'

'With reason. I understand. Make love to me, Ross.' He went very still. The candlelight was golden on the plane of his chest and he seemed to have stopped breathing. 'Not as your mistress, just as the two of us, here, tonight. I don't know about tomorrow, I can't think about that.'

He shook his head as though he did not believe her. 'I am wrong for you. I should never have asked you to be my mistress. You deserve a handsome young man, not a battle-scarred, ghost-haunted—'

'If you say *killer* again I will slap you,' Meg threatened. 'I do not want a handsome boy.' She laid her palms flat on his chest and felt his shuddering intake of breath, breathed in the scent of hot, aroused man and the salt still on his skin. 'I know all about self-centred handsome young men. I want a real man. Tonight I want you.' *And I love you. I love you.*

Ross sat quite still as she slid her hands down his chest towards his waist, her fingers ruffling the dark hair as it narrowed towards his navel. The twisted sheet covered his loins and she let her hand drift further, holding his eyes with hers as she moulded her hand round the hard heat beneath the linen.

'You have such faith in my self-control,' he murmured. 'Just don't… Ah! Don't move your hand.'

'No?' she queried, experimenting with a teasing stroke.

'No,' he growled, moving faster than such a big man should be able to. Meg found herself on her back, her robe and nightgown stripped away and Ross kneeling over her. 'Meg, I do not think I can manage subtlety here, or any self-control. Not now, I want you too much. If you are going to change your mind, say so now.'

'Do you remember telling me on the ship that if you wanted me flat on my back under you, that it would happen?' He paused, his eyes hot on her. 'Well, I have thought about that—often. That is what I want, Ross, and I do not want to wait either.'

In response he simply threw the sheet aside and knelt between her legs, nudging them apart to give himself room. *Oh, my God.* Naked and erect he was as magnificent as she had dreamed he would be.

'Tell me if I hurt you.' Meg closed her eyes for a moment as his weight spread down over her. His erection pressed into the flesh of her belly, branding it, wrenching a gasp from her lips. Then he took some of his weight on one elbow as his hand slid down, teasing into the slick heat between her sea-cold thighs. 'You are ready for me.' It was not a question, she was utterly aroused already and they both knew it.

'Take me, Ross. Please.' She watched his face as he moved against her, nudging, gentle, still unwilling entirely to accept her word. Meg dug her nails into his shoulders and lifted her legs, wrapping them around his hips as he thrust, filling her utterly with one stroke. *'Aah.'* Nothing had ever felt so right, so perfectly *meant*.

Ross dropped his head so his forehead rested against hers, their breath mingling. Then he began to move and she cried out, rising to meet him, surging with him, arms and legs tight in an effort to join with him utterly, be absorbed into him, to take him into her. She looked up into his face, rapt, taut, and she lifted her hands to pull him down to her so their lips met. And then his mouth was ravaging hers, his tongue filling her, his breath sobbing into her as the tension mounted and tightened and he lifted her off the bed, pushing up on to his knees, pulling her with him so he impaled her impossibly, totally, and everything broke around her in a shattering climax and exploding colour was eclipsed by total blackness.

Chapter Sixteen

Ross was lifting her, laying her down. There was a shout of ecstasy as he convulsed against her, then they were still, the only sound in the room their breathing. His hands drifted gently over her flanks, up to touch her face. 'Meg,' he murmured, then his head settled against her shoulder and she realised he was asleep.

Ross was heavy and hot and they were both sticky with salt and sweat and sex. It was, Meg decided as she floated on a hazy dream somewhere between sleep and waking, quite perfect.

She managed to free a hand and stroked his hair, feeling the shape of his skull, elegant under her fingers. 'I love you.' She felt herself slip into sleep. 'I do love you.'

'Meg. Meg, sweetheart, wake up.' She blinked her eyes open and found Ross bending over her.

'Mmm.' She reached for him. Now they could be slow, could explore, discover, linger over their loving.

'It is four. The clock has just struck. You have to get out of here.'

'Oh.' The blissful, sensual mood vanished. Meg sat up amidst the tangled wreckage of the bed and surveyed the room, lit by the morning light through the unshielded glass. Ross, naked, was standing in the middle of it, hands on hips. A sight to stare at quite blatantly.

'What is it?' He smiled at her, his teeth very white against the black morning stubble.

'I like looking at you.' To her delight he blushed.

'Wicked woman.' But he came and leaned down to snatch a hard, fast kiss. 'I like looking at you too.' Then the smile vanished and he knelt by the bed. 'Meg. Are you...is it all right?'

'Our adventure last night or...or what happened afterwards?'

'Both. Meg, would this have happened if it had not been for last night? I should have waited, we were both...emotional. After that nightmare I was not thinking straight.'

'I am...fine.' A very inadequate word for the way she felt. 'I hope it would have happened anyway. I hope I would have had the courage to tell you how I felt, what I needed.' She curled her arm around his neck and tugged him down to find his mouth again. When he pulled back she clung on, using his own strength to rise up and wrap herself around him, bare skin against bare skin.

'Stop it.' Ross untangled her and sat her on the bed. 'I never knew what will-power meant until I met you.' He picked up her wrapper and held it out.

Meg took it, wrapped it around herself and curled up against the head of the bed. Last night she had accepted that she loved this man. She had told him, as he slept, after she had made love with him. Now she had to come to terms with that. She wrapped her arms around her bent knees, rested her chin on them and watched while Ross shook out her nightgown, fingering the rent down the front of it. *How long have I loved him?*

'What is it?' He looked across at her. 'What is wrong, Meg? There won't be consequences, I was careful.'

'No, of course not. I am not worried about that. I am just sleepy.' She managed a smile, and, if she was honest with herself, she reflected, it did not take much pretence to smile at Ross. But there were consequences far beyond what he meant just now. She would not be able to stay here when he married. She was not even sure her conscience would allow it once he began to court a bride.

'Come on.' He bent and kissed her forehead, pushing back the salt-damp tangle of her hair, then pulled her to her feet beside the bed. 'Tonight, come to me again.' His lips quirked into a smile. 'This bed is much bigger than yours.'

'I know.' Her imagination was full, as she was sure he had intended, with visions of what they could do on this wide expanse. Dare she risk another night? A night with time to explore each other, to make gentle, leisurely love. What if he guessed the depth of her feelings? She was not certain she could hide them from him.

'You will come?'

'If I can do so safely.' She only had him for a few weeks, perhaps a month or so. She was not strong enough to gainsay both him and her own feelings.

His gaze rested on her, heavy, sensual, happy as she slid off the bed and tied the robe around her waist. *I have made him happy.* Ross opened the door, holding her gaze until the last moment. *And I have made myself happy too.*

'There were smugglers in the bay last night, Mrs Halgate!' Damaris dumped the hot water cans beside the tin bath, her face alight with her news.

'I know. I had a very lucky escape.' Meg decided that she must tell as much of the truth as she could. 'I had been for a swim—'

'In the sea, ma'am?'

'Yes, in the sea. I heard the shot—someone seems to have frightened them away.'

As she hoped, Damaris put two and two together and made half a dozen. 'So, you'd had your swim and were coming back? How did you know it was smugglers, ma'am?'

'There was a shouted exchange.'

'It was his lordship and old Billy Gillan who saw them off,' the maid confided as she set the screen round the bath. 'Perrott told me this morning. Apparently there was a fight and his lordship came back in ever such a state. You should see his inexpressibles!'

'Damaris!' Meg managed to look suitably shocked at the mention of a man's nether garments. 'But you may imagine my alarm. I had no idea anyone was around.'

'Ooh!' Damaris's eyes were wide. 'They could have been spying on you!'

'I was wearing my shift,' Meg said repressively. 'And it was too dark, just the moon to see by.' She climbed into the bath and reached for the washcloth. 'Pour that jug of water over my head, would you please? I must get all the salt out.'

Ross took a gun and the old pointer dog that haunted the stable yard in the hope that someone was going out shooting and made his way through the woodland towards Billy's cottage. It was remarkable how good a large breakfast—on top of action, danger and a thoroughly satisfactory bout of lovemaking—made a man feel.

He paused and leaned on a fence, narrowed his eyes

against the sunlight and looked out over fields he was beginning to learn the names of. He knew where a hedge bank needed repair, just out of sight to the left, he knew how many cottages needed work on them and what the rents were and he was beginning, much to his own surprise, to enjoy learning these things.

My land. The sun was hot on his back and the gentle thump against his legs of the pointer's tail was all the company he needed just now. *My people, my place. My home, as Meg would say.* He climbed the fence and plunged, whistling, into the coppice that sheltered Billy's cottage, a piece of no-man's land, its ownership lost in time.

'You make enough noise, boy.' Billy was leaning against a tree trunk, almost invisible until he moved. 'Not a bird left, here to Truro, you and your big feet.'

'We don't all have to creep about on unlawful business, Billy.'

'Aar, well. Suppose you don't, not being lord and master, hereabouts.' The old man shifted a plug of chewing tobacco in his mouth and spat.

'Why the devil are you getting mixed up with smugglers?' Ross hitched one hip against a fallen tree. 'Tregarne told me he suspected you were at it.' Silence. 'Do you need the money?' This stubborn man had taught him patience when he was a child; now he was prepared to wait it out. 'I've got all day.'

Billy scowled at him. 'Interfering cursed keepers. The boy's growing, got a good brain. Lily's worried.'

'So you wanted money for William? Has Lily told you what I am doing about him? You don't need to worry.'

'Fool of a maid's got it wrong—you'll not be acknowledging your own father's base cheel.'

'I will and I am. He's my brother, Billy. And I'm giving

them a cottage on the estate and an allowance. You can have one, too, if you want.'

'Who, me? In one of them cottages with a garden all round so all the neighbourhood can see you and what you're about? Not me.' He shifted against the tree. 'But if you mean it, that's a good thing you're doing for Lily and the boy.'

'You know he wants to be a lawyer?' The old man nodded. 'Can't have his grandfather taken up for smuggling then, can he? Or poaching? You think of that. Kimber will take him to train, but not if you're in Truro gaol.'

'What'll I eat then, if I can't go after game?'

'I'll tell Tregarne that as my brother's grandfather you may shoot and trap what you like on my land. And don't look like that,' Ross added as Billy scowled at him. 'I don't care if it spoils your fun—think about William. And don't you go sneaking off on to anyone else's land—I can't help you there.'

'You've grown up into a hard man, Ross Brandon.' It was, he knew, both praise and an apology.

'I had a good teacher.'

'What you doing with that 'ansum maid?' Billy demanded, obviously happier now he could catch Ross in the wrong.

''Ansum? I suppose Mrs Halgate might be described as attractive, yes. Trying to keep her out of trouble with old rogues like you around, that's what I'm doing with her. She's my housekeeper.'

'Then what's she about, capering in the scroff?'

'Swimming, apparently. She'll not do it again.'

'Huh.' Billy slung his shotgun over his shoulder and snapped his fingers. The black-and-white dog slid out of the undergrowth and came to heel. 'If you've finished giving me a slice of tongue pie, you can come and have some rabbit stew and tell me about this here courting you're doing.'

'Who says I'm courting?' Ross fell into step beside him.

'I see them carriages and all those fancy pieces getting out of them. Some people can't see behind the end of their nose, if you ask me.'

'I should get a wife. And an heir.' Ross said it with outward confidence, wondering at the hollow feeling in his stomach. It was almost like apprehension, or the sensation that he had done something wrong, but couldn't work out what. He shrugged. Not enough sleep, obviously.

'That you should,' Billy agreed. 'Just get on with it, boy, and try to think with your head for once.'

Meg stood with Damaris in the middle of Ross's bedchamber and sighed.

'I know, ma'am. It's enough to make you fall into a melancholy, isn't it? It's that dark and sort of quiet-like.'

'That's because of all the curtains.' Meg turned slowly round, avoiding looking at the bed. 'The dark mulberry velvet is dignified, but with the dark blue walls and all this heavy furniture, and those paintings, it is just depressing.' She turned again. 'These windows match the big room on the other side of the stairs, don't they? Come along, Damaris, I have an idea.'

An hour later she left the maids exchanging the pale blue silk hangings from the main guest chamber for the mulberry velvet in Ross's room and went to see what she could find to substitute for the collection of disapproving seventeenth-century portraits on the walls. She was sure there were some seascapes somewhere. She found that her cheeks were growing warm at the thought of the sea. It was going to be impossible if everything she thought about made her recollect Ross and last night. She was still smiling as she passed the door to the library.

'Ow!' There was a thud and a muffled curse from inside. Not Ross, he was out and that was not his voice. The maids had finished this part of the house for the day and the footmen were all up ladders wrestling with curtain poles.

Meg pushed open the door with some caution. A young man was crouched, gathering up a pile of fallen books. As he heard her he straightened: six foot of gangling, black-haired, strong-jawed young male Brandon—Ross's portrait come to life.

They stared at each other. 'They aren't damaged,' the youth said and at the sound of the Cornish burr in his voice the spell was broken.

'I can see it was an accident.' *But who is he?* Then she saw his eyes were an unusual amber and realised. 'You are Billy's grandson, aren't you?' *And Ross's brother.*

'Yes, ma'am. William. His lordship…Ross, I mean, said I could borrow books.'

'You may call me Mrs Halgate,' Meg said. 'I am house-keeper here.' He was family, and should be treated as such. But did Ross mean to acknowledge him? 'Can I help you find something?'

'I don't know. I've never seen so many books all in one place.'

'What do you like to read?' Meg asked, wondering how well he had mastered his letters. Had he been to school?

'Anything,' he said with a smile, so very like Ross that she smiled back. 'Newspapers, the Bible… Anything.'

'I know.' She took *Gulliver's Travels* from the shelf. 'Your brother likes this one.' He showed no surprise at her description of Ross. 'And I looked at this the other day, it is Cornish legends, the engravings are fascinating.' She put them on the table and gestured to the seat next to her. 'Come and see.'

One book led to another. Soon the table was littered with open volumes as they delved into the collection, reading snatches to each other. 'Look at this, Mrs Halgate,' William said and she came to look over his shoulder at an illustration of a whale, just as there was a sound behind them.

Meg turned. It was Ross, one hand on the window frame he had just stepped through, staring at the pair of them as though he had seen a ghost.

'Good afternoon, my lord,' Meg said, summoning up all her composure. 'I will clear up directly.' Beside her William scrambled to his feet.

'That is all right,' Ross said. 'I told my brother he may use the library.'

'But you did not tell me I could turn out half the bookshelves.' Meg cast a rueful look at the table.

'I'll put them away,' William said. 'Mrs Halgate was helping me.' She could feel his tension in case Ross was angry.

'I know.' Ross smiled at her. Meg felt light-headed. There was so much meaning in that smile, so much warmth in the caress of his eyes.

'I will just go and see whether they have finished in your bed…bedchamber.' She stumbled over the word. 'We changed the curtains for something lighter. But I haven't found the seascapes I was going to replace the portraits with yet. Excuse me.'

Ross watched as Meg whisked out of the door, her cheeks pink. He had never seen her so flurried before and it was both charming and, he was amused to discover, flattering, that he could put her in such a state.

But she was not the only one feeling disconcerted. He

had stood at the window watching them—the woman who was his lover, the boy who could pass as his son—and had felt a shock of recognition, a premonition almost. They had looked right together, companionable, sharing and enjoying the books without the need to say very much. She must have known who William was, but she accepted him.

'I like her,' William said as Ross continued to stand looking at the closed door. 'Mrs Halgate. I like her a lot.'

'Yes.' Ross turned back to the table and picked up *Gulliver's Travels*, running his fingers over the leather binding as he pictured Meg sitting on the trunk in the cabin with it open in her hands. 'So do I.'

Chapter Seventeen

Patrick Jago's letter was short and brutally clear.

Dear Mrs Halgate,

I regret that I have been unable to find any clues as to the whereabouts of your sisters. I can be clear on only three points: the facts that I communicated to you in my last letter, the fact that nothing is recorded under their names in any parish register for ten miles around and the certainty that they are nowhere in the vicarage or its adjoining buildings, which I must confess to entering and searching on Sunday last during morning service.

I am in London now. I enquired at all the coaching inns receiving passengers from East Anglia, in case one or both went to London. However, at such a distance in time I have not been surprised to find no one remembers two young ladies amongst so many.

I find myself detained by another, personal, matter, and will remain here at the *Belle Sauvage*

on Ludgate Hill, where any correspondence will find
me, for the foreseeable future.

   Yours etc…

'Et cetera, et cetera,' Meg murmured, refolding the
letter.

'Not good news?' Mrs Harris topped up Meg's tea cup.

'No. Not bad, either.' She knew what Jago had meant by
that reference to parish registers. He had been searching
for burials.

'Bless your heart.' The cook's homely face creased with
concern. 'And on top of the fright you had last night with
those wicked smugglers, too. What a mercy you were on
your way back to the house before they landed.'

'I should never have gone swimming,' Meg confessed.
'I was feeling a trifle…agitated and thought it would be
calming.'

'And no wonder you were,' Mrs Harris said comfortably.
'All that worry about your sisters and then that big party
to prepare for. Not that his lordship found anyone he likes
the look of, not that I can see. I'd have heard if he'd gone
calling on the ladies afterwards. We'll be having another
dinner party soon with another selection, mark my words.'

'You can't be wondering at it, Mrs Harris,' Heneage
observed. 'He's a man in his prime and he needs to be
settling down and starting a family.'

'Got more of one than I realised.' Perrott piled clotted
cream on one of Mrs Harris's scones. 'There's a brother,
I hear, and a serving of scandal with him.'

'Half-brother,' Mrs Harris corrected. 'William Gillan,
and a nice lad he is too, even if that old rogue Billy's his
grandfather. Lily, his ma, is a good woman and brought
him up decent—no shame to her what his late lordship
did, poor lass.'

'Still, there's not a lot of gentlemen who would acknowledge the family by-blows like that,' Perrott observed, the jam and cream-laden scone halfway to his lips. 'Getting a tutor for him and setting him up for the law and giving him the run of the house.'

'Might make difficulties with a new wife,' Heneage said. 'What if she disapproves, which many might? Or thinks the boy's his? He was wild enough as a lad, as I recall.'

'Then his lordship would be better off without her.' Meg replaced her cup in the saucer with a clatter and got to her feet. 'If she puts appearance over family affection and doing the right thing and if she cannot take his word, she does not deserve him, whoever she is. Excuse me, I must go and think about Mr Jago's letter.'

She was out into the passage, the door almost closed, when Perrott's low whistle made her pause, hand on the knob. 'That was a trifle vehement! You don't think—'

'I try very hard not to think, Perrott,' Heneage said repressively. 'It just leads to imaginings, and I don't hold with that. Not about the family.'

Meg eased the door closed and walked blindly away from the kitchen. When she pulled herself together she was sitting in the shelter of the rustic arbour looking out over the rose garden. A light drizzle had begun to drift in from the sea, darkening the flagstones at her feet. Meg curled up on the seat and thought grimly that it provided a counterpoint to her mood that had slipped, in less than an hour, from confused happiness into miserable uncertainty.

It was easy to fall in love again, it seemed. Or had what she felt for James ever been real love? Was that why it had been so quick to turn into affectionate exasperation? She had been very young, besotted, romantic. And the man she had left her sisters for had always been younger than her in every way except years. It was easy to see that now, when she loved a man, not a handsome, gallant, heedless boy.

So, where am I now? Meg broke off a pink rosebud and fretted at the tight petals with her fingernail, peeling them back with painful concentration. She loved Ross and she had made love with him and now, soon, she must leave him. Sooner than she had hoped, if she was to avoid bringing gossip down on the household. She had betrayed herself to the upper servants, it seemed. They would be loyal and discreet, but it would only take a whisper and the local families would think twice about their precious daughters. It was bad enough, the less charitable would think, that Ross acknowledged his half-brother, but an *affaire* with his housekeeper really would put the cat amongst the pigeons.

And what of Bella and Lina? She had carried out her plan and now the unthinkable had happened: her agent had not found them. Perhaps if she went to London, found some occupation there, she could advertise for them. If she could only think straight, work out how much money she had left, how long she dared remain here. Meg shivered; she was becoming cold, but it was hard to move. The rosebud, ruined, lay in her palm, the fragments of petal scattered over her dark skirts, clinging as the sea fret dampened the fabric. But the golden heart of the flower was revealed in all its complex beauty and when she lifted it to her lips the rich perfume still filled her nostrils with sensual delight.

She would go to Ross tonight and every night that he wanted her for one week. That was all she could permit herself, the gift of loving him for seven nights. Then she would go before she harmed him, go and devote herself to finding her sisters and making her own life.

* * *

The clock on the landing, five minutes out of time with the others in the house, struck one. Meg started, her fingertips sliding across the oak panel of Ross's bedchamber door. Every sensation, the smell of the beeswax polish, the faint graining in the wood, the creak of the clock settling down again, was magnified by the sensual tension that had been gripping her ever since she had come in, damp and shivering, from the rose garden.

She had made a decision, set a limit, now she had only these days to create the memories that had to sustain her for all the years without Ross. Meg turned the handle and slipped inside, uncertain what to expect.

'Meg.' Ross got up from the chair by the fireplace, dropping his book unheeded on the floor. He was dressed in the splendour of a robe made from some exotic eastern brocade, gold and silver mingling and gleaming in the light of the candles that were blazing all around the room. 'Thank you for this room,' he said as she stood there, staring at him. 'It is full of the sea—it reminds me of our voyage.'

'Pain and boredom and a distressing break with the past?' Her back was still flat against the door.

'Never boredom. How could I be bored with you, Meg?' He stayed where he was on the hearthrug, watching her. 'What is wrong?'

'Nothing.' How could she touch him without letting him see how she felt? How could she explain to herself that she was staring at the most handsome man she had ever seen? Was it love that turned those harsh features into beauty? Then she realised. He was happy, home at last, and that contentment transformed him, even if perhaps it was only her eyes that could see it.

'That is a very fine robe.' Something safe to say.

'An antique. Perrott has been delving deep into the wardrobes around the house.'

Under the hem of the robe his feet were bare and dark hair showed at the open neck. Beneath the heavy silk brocade he was naked, and the breath caught in her throat at the memory of his body last night. 'Meg?' Ross held out a hand and she understood. It was her choice. If she turned around and left, he would not pursue her.

Seven nights, my love. She walked forwards and put her hand in his, letting him draw her close so she could rest her cheek against the cool fabric. Ross smelled faintly of the sandalwood the robe had been stored in. Meg burrowed her face closer, searching for the real, familiar, scent of him, parting the lapels until she could press her lips against his shoulder. *Oh, yes.* 'Mmm.'

'Mmm?' he queried, his lips vibrating where he was running them down the exposed curve of her neck.

'You taste good.' Meg touched the top of her tongue to the hot skin, then licked, drawing her tongue along the carved line of his collarbone.

'So do you, and even better for an absence of salt and sand.' Ross's tongue was doing intricate, tormenting, delicious things to the whorls of her ear. Meg wriggled closer, insinuated her hand between them to search for the knot holding the robe closed, then tugged knot and robe open. He was hot, she found, stepping close so her whole length was against him. His skin was hot, his hands were warm, pressing against her shoulder blades through the fine muslin of her nightgown and the cotton of her robe, and the arrogant, heated thrust of his erection against her stomach made her gasp. Was he always so easy to arouse or could she dream there was something about her that brought him to this state?

Her own heat was flooding her belly, aching between

her thighs, stinging her breasts as she rubbed, shameless, against him. But she dared not lower her hands from his chest, dared not let them slide over the bronzed skin, down to touch him as she yearned to.

'This is unequal.' Ross lifted his head to untie the cord around her robe. He pushed it off her shoulders and then attacked the simple ties fastening her plain and practical nightgown. His fingers were deft with the dexterity of a man able to load and fire a rifle at high speed, and when she stepped back and gave a wriggle the garment slid from her shoulders to her feet.

'Let me look at you.' He gestured for her to be still as her hands lifted in the instinctive feminine gesture to shield the delta of her thighs, the erect buds of her nipples. 'You are so delicate. Why did I not realise that? You held my weight in the river, you coped with all the privations of camp life. Even last night when you were naked, I did not see.' Ross reached out, stroked gently over the modest curve of her breast, down to the swell of her hip. 'And I took you, hard and fast and without care.'

'No. Not without care.' Meg caught his hand and lifted it to cup one aching breast again. 'I wanted you just as urgently and you made me feel so good, so very good.' She had never felt that passion, that rightness before, but she could not say so, it felt so disloyal to the man who had, it proved, shown her no loyalty. She reached out and circled Ross's erection with one hand, loving the way he closed his eyes at the touch, the sharp intake of breath as she caressed down and then up again using the flat of her thumb to tease the head until he moaned.

'It will be fast and urgent again if you do that.' He opened his eyes, dark and hot and full of wicked thoughts that spoke to her own desire.

'We have all night.' Meg sank to her knees on the discarded nightclothes and placed her hands firmly on his slim hips. She had never done this before, never wanted to; now all she desired was to pleasure Ross, show him, without words, how she felt.

'Meg! Oh, my... Meg, stop that.' Ross's voice trailed off into a husky groan as she took him fully into her mouth to torment him, tongue and lips and teeth merciless. His hands locked into her hair as she gave herself up to wringing groan after groan from him. His breath was panting now, she could sense his fight to control himself, not to thrust. She was determined to overwhelm him, thought she had succeeded until his hands fastened over hers and he pulled himself free, dragged her to her feet and fastened his mouth over hers.

He lifted her without stopping the kiss, carried her, hands tight at her waist, until he lowered her to the bed, coming down with her to pin her to the heavy satin of the coverlet before sliding down between her legs, angling her with implacable gentleness until he could kneel and part her legs to kiss her, deeply, intimately, while she writhed and sobbed and begged for mercy.

But she had shown him none and now that he had her, Ross was the stronger. Meg gave up struggling, let him take her and drive her into a completely mindless frenzy of delight, once, twice, before she was dizzily aware that his weight was over her again.

'Ross.' Somehow she forced her eyes open, looked into his.

'You are a wicked woman.' He settled himself between her legs, teasing her with small thrusts of his pelvis that sent shock waves through the sensitised folds he had been tormenting so exquisitely.

'Stop teasing me,' she managed to gasp, curling her legs around him to hold him close.

'Tell me what you want.' He nudged, pressing just a little, withdrawing, bringing her to the brink again and again.

'You know what... Ross, please!'

'Please what?' Now she could hear the strain in his voice, see the veins standing out on his temples, feel the tension racking him.

'Fill me. I need you, all of you.'

And then he gave her all, surging into the warm, wet heat that was aching for him, sobbing her name as she clenched around him, hungry for him, sheathing him as he drove her up and over the edge into mindless pleasure, staying with her until she screamed his name and somehow, despite her limbs locked around him, managing to pull free and find his own release, shuddering against her.

Ross heard the clock strike three and stirred, feeling the weight of Meg's head on his shoulder, enjoying the tickle of her hair as it slid over his chest. His right arm had lost all feeling, her elbow was digging into his side and his body ached. He felt wonderful. And his thoughts were clear, not at all like those of a man who had just roused from the deep, dreamless sleep that follows passionate lovemaking.

He knew what he wanted, he realised, and it was obvious that it was just under his nose. Literally. It was madness to make himself miserable by marrying a young woman with whom he had nothing in common simply for the sake of marriage and equally foolish to stay unmarried in the hope of falling in love. He was not convinced such a state was anything but a temporary brainstorm in any case.

Ross untangled himself with care. Meg grumbled in her sleep, then settled again as he slid from the bed, pulled on his robe and poured two glasses of claret from the decanter on the chest of drawers. He put one on the nightstand beside Meg, then pulled the coverlet up over her; he did not want those slender curves or the shadowed mysteries he had explored with such dedication to distract him.

Then he sat with his back against the bedpost at the foot of the bed and watched her sleep until the clock struck the half-hour.

'Meg.' It took a while, but eventually she woke, one sleepy eye peering at him over the sheet beneath a tousle of hair.

'Ross.' She scooted up in the bed and smiled, a ravishing smile of pleasure at seeing him that took his breath. 'Come back to bed.' The throaty invitation in her voice had him hardening on the instant.

He shook his head. 'No. We need to talk.' Immediately the warmth vanished and she regarded him warily. 'There's a glass of wine beside you.' He raised his and toasted her with it. 'To my lady.'

Her lips opened, she hesitated, then whispered, 'To my lord,' and drank.

'I need to go to London.'

Meg choked and put down the wine glass. 'When?'

'The day after tomorrow.' She closed her eyes and he thought she murmured, *Just two after all.* 'I've had yet another letter from my man of business up there about decisions I need to make. It is complex, so better that I speak direct with him and I cannot leave it any longer. Meg, come with me.'

She sat bolt upright, eyes wide open. 'To London?'

'Yes.' Now he had to get this right, this question he had never asked before. 'Meg, I want you to be—'

'Your mistress,' she finished and to his horror Ross saw the glint of tears in her eyes. 'You want to set me up in a house in London.'

'No! Meg, listen and do not interrupt me.' The tears vanished as she glared at him and he almost laughed. 'Meg, will you come to London and marry me?'

Chapter Eighteen

'Ma...marry you?' Meg groped for the wine glass and emptied it in one gulp. It might as well have been water. She said the first thing that came into her head. 'Why?'

'Because I think we would suit.' Ross frowned, but remained remarkably calm in the face of this less than rapturous reception of his proposal. 'I need a wife, we get on well together, and not just in bed. You had no other plans, had you?'

'Other plans? Not plans like that, certainly.' Meg gave herself a little shake. She was not dreaming, there was no need to pinch herself. 'Ross, you do not have to marry me because you have made love to me and I turned down your offer to be your mistress. I was not a virgin, for goodness' sake! You did not seduce me. Surely your sense of honour does not demand that you marry me?'

'My honour be damned.' He was becoming angry now. 'Is a title, comfort, a home—and let us not forget the damn good sex while we are about it—not enough for you?'

'Damn good....?'

'You seemed to be expressing your enjoyment freely enough a while ago.'

'Yes.' Meg nodded. Her body still glowed and ached and tingled with the after-effects of this man's lips and tongue and hands and… 'It is good,' she agreed before her heated memories made her blush like a peony. 'I was just taken aback at hearing it listed so frankly with the other benefits you offer.' She managed a smile and saw the anger leave him as swiftly as it had come. 'Have you not thought that you will fall in love one day, Ross? And then what will you think of the imprudence of marrying your housekeeper?'

'I fell into lust with you. And then I fell into liking. Is that not a good basis for a marriage? If I was married to you, Meg, I would not be looking for young ladies to fall in love with, you should never fear that.'

'You mean if your belly was full with a good plain dinner you would not be out looking for a banquet?' She tried to joke while her brain was spinning. Marriage to Ross. A dream, a fantasy she had not even dared contemplate. 'One day you would hanker for someone to love.' *And my heart would break.*

'I know you married for love before, Meg. I cannot give you that—the innocence of first love, the devotion of a young man off to war, pledging everything to you.' She flinched and saw him register the reaction. 'But we have much already, more than many couples going into marriage. I will never betray you, Meg. Not in thought and not in act. You have my word.'

She saw that he was serious and her certainty that she should refuse him, regardless of pain, faltered. But could she tell him the truth about James and watch his face change when he realised what she was?

Could she tell him that she had lived as his wife with a man who was already married, a man who had deceived

her up to the day he died? That she had only discovered
the truth when the will was opened and she found James
Halgate had a wife that he had abandoned, the result of a
foolish, drink-fuelled episode when he had left home to
sow his wild oats in London?

Thank you for your honourable proposal, she could
say. *But my marriage was bigamous. I am ruined, I was
already ruined, shunned by the ladies of the regiment,
when I accepted Dr Ferguson's protection.* No. She found
she could not say it. Even thinking of that shame and the
betrayal and the shock brought tears swimming to blur her
vision.

'You have a title, a position in society.' She tried for
the rational arguments. 'I am the second daughter of an
obscure Suffolk vicar. I can bring you neither connections
nor dowry.'

'Have I given you the impression that I am hanging out
for a rich wife or that I yearn to mingle with the *haut ton*?'
Ross enquired. His gaze was steady on her face, assessing,
listening to what was below the surface of her words. He
was an experienced officer, she must never forget that. He
had years of talking to his men and hearing the truth under
bravado and lies, confessions and prevarication.

'No. You have not.' But he had a strong sense of what
was due to his name, an innate pride of lineage, a natural
arrogance, whether he realised it or not.

'Then come with me to London, Meg. Bring Damaris
for respectability. Leave here as my housekeeper, coming
with me to assess the town house. Think about it for as
long as you need—and then come back as my wife.'

She must say *no.* It would cause enough talk hereabouts
once word got out that Lord Brandon had married his
housekeeper, but sooner or later the gossip would reach
London and the ears of someone who knew what had been

revealed in Spain. And then the story would come back to Cornwall with all the embellishments such a titillating tale was sure to attract. Ross was a proud man with a strong sense of duty that had brought him back here against all his desires and instincts. He would not tolerate his wife's scandalous past being common knowledge.

Her choices seemed to be to refuse him without explanation or to tell him the truth and then refuse, for as a man of honour he would not withdraw his offer. But she must speak now, at once and put an end to this.

'I must…' The right words would not come. She tried again. 'I must think about it.' Where had that come from? It was not what she had meant to say. And yet there was this nagging feeling inside that somehow it could be all right, that somehow she could marry Ross. *But how?* Meg demanded of herself. *How can it ever be right? And he doesn't love me anyway, and I need to be loved, I cannot live with a man without love.*

'You will come with me to London while you think?' Ross maintained his composure, his dark, harsh face as expressionless. He would not show hurt or rejection, even to her. Least of all to her.

You love him. Love will find a way. That was what Bella had said when she had helped Meg elope. 'Yes,' Meg said, recklessly following instinct, grasping the romantic dream. 'I will come to London and we will take Damaris and we will see what you want to do with the town house. It is a long time since I was in London.'

'Was that where you married?'

'Yes. James got the money for a licence somehow and lied about my father's permission. Looking back, he must have known Papa would not deny it if it were ever challenged, not with the scandal that it would bring.' The clergyman must have guessed, she realised that now. The way he took the money James handed him, the sly smile as he slid it into the pocket of his threadbare cassock would have alerted a girl more worldly-wise than innocent Miss Margaret Shelley had been.

'I did not see much of the town, though.' Just a cramped and shabby inn room for their wedding night, the maze of narrow City streets. There had been a child selling oranges from a basket, brilliant against the grey stone as they passed on their way to the church and the inn sign had creaked all night outside their room. She had thought she was in heaven, there in James's arms. She hadn't known what bliss really was, had not known until she had lain with this man.

'We can explore together. I have never been there. My parents did not believe in taking us up to London as children.'

'Never? No, of course, if you ran away when you were seventeen you had no chance as a young man either. Will you take Perrott? He will enjoy sending you to tailors and hatters and bootmakers. But I expect you will disappoint him and refuse to be measured and fussed over.'

'Perhaps not.' Ross shot her an enigmatic look before getting off the bed. 'A married man should be well turned out, don't you agree?'

'Ross…' Meg stretched out a hand to him. 'Please do not assume what my answer will be. I do not know my own mind, truly I do not. I cannot promise you anything.'

'Not even hope?'

'No.' Meg threw back the covers and pulled her night-gown over her head. 'I am sorry. Not even that.'

However ambivalent the feelings of their employer and his housekeeper it was clear that Damaris and Perrott regarded the entire trip to London as a holiday. Even the action of the post chaise, one of the infamous yellow bounders, was not enough to dampen Damaris's spirits. 'Just like being at sea in Uncle Henry's fishing boat,' she said cheerily as Meg stared fixedly out of the window and tried to settle her mind on something other than her stomach or Ross.

They spent the first night at Ashburton, the second at Andover. On both occasions Meg and Damaris chastely shared one room and Ross and Perrott another and they dined together in a private parlour. Ross kept all conversation at meals strictly impersonal and passed the time in the post chaise reading a fat file of correspondence and making notes. Damaris and Perrott played cards or watched the world go by and Meg brooded. She felt oddly lonely, despite having three companions.

Her deep thought had brought no answers by the time the carriage drew up in front of a house in Clarges Street. They were in Mayfair, Ross told them, and she needed no more than that and one glimpse of the house to know they were in the very heart of fashionable London. The railings were ornate, the front door with its brass work was wide and the passers-by had a certain air about them that reduced Damaris to nervous giggles until Perrott elbowed her sharply.

'The knocker is on the door.' It gleamed, as did the paintwork and the windows. There was a cook who doubled as housekeeper when the family was away and it appeared she knew her business.

'I wrote to warn them to expect us,' Ross said as the door opened.

'My lord.' The butler at the door was younger than Heneage, his tail coat of a sharper cut, his bow more precise. *The London touch,* Meg thought with an inward smile. Ross looked back as though waiting for her to precede him, then must have recalled her status, for he went through the door leaving his little entourage of country servants to follow in his wake.

I could walk up these steps on his arm. Lady Brandon entering her smart town house. Fantasy. And besides, she loved him for himself, not for possessions or title.

'Woodward.' Ross nodded to the butler as two tall footmen went to retrieve the bags. 'This is Mrs Halgate, the new housekeeper at the Court, Perrott, my valet, and Damaris, Mrs Halgate's maid. You will see to their comfort, I am sure. Mrs Halgate, would you be so good as to take tea with me tomorrow afternoon so we can discuss any changes you wish to make here?'

'My lord.' Meg bowed her head. 'I will make a list.'

'Well?' Ross enquired as Meg curtsied and took her place behind the tea tray. 'Thank you, Felton, that will be all.' The footman took himself off and Meg set out the tea cups looking delightfully domestic. But she was pale. How was she feeling? He had missed her in his bed and to talk to, but he was wary of giving the servants here any cause for suspicion about her status.

'Very well, my lord. This is a pleasant house, if somewhat dark and cluttered.'

'That was not what I meant, Meg. Have you been giving any thought to my proposal?'

'I have thought of little else.' She poured the tea, then skimmed the surface of both cups with the mote spoon, concentrating, it seemed to Ross, on the simple task to avoid looking at him. 'Milk or lemon, my lord?'

'Lemon. Meg, have you an answer for me?'

'No.' She passed him the fragile Worcester cup. Her hand appeared steady until he saw that the surface of amber liquid trembled. 'My thoughts run in circles, my

conscience keeps me awake at night and—I ache for you.'
She put her own cup down with a clatter. Her composed
face crumpled and Ross was half out of his chair before
she waved him back.

'No, it is all right. I am tired from the journey and
learning about a new household, that is all.'

'They treat you with respect?' He wanted to hold her,
tell her to weep if she wanted. He was doing this to her
and he hated himself. But not enough to stop. 'I spoke to
Woodward and Mrs Richmond, told them that you were
an officer's widow, a lady forced by circumstances to take
this post.'

'They are most respectful. But, no, Ross. I do not have
an answer for you.'

'Come with me tomorrow,' he said on an impulse,
fighting not to show disappointment or impatience. He
wanted to take her in his arms, kiss her until all her rational thought, her conscience, her modesty, flew out of the
window and all that was left was a quivering, yearning
woman in his arms. But that was not his Meg. That was
not who he needed. 'I have to go into the City first to sign
papers, but today's meeting has dealt with most of the
important matters, I will not take long. Then we can see
the sights together.'

'Alone?'

'In an open carriage with a footman up behind. I believe
there is a barouche in the mews. Surely there is sufficient
excuse on a first visit to London to make such an expedition unexceptionable?'

'Yes, I expect there is,' Meg said, an edge to her voice
that was either anger or tears. 'You are a master of temptation, Ross.'

He had to be content with that, he thought later,
spreading out the paperwork from his London lawyer

and attempting to concentrate on the knotty question of lease renewals on a row of speculative houses towards Tavistock Square. But Meg's face kept coming back to him. There had been dark shadows under her eyes, she had lost weight—and she had little enough to lose in the first place—and when she spoke there was strain in her voice, even when she said something light.

Am I bullying her? He dropped his pen, heedless of splashes, rubbing his hands over his face to try to clear his head. But she had not feigned passion when they made love and she was a strong woman, strong enough to say *no* if she meant it. If she was certain. Which meant she was not certain and that was cutting into her sleep and her peace. While she was still unsure, then there was hope.

Ross flattened the architect's drawings under his hand and made himself study them. After five minutes he realised they would make more sense the right way up. Why was he feeling like this? The world was full of women: attractive, intelligent, eligible women. Women who would be passionate in bed. Women who could make him smile. If Meg turned him down, he had to find only one of those women. There was no need to feel as though her refusal would be a tragedy. None whatsoever.

Chapter Nineteen

'I found a guidebook in the library. And as we are in the City I suggest we start here. There is the Tower of London, the Guildhall, St Paul's Cathedral, the Bank of England—where shall we begin?'

'The Tower, if you please, my lord,' Meg said, aware of the footman up behind the open barouche. 'It sounds most romantical. I feel a complete country bumpkin—wide-eyed and dependent on the guidebook.'

'Which is all of fifteen years out of date,' Ross admitted with a grin. 'The Tower, Jenkins,' he told the driver then settled back in the seat beside Meg.

She caught her breath at the sight of the White Tower when it came into view and stared with awe at the moat and the towering bastions. 'It is so old. Think of all the historical events that have taken place within those walls.'

'What would you like to see, Mrs Halgate?' Ross handed her down at the West Gate.

'The Menagerie and the Jewel House,' Meg decided. 'And you, my lord?'

'The Menagerie by all means and the Armoury. Jenkins, you may have a while to wait. Walk the horses, if you please.'

Ross waited until they were through the gates and he had paid their shillings, before tucking Meg's hand through his arm. 'There, you may now stop calling me my lord, at every sentence.'

'We must be discreet.' She tried not to think about the warmth of his body through her glove and against her arm. It seemed so long since they had last kissed, since she had lain in his arms. 'Look,' she said with a bright smile, 'Here is the Menagerie.'

The Keeper, on payment of another shilling each, walked them along the row of cages. Meg had been prepared to see cramped conditions and to regret her desire to visit, but they were spacious and clean so she was able to enjoy admiring Young Hector, Miss Jenny and Miss Fanny Howe, the lions, and the sinister elegance of Miss Peggy, a black leopardess. The laughing hyena made her recoil, but they both admired the antics of the racoons.

The armour and weapons took rather longer. Meg found a bench to perch on in the end and smiled while she watched Ross inspect every item with close professional attention, hands clasped behind his back, face severe. The keeper hovered at his side, apparently expecting a reprimand for a speck of rust or an improperly polished barrel at any moment.

'I do beg your pardon for keeping you waiting, this must be intolerably boring for you.' Ross came back to her side with an expression of contrition. Meg knew perfectly well he had entirely forgotten her.

'Not at all. She put her hand on his arm as they went to find the Jewel House. 'I was just thinking how much William would enjoy this.'

'He would, indeed. Meg, you do not mind about William?'

'That you acknowledge him and are sponsoring his career? No, of course not. I think it admirable and he is a charming and deserving young man.'

'I mean that there will always be people who think he may be my son, not my brother.'

'I know they are wrong, and so does anyone who knows you. There will always be unpleasant gossip from some people.'

'I am Brandon,' Ross said, his voice suddenly hard, 'And I will not have my honour smirched or my future wife distressed by rumour and scandal.'

'You do all you can.' Meg's stomach sank in a most unpleasant manner. *I will not have my honour smirched.* 'Your very openness will kill rumour.' But the scandal around *her* name was real and could not be denied. She must confess it all to him. But not yet, not until today was over.

More shillings were needed for the Jewel House and the glitter of crowns and orb, sceptre and Sword of State took Meg's mind off her problems for a while.

'Shockingly vulgar, was it not?' Ross remarked as they strolled along the gun platform looking at the crush of river traffic.

'So close up, it is a trifle overwhelming,' Meg agreed. 'But at a distance, as part of the pomp of royalty, it would look spectacular.'

'When will you give me the right to buy you jewels, Meg?' Ross stopped, catching both her hands in his. 'I want to buy you pearls and diamonds and sapphires.' He lifted her knuckles to his lips and held her eyes with his own as she blushed and stammered.

'Oh, no.' Meg snatched back her hands. 'I do not want you to buy me anything.'

'You will not give me that pleasure?'

'No.' She shook her head, not looking at him, imagining the warmth of his fingers on the nape of her neck as he fastened a necklace, the cool slide of metal and gems over her breast. Ross placing a ring on her finger. 'Please, can we go on? The breeze from the river is chilly.'

'As you wish.'

His face was shuttered and the smile gone from his lips and his eyes as they walked back to the carriage. She might think she had hurt him if she believed that his feelings were very deeply engaged. If he loved her. But he did not, so it was his pride that was hurt. He was Brandon, and he wanted to mark her as his with gemstones when all she wanted was to be branded by his kisses.

When they found the barouche again Ross gave Jenkins a list of locations to form a route. He did not intend to walk around any of them, so they must maintain their formal distance in front of the footman. It would be safer, she told herself. Then their fingertips brushed as they lay on the leather upholstery. Ross shifted slightly and the edge of his coat fell over their hands so she left hers just touching his, while they made polite and distant conversation about the sights that unfolded on either side of the barouche.

They drove past the Bank of England and the Guildhall, exclaimed over the herds of cattle and sheep being driven through the crowded streets on their way to market at Smithfield. They stared up at St Paul's, passed the Inns of Court so they could tell William that they had seen his future place of study and the British Museum because Meg thought they ought to at least see it.

And then they drove through St James's Park, saw the Queen's House and the lake, passed into the informality of Green Park with its herd of cows and milkmaids selling glasses of fresh milk and into Piccadilly. Meg knew they were almost back.

Ross's fingers slid under hers, curling until their hands were clasped. Meg returned the pressure, and his thumb found the bare skin below the button of her glove, stroking against the pulse point. 'I have made a decision, my lord. About the matter we discussed in Cornwall.'

He went very still, just as a man might who had been waiting with desperate patience for the answer of a woman he loved. But he did not love her, only desired her and, it seemed, he enjoyed her company. Was that enough to sustain her need to love and be loved? Perhaps it would be enough to overcome the revulsion he must surely feel when she told him her story as she was determined to do, now, before she lost her nerve.

They maintained a flow of innocuous conversation up to the house in Clarges Street, in through the front door while Ross handed his hat, gloves and cane to the butler and Meg untied her bonnet strings.

'Could you join me in the study, Mrs Halgate?'

'Of course, my lord.' She followed him, her heart thudding, telling herself over and over again that this was right and she would release him first from the offer he had made. Then, when he understood just who and what she was, he could make up his own mind.

'Excuse me, your lordship.' Woodward clear his throat. 'A lady and gentleman are waiting for your return. I explained you were not at home, but they intimated that it was a matter of some urgency.'

'I will come to the study later, shall I, my lord?' Meg was already at the foot of the stairs, shaky with relief at the postponement of the fateful interview. She should not speak on the spur of the moment; she would collect herself, compose what she was going to say.

'Thank you, Mrs Halgate.' Frowning, Ross reached for the card on the salver Woodward held, but she was already up the stairs and away.

Ross picked up the card, smiling at his own disappointment. *Like a child deprived of a sweetmeat.* Meg was going to say *yes*, he knew it. Her fingers curling into his for those last few minutes, the touches of colour on her cheek-bones, the flustered way she had fled up the stairs. *Yes*, he told himself. *Yes*.

And then he looked at the rectangle of pasteboard in his hand. *Mr James Walton Halgate, The Grove, Martinsdene Parva.* 'Halgate?' he demanded.

'Yes, my lord. But as they did not enquire for our Mrs Halgate I assumed it was a coincidence.' The butler looked a trifle uncertain. 'I took in refreshments.'

'Very well.' With something unpleasantly like apprehension knotting his stomach Ross opened the drawing room door and went in.

A tall man, his once-blond hair now pepper and salt, stood up. Slightly faded blue eyes fixed on Ross as the woman by his side came to her feet. *A good-looking couple,* he thought, with the sensation of time slowing that happened just before an encounter with the enemy.

'Lord Brandon?'

'I am Brandon. Mr and Mrs Halgate, please, sit down. How may I help you?'

He was managing to sound calm, if not particularly cordial, some remote part of his mind observed.

'We feel it our duty to inform you of a certain most delicate matter,' Mrs Halgate said, her lips tightening into an expression of righteous indignation. 'We understand from

Sir Edmund Keay, an old family friend who has recently moved to Falmouth, that you have employed a new house-keeper.'

'Sir Edmund, whose acquaintance I have not had the pleasure of making, is correct, although, forgive me, I am not clear how it is any concern of his.' So, it *was* about Meg and the names were no coincidence.

Mr Halgate flushed at the ice in Ross's voice. 'He felt it his duty to tell us that Margaret Shelley is fraudulently continuing to call herself Mrs Halgate and is representing herself as our late son's wife.'

'Fraudulently?' Ross realised he was staring blankly. He had expected—feared—they were going to say that James Halgate had not been killed but had gone missing and had now managed to get back to English assistance. He had feared discovering that Meg was still married, even as he hated himself for wishing a fellow officer dead. 'Fraudulently?' he repeated.

'She prevailed upon our poor James to run off with her,' Mrs Halgate burst out. 'He was already married, the foolish boy. Most imprudently, I fear. But then that little trollop—'

'Madam,' Ross interjected, 'I am aware that your feelings are agitated but Mrs…Meg is in my employ, I will not have her so described under my roof.'

'She was always wild,' Mrs Halgate said. 'Wild and wicked and out of control. She seduced poor James into a bigamous marriage and now she has the effrontery to continue to use our name. His name.' She buried her face in a handkerchief and gave way to her feelings.

'And your son's true widow?' Ross felt rather as he had the first time he had been wounded. Strangely breathless, but numb, although he knew something should be hurting very badly indeed. The pain had come later. Then he had wanted to scream, although he had not.

'Dead.' Mr Halgate said grimly. 'And the child too. An imprudent match, I fear. Not at all the wife we would have chosen for him—a tavern owner's daughter. They became lovers, he married her when they learned a child was on its way, but then he received his orders so he left, telling her he was coming home to make his peace with us. Of course, we would have done what we could to buy the unfortunate creature off and take the child to rear properly ourselves once we had known.

'But then that hussy got her hands on him, persuaded him to abandon a marriage he was already regretting and the child with it. Of course we knew nothing of the real wife until the letter from his commanding officer enclosing his will, by which time it was too late, some fever had carried them both off. But the fact remains, Margaret Shelley seduced our son away. And we heard what happened after his death. He was scarce cold when she had taken up with another man, living with him brazenly, acting as a common nurse.'

'She was not his mistress.'

'She would say that, no doubt.' Mrs Halgate sniffed. 'I do not suppose she told you the truth about her marriage, did she?' When he did not reply she nodded sharply. 'Then why do you believe her about the other man?'

Because she is Meg. Because I would trust her with my life. But why did she not tell me all this when I asked her to marry me?

'You are saying that Meg Shelley knew of your son's prior marriage but persuaded him to elope with her regardless of that?' he demanded, ignoring the question.

'Of course. His letters made reference to Meg *knowing all about him, understanding his problems*, wanting him *anyway.* James could never keep a secret,' his mother said bitterly.

'What, precisely, do you expect me to do with this information?' Ross asked. He knew what he wanted to do. He wanted to find Meg and shake her. He wanted to lose his temper and shout at her. He wanted to drag her to his bed, use her until he was sated with her. He wanted her to feel as bad as he did. Instead he sat back, steepled his fingers and regarded the Halgates over the top.

'Why, cast her out! Surely no decent gentleman would employ her.'

'So you wish not only that she stop using your name, but you desire to punish her also?' Ross found it was not only Meg he wanted to shout at.

'Of course.' Mrs Halgate looked taken aback that he should need to ask. 'Her own father has disowned her, naturally.'

'I imagine he did that when she eloped,' Ross said, thinking of what Meg had told him of her father. 'And what of her sisters?'

'Vanished. Gone to the bad, all three of them. We have no idea where Celina or Arabella are.'

'I see.' Ross stood up and waited, silent, until the Halgates realised this was the end of their interview.

'So what are you going to do about her?' Mr Halgate demanded as Ross rang for Woodward.

'I do not discuss my domestic arrangements with anyone, sir. But I will suggest to Meg that she uses another surname. I do not imagine that she would wish to retain yours once she hears of your attitude.'

'Ha! She knows it well enough. Believe me, we made it very plain when she had the effrontery to write and condole with us on our loss. Wanting money, more like.

We wrote straight back and told her that we refused to acknowledge her existence.'

'In that case, I wish you good day. Woodward, show Mr and Mrs Halgate out.'

Meg had never been married. And she had, according to the Halgates, gone through a form of marriage with their son knowing he was already wed, however unfortunately. She had lied to him about her marriage, persisted in the lie when he thought that she would have trusted him with any secret. Pride, and the fatalistic expectation that the worst would happen just when he was happy again, nagged at him. He could feel his temper rising, and with it pain that Meg was not all he had thought her. He curbed it, hard.

'Woodward.' The butler stopped in his progress across the hall. 'Kindly ask Mrs Halgate to come to the study.' He would not tolerate being lied to. Ross fixed that thought in the forefront of his mind and clung to it. Anything rather than examine the puzzled hurt that seethed beneath his anger.

Meg tapped on the study door, then let herself in. Her stomach was fluttering with nerves, but she knew what she was going to do. She would sit down and tell Ross the story of how she had come to fall into what she had believed was love with James, the long, silent months when he was in London, the delight of finding he still cared for her, her misery at home, the elopement—everything. Then he would understand.

Her courage failed a little as Ross turned from the window to face her. His face was stony, but his eyes burned dark. Meg opened her mouth, but no words came out.

'I have just had the dubious pleasure of entertaining Mrs Halgate,' he remarked.

The tone was so at odds with the words that she blinked

at him, failing to understand. 'Mrs… James's *wife*? She is alive?'

'I understand that both his wife and child are dead.'

Child? Meg's knees gave way and she sat down with a thump. 'Then who…?'

'The late Lieutenant Halgate's parents. The people who, hardly surprisingly, failed to acknowledge you when Halgate was killed.' Ross hitched his hip on one corner of the desk and studied her face. 'They felt I should throw you out.'

'I was going to tell you. To explain.'

'Yes? Meg—I wish you had told me sooner. It appears to me that you were intent on deception when you boarded that ship and you have kept it up ever since. Why call yourself by a married name you had no right to?'

'Because it was my identity for five and a half years! I was James's wife for five and a half years and I—'

All the blood in her head seemed to have ebbed away. The room spun, the only fixed thing in it was Ross's hard, implacable face, the only reality the pain and suspicion in his voice. 'I did *not* know when I married him and I was going to tell you this afternoon.'

'You did not tell me on the ship, or when I offered you employment. You did not tell me when I asked you to be my mistress.' He paused and for a moment Meg thought he needed to control his breathing, but his voice as he went on was steady. 'You did not tell me when I asked you to be my wife.'

'I did not know how to.' It was the truth. Even thinking about it had hurt too much.

'Could you not trust me?' He picked up the pen from the ink stand and began to roll it between his fingers. 'Do you know how the Halgates found me? One of my neighbours knows them and wrote them a letter warning that you were back in England, still masquerading as their son's wife and apparently pulling the wool over the eyes of a certain Lord Brandon. Or perhaps he thought I did know and did not care.'

Everything was mercifully numb now, just as it had been when they told her James was dead. The numbness had begun to melt into regret by the time they showed her his will and the document folded inside it and then the pain had come like a slash from a knife, all consuming. It would again, very soon, but not yet.

'I did not know when I married him,' she repeated finally as the silence dragged on. 'I had no idea.'

'You say you loved the man, yet you suspected nothing?' There was a sharp crack and Ross tossed the splintered halves of the pen on to the desk.

'I was an innocent. A romantic innocent. I thought I loved him.' *I love you. Please do not kill that, please,* the voice in her head clamoured.

'Then you have changed, Meg. These days you are all practicality. You seized on my unconscious body quickly enough as a means to get you back to England. I wonder what would have been my fate if that plan had not occurred to you? I would be feeding the crabs on some sandbar in the Gironde, I suppose.'

It seemed her legs would support her after all and that pain and hurt could be turned into anger. Meg stood up, so close that her skirts brushed Ross's knee. 'I had years to learn to be practical, years to learn to look after myself and a man who was not the model of perfection a foolish girl thought him to be. And afterwards? When I learned that he had betrayed me and that poor woman? I could have just given up and died, I suppose. Or sold myself. Either would have been convenient for others, I am sure.

But I chose to live. It is hard to be a woman alone, Ross; a married title is some little protection, although not much.

'I was coming to tell you the truth today, give you the opportunity to withdraw your offer. You can believe instead two people who were deeply hurt by their only son's behaviour. They need to blame someone, poor things, especially if they have lost a grandchild as well as a son.' Meg fought for composure as Ross straightened up, his eyes fixed on her face. 'If I may go now?'

'In a moment,' he said as he reached for her and pulled her into his arms. His mouth was hot and hard, but his control was complete as he plundered her mouth, holding her with one hand cupping the back of her head, the other at her waist. Meg tasted anger and need and confusion and fought her own wildly conflicting instincts, to claw at his eyes and to melt into his arms.

It was the last time they would kiss, the last time her nostrils would be full of the spicy scent of his skin, the last time his body would heat hers with demands that her own flesh leapt to answer.

Then Ross released her. 'Meg, I want to trust you, I want you. But—'

She knew him now, saw the pulse beating in his throat, the vein blue on his temple and the rise and fall of rigidly controlled breathing. That demonstration of male dominance had been as hard for him as it had been for her. But if he could not trust her, there was nothing, could be nothing. He would never be sure of her again.

'But?' she asked rhetorically, turned on her heel and walked out, up the stairs and into her room. She turned the key in the lock and then simply slid down the door until she sat crumpled at the foot of it.

She loved Ross and she had lost him, not because she had refused him, not because he had heard her explanation and acknowledged that Lord Brandon could not marry a woman in her situation. No, she had lost him because, it seemed, she had never truly had him. Perhaps he could not trust, perhaps his past had killed that in him. She did not know, all she knew was that she hurt.

He did not trust her or he would have shown the Halgates the door, she told herself. He did not love her or he would have fought for her. Meg drew up her knees, wrapped her arms around them and sat, face buried in her skirts, and sobbed.

Chapter Twenty

'Mrs Halgate!' The knocking shook Meg out of a cramped sleep. She was still huddled against the door, her face sticky with half-dried tears, her skirts rumpled, her back aching. She scrambled to her feet and went to sit on the edge of the bed.

'Mrs Halgate, ma'am!'

'Damaris, I have a sick headache,' she called back, her voice convincingly shaky.

'Oh. I'm sorry, ma'am. Can I get you anything? Some tea? A tisane?'

'No. Thank you.'

'I'll leave you in peace to sleep, then. Only, you don't know where his lordship's gone, do you? He went out, very suddenly without saying and Perrott was wondering what clothes to lay out for him this evening.'

'I'm sorry, Damaris. I have no idea.'

He may go to the devil, for all I care, she thought, knowing it was not true. But she was angry, she realised, as she splashed water on her blotchy face and dragged a brush through her hair. Furious with Ross and the Halgates and James. The only people in the world who loved and trusted her and always would, whatever anyone said about her, were her sisters. And she was going to find them. If the villagers would not talk to Jago, perhaps they would talk to her.

Meg dragged open drawers and threw wide the clothes press. Out of old habit she had simply packed everything she owned—it was little enough—when she came to London. Now she stripped to her skin and folded each item she had bought with Ross's money on the bed. She dressed in her old gown and underthings and shook every penny she had out of her purse and the money bag that contained her savings and the salary Ross had advanced.

She knew how much she possessed on the day she met Ross. She put that to one side. He owned her nothing for the voyage; she had exchanged her care of him for food and the cabin. She totalled the days she had been employed and counted out the money for those and added it to her own cash. Then she wrote a careful sum out on a piece of paper and piled the remaining money with that on top of the clothes.

Meg packed everything else she owned back into the valise, put her old bonnet on her head, wrapped her shawl around her shoulders and unlocked the door.

The hall was deserted when she leaned over the banister. Meg eased her way down the remaining flight of steps, ran across the hall and opened the door. The street was busy and there, coming towards her from Piccadilly, was a hackney carriage. She hailed it. 'Ludgate Hill, the Belle Sauvage.'

Ross woke with a blinding hangover and lay staring at the ceiling while he tried to remember how much he had drunk, and why. Meg. He sat up, winced and reached out an arm for the bell. He had gone out, fully intending to get drunk and make someone else's life miserable. He had found a gaming hell off St James's—Pickering Place, he seemed to recall—and had proceeded to win a great deal of money at cards while drinking an inordinate amount of very bad, very expensive claret.

'Good afternoon, my lord.' Perrott came in with cat-like tread and proffered a salver with a small glass of an unpleasant milky-brown liquid on it. 'My previous employer used to swear by this.'

It could only kill him. Ross swigged it back, gasped and collapsed on to the pillows while his head spun and his stomach churned. Then, by some miracle, he felt marginally better.

'What time is it?'

'Two, my lord. Shall I send for your bath?'

'The bath and cold water. Then coffee.'

He forced himself out of bed when the shallow tub was manhandled into the dressing room and stood there stark naked while Perrott poured cold water over him. It was vicious, but effective. By the time he had drunk two cups of coffee his brain was working again, which was unfortunate as he was then able to recall, in unpleasant detail, just why he had gone out to get drunk yesterday.

He had to go to Meg, speak to her, try to convince her that he did trust her. Yesterday the shock and anger had overwhelmed him and the cold temper that was his inheritance had ridden him. She had seemed so shaken by his disbelief, so angry when he kissed her. She was as hurt by his lack of trust in her as he had been that she had lied to him.

Something was nagging him, some turn of phrase. Ross

rang for food and poured more coffee, forcing his memory
back over every word they had exchanged.

*I was coming to tell you the truth, give you the oppor-
tunity to withdraw your offer.*

Before... That was the unsaid word in that sentence. Meg
had been going to tell him the truth so he could withdraw,
because if he did not she would accept him. If he believed
that, then other things made sense. She was not trying to
trap him, or she would not tell him the truth—not until
she had accepted him, by which point his sense of honour
would probably bar him from withdrawing.

And if she was prepared to marry him, at the cost of
confessing her whole painful history—what did that prove?
That she loved him?

Perrott put a veal chop coated in steaming onion gravy
in front of him. Ross cut into it and chewed. What had she
said to him when they had had that furious argument?
*Don't men realise that it is not the lying together that is
important to women—however good that is—it is all the
other things. Friendship, companionship, trust, give and
take between two people...*

And he had sneered at her about love and she had gone
white. If she loved him, and thought she would lose him
by telling him about her sham marriage, then that would
explain her reluctance, the time it had taken her to pluck
up courage.

Love. Did he want love? Of course he did. He wanted
Billy's love, as the grandfather he had never known, Lily's
love, the sister he never had, William's love, another
brother. And Meg's love. A wife and lover's love.

'You damned idiot.' He stared at the half-eaten chop.

'My lord?'

'Not you, Perrott. Me. Where is Mrs Halgate?'

'In her room, I believe, my lord. Damaris said she was unwell yesterday afternoon and I have not seen her since.'

Something trailed one icy fingertip down Ross's spine. He shoved back his chair and strode out of the door, up the stairs, two at a time. There was no answer as he hammered on Meg's door, only the silence of an empty room. When he opened the door the bedchamber was immaculate and on the end of the bed was a neat pile of clothing and money. Money and paper.

Ross snatched at it.

'Oh, my lord.' Damaris arrived flustered in the doorway. 'Mrs Halgate said she had a sick headache, my lord. I left her to sleep until she rang.' She stared about the room, then at Ross's hand. 'She's gone? And left a note?'

'She has gone and left a precise accounting of her wages.' Ross strode to the landing. 'Woodward!'

'My lord.' The butler appeared below him in the hall.

'When did Mrs Halgate leave?'

'I was not aware that she had, my lord.'

Ross closed his fist and felt the painful scrunch of the paper against his palm. *Where have you gone, Meg? Back to Cornwall?* No, there was nothing for her there. So where? Where could a young woman without friends, without references and with virtually no resources, go?

Meg climbed down from the farmer's cart, stiff in every joint. The journey had seemed to last for ever. The stage from Ludgate Hill had been cramped and smelly and it had been a relief to climb down at the Falcon in Ipswich, even though she then had to find a carrier's cart to take her as far as Framlingham. When they finally arrived she had given up for the day and went to seek a room at the inn, too tired and hungry to face finding someone to carry her the remaining six or so miles to Martinsdene.

Discomfort was a blessing sometimes, Meg decided, buttering bread in one corner of the dining room of the Blue Boar. It was difficult to think too hard when you were uncomfortable. Now with a chair beneath her bruised behind and good food in front of her it was all too easy to think about Ross and to mourn what she had so nearly shared with him. He might even have come to love her, one day. Just a little.

She no longer even wanted to throw things at him, exasperating, proud, private man that he was. She just ached for him and the challenge of teasing the faintest twitch of a smile from that gorgeous, wicked mouth.

Meg finished her roast gammon and found she even had appetite for the apple pie the waiting girl was bringing out from the kitchens. She had learned in the Peninsula that it was no good picking at food, however miserable she was. Food was strength and she needed that.

Now, as she turned up the lane towards Martinsdene, the church tower was visible ahead, the slopes of the hills and the angles of the copses as they met the fields were all achingly familiar. Life had gone on while she had been away and the place that had once been the centre of her world had got along perfectly well without her. Meg shifted the valise from one hand to another.

Jago had found nothing here but a wall of silence. It was only her anger and the hope born of desperation that made her even try. But try she would. There was even the faint, forlorn hope that her father would welcome her back, that after all these years apart they might find a way to reach each other. Meg walked into the Royal George inn. 'Good morning, Mr Wilkins. I require a room for two nights.'

'Yes, ma'am.' Ben Wilkins put down the cloth he had been polishing tankards with and smiled his familiar gap-toothed smile. 'We've a nice one overlooking the green.' Then he blinked, stared and Meg smiled back. 'Miss Margaret! Why, they said you'd run off with young Mr Halgate, so they did—and here you are, home again.'

Meg winced inwardly at the word *home*, but kept her smile bright. 'Yes, here I am. It is good to see you looking so well, Mr Wilkins.'

'I've been married to Jenny North—you remember her?—for five years now and we've three nippers, all bright boys too. And Jenny, she's smartened this old place up wonderful fine...'

Meg nodded and smiled and waited until Ben ran out of news and started thinking. 'But, Miss Margaret, why do you want to stay here?'

'I may not be very welcome at the vicarage,' she said frankly. His expression showed embarrassment and comprehension and an obvious question. 'But I need to find my sisters.'

'I don't know, Miss Margaret. It's a mystery, certain sure.' All she got after half an hour of speculation and gossip were the dates that Jago had gleaned.

'I will visit my father, of course,' she told Wilkins as he carried her bag upstairs, ducking under the low beams in the room he showed her to. There was no point in trying to be secretive. Better to be frank and give the village gossips something accurate to clack their tongues over.

And there was no point in putting things off either, she decided after eating the luncheon that Jenny Wilkins had provided along with five years' worth of village news.

The vicarage looked just as it had when she had left. She walked in at the side gate and cut across the yard to the kitchen door. The garden was clipped and regimented, the door knocker shining, the white curtains starched. Everything as upright as its inhabitants, Meg thought with an attempt at humour.

The back door was open so she went right in. *I am a grown woman now. He can neither control me nor harm me.* So why was she feeling sick?

Mrs Philpott the cook, greyer and stouter than Meg remembered, was standing with her back to the door at the range. 'Good afternoon, Mrs Philpott.'

The cook turned stared, gasped, 'Miss Margaret!' and went into strong hysterics, throwing her apron over her face and shrieking.

'Oh, be quiet and pull yourself together!' Meg gave her a little shake and the hysterics turned into gasps. 'I have come to find out where my sisters are,' she said as calmly as she could.

'What is this racket?' The door opened to reveal the Reverend Shelley, spectacles on his nose. 'I am attempting to write tomorrow's sermon—' He stopped dead. 'Margaret!'

'Father.' Once, long ago, there had been laughter, once he had loved her, she thought, reaching back into childhood memories and the hazy recollections of the time before Mama died. She had wanted so much when she was growing up to please him, make him proud of her, find that vanished love again. She held her breath—she was home again, the prodigal daughter. Would he forgive her? Could she learn to love him again?

'What are you doing here, you sinful girl?' The pain twisted in her stomach. Rejection, not forgiveness. But she would not weep, there were her sisters to think of.

'Where are Arabella and Celina?' Meg demanded, her eyes fixed on her father's face, searching for some hint that he knew as avidly as she had searched for some spark of welcome. But there was only baffled anger and righteous indignation on the vicar's lean features.

'I do not know and I do not care. They have fallen into sin as you did, I have no doubt. I failed to drive the wickedness out of you all, now I must bear the burden of it.'

Meg stood her ground for a long minute. She was not going to allow him to intimidate her, or to hurt her, ever again. It was worth coming back, worth the pain of the last few minutes, just to know that. Without a word she turned on her heel and walked away.

Sunday dawned bright and sunny. Meg lay listening to the sounds of the inn and the village starting the day, then got out of bed and began to wash and dress. She had one more idea, one more faint hope. If that did not work then she would go back to London, find whatever employment she could with no references, and advertise for her sisters. And she would forget Ross Brandon. The last resolution seemed impossible. How could she forget him when she ached for him, worried about him, thought about him every moment?

She timed her arrival at church for Matins just as the organist lifted his hands from the keyboard and the vicar emerged from the vestry. Her veil down, Meg slipped into the rear pew. It was strange to be back here. The view was different from here and not from the high-sided Vicarage box pew. But there were the familiar monuments on the walls and the familiar hymn boards hanging on the pillars. The same vases held greenery around the font and the organ still wheezed on the high notes.

The ritual was soothing, although her father's sermon was both dull and uninspiring after the warmth of Reverend Hawkins's words.

* * *

She waited until the service was over and the congregation got to its feet, then stood out in the aisle and threw back her veil.

'Please, may I have a moment of your time?' She pitched her voice to carry and they stopped talking. Heads turned, she saw some she knew, saw recognition dawn. 'My name is Margaret Shelley and I am trying to trace my sisters. Can anyone help me? If you know anything, however insignificant it might be, I beg you to tell me. I will be at the Royal George until tomorrow. I would be so grateful if you—'

She had lost them. They were all still staring up the aisle, but not at her. The breeze from the open door caught at her veil as she turned. A big man was standing beside the font, his face expressionless under a shock of black hair. It needed cutting. Perrott should have... *'Ross.'*

Someone gasped, then the spell was broken as her father emerged from the vestry, still in his cassock. 'What is this? Margaret, you will leave this church immediately!'

'This is not your house to order anyone from,' Ross observed, his deep voice echoing around the stone walls in the shocked silence. 'It belongs to a higher authority.' Someone giggled nervously and the vicar turned a furious glare towards the sound. Ross ignored him, addressing himself directly to the congregation. 'Miss Shelley has not received any reply to her question. As she said, we will be at the inn and will be most appreciative of any assistance you may give us.'

'And who are you, to make a disturbance in this place?' the Reverend Shelley demanded, striding down the aisle, cassock flapping around his legs.

'I am Brandon,' Ross said with the arrogance that always made Meg smile. *He is real,* she thought, grasping one of the poppy-head carvings at the end of the pew.

And he was here. 'And this lady, I trust, is about to consent to be my wife.'

'I…' He was here, talking of marriage after all that he had discovered about her, after all he had said? 'After the last time we met, my lord,' Meg said, finding her voice, forgetting their audience, 'I was left with the impression that you had mistaken your feelings for me.'

'I was not aware of the truth of them.' His eyes were dark and intent on her face. 'I had thought of a number of very good reasons why we should marry, but the fact that I love you had not occurred to me.'

'You love me?' A sentimental sigh from the verger standing a few yards away brought Meg to her senses. 'My lord, we are not alone. We should discuss this…elsewhere.' *He loves me?*

'By no means. I feel the need to declare my intentions before witnesses.' Ross thrust his tall hat and his gloves into the verger's hands, walked forwards and went down on one knee in front of her, lifting her hand to his lips. The little church and all in it fell entirely silent, holding their breath, just as she was. 'Margaret Shelley, will you do me the inestimable honour of becoming my wife? I love you with all my heart and soul.'

Someone burst into tears. Meg could hear her father spluttering, but all she could see was Ross's smile, the passion in his eyes, the utter truth of what he said, written on his face.

'Oh, yes. Yes, I will marry you, Ross Brandon. I love you too much not to.'

He came to his feet, her hand still in his, and drew it through his arm. 'Then you have made me far happier than I ever deserve to be.' He turned them both to face the vicar. 'Do you wish to be married by your father?'

She looked across at her father, hoping against hope for

the slightest softening, at least the faintest hint of approval or forgiveness, but there was nothing. 'No,' she said after a moment. She could not go back, only forwards. 'I would like to go home. Home to Cornwall. And I would like to be married in our little church by dear Mr Hawkins, with Miss Hawkins playing the organ out of tune, with Lily as my bridesmaid and old Billy to give me away.'

'And William can be best man.' Ross laughed, his rare, rich laugh that made her want to laugh too. 'We will go home tomorrow, my love.' He looked round the church. 'Thank you, my friends. If you can help my fiancée, we will be in your debt.'

Chapter Twenty-One

'All it amounts to is that Bella was seen weeping in the woods, in a place known as The Dell, on a Saturday and came to church the next day looking wan and not her usual self and that was the last anyone saw of her. Oh yes, and was wearing no bonnet when she was seen crying,' Meg said. 'And everyone was adamant that there was no man courting Lina.' She looked at the sheet of notes in Ross's surprisingly neat handwriting that lay on the table in the corner of the inn's public tap room.

They had been there all afternoon, where they could be easily found, had eaten their luncheon there, spoken to the parishioners who slipped in, mostly by the back entrance to avoid the vicar's eye. It had been many hours, hours when she could not kiss him, touch him, ask him how he had found her or how his mistrust had turned to love. But they could exchange looks and the anticipation was sweet.

'I think we must give up, my love,' Ross said as he gathered up the sheets of paper. 'I will leave our direction with the landlord and promise a good reward for any more news he can gather. Here he comes now, with word of our dinner and the parlour I asked him for, I hope.'

It was snug and private and she went straight into Ross's arms as the door closed behind them. 'Oh, Ross. You truly love me? After what happened in London? After what you found out about me?'

'Let me kiss you.' He bent his head and took her mouth gently, passionately, a slow, lingering caress. 'I feared I would never be able to do that again.'

Meg curled her arms around his neck and looked up into his face. His dark, smiling face. 'When did you realise you loved me?'

'When I thought I had lost you.' Behind Ross the door opened, banged into his back. 'That must be our dinner.' Meg disentangled herself and went to sit at the table, trying to look as though she was not tingling from head to toe with his kiss. Jenny Wilkins bustled in and out until the table was laden and then stood back, gazed at them, gave a gusty sigh and took herself off.

'Oh, Ross. Everyone is enjoying this so much, bless them.' All except her father, of course. At least he could congratulate himself on being entirely correct about her. First she eloped with a married man and then she made a disgraceful scene in church.

'But not as much as I am.' Ross carved the chicken while he talked. 'I thought I had lost you and I did not understand why I felt so bad. It wasn't anger at you keeping your secret, it was a sensation I had never experienced before. And then I realised why I had been feeling like that for weeks.'

'Weeks?' Meg helped him to vegetables, feeling ridiculously wifely as she did so. She wanted to be in his arms and in his bed, but first they must talk, and she was content to wait and anticipate.

'Weeks. I just thought it was part of the confusion of coming back home again. Home,' he repeated, savouring the word. 'You made it a home for me, Meg.'

'I changed a few pictures, picked a few flowers,' she protested as he poured her wine.

'No, I mean that by being there you made it a home. You brought life and warmth and love.' His face was shadowed by more than the curtain across the window. 'You accepted William. You cared, you took me out of my nightmares and made me stop thinking of death and killing and pain.'

'When I saw you first,' she admitted, 'I thought you were Death. You looked so dark, so implacable, so utterly without hope to have or to give. And then you saved that child and you sheltered me and I knew I was wrong.'

'I had lost hope.' Ross cradled his wine glass in his hand and stared into the red depths. 'All I could see was duty and guilt and living the reality of memories that haunted me and spending the rest of my life as a cripple.'

'You left it all in the hands of Fate?'

'And Fate turned out to be five foot five inches of brown-haired, grey-eyed female with a sharp tongue and a kiss that tastes of fresh raspberries.' He looked up from his wine and his eyes were smiling. 'And there I was picturing her as a wicked old hag with no teeth and a rusty pair of scissors waiting to snip the thread of my life at the worst possible moment.'

The silence was good between them, companionable and healing. They would never have to make conversation, chatter of nothings, to break it. It was enough to be together, enjoying this honest food and drink.

But there were things that had to be said. 'I did not tell you about James and our marriage that was no marriage because, at first, it hurt too much. No one ever asked me for the truth about it, how it had felt to run away with him, how our marriage had been. So I hugged that inside me and the more time passed, the harder it was to speak of it. I called myself Mrs Halgate because otherwise, who was I? Those five years had been…nothing.' It was harder to say than she had imagined, even to Ross, who sat watching her face, his eyes soft with an emotion that made it hard not to cry.

'It never occurred to me anyone would know who I was, down there in Cornwall. We met no one with army connections. I thought, as your housekeeper, I was safe.'

'And then I asked you to marry me.'

'And London—anyone might know the story there. And you are hardly nobody, despite your pretence of being just a country squire. One day you would want to take your seat in the Lords, do something that would make me an embarrassment to you.' Realisation hit her. 'What am I thinking of, saying *yes*? Nothing has happened that makes the scandal any less.'

'Nothing except that I had hoped I had convinced you that I do not care that my romantic love once eloped and was misled by the man she trusted. I was angry and shocked by the story and I should have mastered those feelings before I spoke to you. Forgive me. Meg, with your permission I will see that the story is spread far and wide. You were young, impetuous and entirely innocent. Anyone who shuns us because of that, we can live without. Anyone who criticises you will have to deal with me. I will be open, you will hold your head up and the gossips will see there is no sport to be had from us.'

'You truly do not mind?' His shoulders were reassuringly broad and strong when she got up and wrapped her arms around them from the back. His neck, where she nuzzled her mouth, needing the comfort of the scent and taste of him, was warm and his over-long hair tickled her nose.

'I confess that were Lieutenant Halgate alive, poor devil, I would kick his sorry backside from here to Oporto. But, no, I do not mind.' Ross twisted in his seat so she ended up on his lap. 'Are you by any chance making advances to me, madam? With our dinner half-eaten and in broad daylight?'

'You do not want to wait until we are married?' The very thought was agonising. The proof that he would find it difficult indeed was reassuringly evident as she wriggled round on his lap to regard him anxiously.

'It will be at least a month, six weeks, will it not? I would like a proper country wedding and that will take some planning. And you have your bride clothes to buy. I think we should be celibate, don't you, Meg?'

He said it so solemnly that she was quite taken in for a moment, then the teasing sparkle in his eyes gave him away. 'Ross Brandon, you are a very wicked man.'

'I could be,' he admitted. The room swooped and swayed as he got to his feet with her in his arms. 'Shall we go and be wicked together?'

'Yes, please.' It was ridiculous how feminine and fragile he made her feel, carrying her up those stairs, even when he bumped his head on the low beams and swore as he clouted his elbow on the rail. They were both laughing when he dropped her on the bed and went to turn the lock in the door, but as he turned back the laughter died away and she saw the same aching need in him that filled her own chest and made her throat dry.

Ross undressed with his eyes never leaving hers while she sat in the tangle of her skirts. She looked at his body in the evening sunlight that filtered through the thin old chintz curtains. 'When they brought you on board and stripped your clothing off I did all the things I needed to do for a patient. You were another wounded man, a matter of damaged muscles and torn skin. And then I went to draw the sheet over your body and I found myself looking at you, shamefully aroused because you are so very male and so very beautiful. I was ashamed of myself, but I could not get the image out of my mind.'

'And I fixed the feel of your body when I lifted you into bed in my memory and the heat and softness of you that night as you lay close to me,' he confessed. 'Undress for me, Meg.'

It was slow and languorous to slip out of each item of clothing, to toss them aside until she was naked for him. It felt good and powerful to see the effect she had on his body and watch him as he watched her, the heat and the tenderness mingling into an expression she thought never to see on that strong, harsh face.

She had plans for later, but she let him push her gently back on to the pillows, lay still, her hands fisted in the patchwork counterpane as he licked and kissed his way from ankle to knee, up the inside of her aching thighs to the wet, quivering, needy core of her.

Plans fled, thought dissolved into instinct and reaction as he kissed the intimate folds, used his tongue to lash her into frenzy and soothe her into whimpering yearning. He held her with those big, calloused rifleman's hands, open to every sinfully loving thing he did, held her until she cried out and reached for him and he came to her, sinking into the heart of her, driving her over the edge into the swirling pleasure-filled oblivion.

He was still sheathed in her as she came to herself, still moving gently, just enough to send aftershocks of delight whipping through her. Meg tightened herself around him and he closed his eyes, off guard for a second as she twist-

ed beneath him and came up straddling the narrow hips,
her hands flat on his chest, her palms rubbing over the
hard knots of his nipples.

'You want to ride?' He sounded interested, if rather
breathless. He was hard as iron within her.

Oh, yes. Meg rose and fell, slowly, by half an inch of
exquisite torture. Up, down, gripping, teasing and then as
the tendons in his neck became rigid and his head began
to move on the pillow she rose higher, down harder, riding
him, driving them both while he gripped her hips and gave
her back every thrust so when she shattered again he was
with her, crying out her name, pulsing his heat into her as
he filled her with love and delight and promises.

'For ever, Meg. For ever.'

The sun shone as they stepped out of the granite porch
into the dappled shade of the churchyard. The waves in the
creek lapped at the mossy edge of the greensward and the
ancient tombstones that lined every path that wound down
the little valley to the church spoke of ages of families and
community and love in this place.

And the community of their times was there in force,
lining the paths, throwing rose petals and rice, clapping
their hands and calling their names. At the point where
one path led off to the ancient sacred springs there were
girls with roses in their hair and garlands in their hands.

Meg paused and turned, one hand fast in Ross's grip,
and smiled at the guests following them. William, as smart
as any London gentleman, bursting with pride as best man,
Lily, serene and lovely with tears in her eyes and old Billy,
startlingly clean and besuited with his dog at his side, its
collar tied with flowers.

'Our family, Lady Brandon,' Ross murmured. Together
they glanced up to where Giles lay under the flowery turf,

then she turned again and threw her flowers up and over her head, aiming for Lily, thinking of rumours that she was courting. 'Your sisters are with you in spirit. We'll never give up on them.'

'Not quite all of our family,' she murmured back, bringing his hand down to rest on her belly. 'Just all the ones you can see.'

'Meg? A baby?'

'Yes, I think so.' She tucked her hand more securely into the crook of his arm as he stared at her, an incredulous smile spreading over his face.

'Then let us go home and start filling that old house with love for her to come home to.'

'Or for him,' Meg pointed out as they began to climb to where the carriages waited.

'For all of us,' Ross said and stopped and took her face between his palms and kissed her until the cheers of the guests sent the jackdaws spiralling into the sky in panic and Meg's happy tears ran over his fingers like soft Cornish rain.

Afterword

Readers who know the Roseland Peninsula will guess that the lovely St Just in Roseland has been very loosely disguised as the church that Meg and Ross marry in. Trevarras Court and all the parishioners are, however, entirely imaginary.

*   *   *   *   *

COMING NEXT MONTH FROM

HARLEQUIN®
HISTORICAL

Available August 30, 2011

- **GOLD RUSH GROOM**
  by **Jenna Kernan**
  (Western)

- **VICAR'S DAUGHTER TO VISCOUNT'S LADY**
  by **Louise Allen**
  (Regency)
  Second in *The Transformation of the Shelley Sisters* trilogy

- **VALIANT SOLDIER, BEAUTIFUL ENEMY**
  by **Diane Gaston**
  (Regency)
  Third in *Three Soldiers* miniseries

- **SECRET LIFE OF A SCANDALOUS DEBUTANTE**
  by **Bronwyn Scott**
  (1830s)

HHCNM0811

REQUEST YOUR FREE BOOKS!

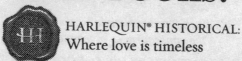

HARLEQUIN® HISTORICAL:
Where love is timeless

2 FREE NOVELS PLUS 2 FREE GIFTS!

YES! Please send me 2 FREE Harlequin® Historical novels and my 2 FREE gifts (gifts are worth about $10). After receiving them, if I don't wish to receive any more books, I can return the shipping statement marked "cancel." If I don't cancel, I will receive 6 brand-new novels every month and be billed just $5.19 per book in the U.S. or $5.74 per book in Canada. That's a savings of at least 17% off the cover price! It's quite a bargain! Shipping and handling is just 50¢ per book in the U.S. and 75¢ per book in Canada.* I understand that accepting the 2 free books and gifts places me under no obligation to buy anything. I can always return a shipment and cancel at any time. Even if I never buy another book, the two free books and gifts are mine to keep forever.

246/349 HDN FEQQ

Name _____
                                (PLEASE PRINT)

Address _____ Apt. # _____

City _____ State/Prov. _____ Zip/Postal Code _____

Signature (if under 18, a parent or guardian must sign) _____

Mail to the **Reader Service:**
IN U.S.A.: P.O. Box 1867, Buffalo, NY 14240-1867
IN CANADA: P.O. Box 609, Fort Erie, Ontario L2A 5X3

Not valid for current subscribers to Harlequin Historical books.

Want to try two free books from another line?
Call 1-800-873-8635 or visit www.ReaderService.com.

* Terms and prices subject to change without notice. Prices do not include applicable taxes. Sales tax applicable in N.Y. Canadian residents will be charged applicable taxes. Offer not valid in Quebec. This offer is limited to one order per household. All orders subject to credit approval. Credit or debit balances in a customer's account(s) may be offset by any other outstanding balance owed by or to the customer. Please allow 4 to 6 weeks for delivery. Offer available while quantities last.

HHI1B

New York Times *and* USA TODAY *bestselling author*
Maya Banks presents a brand-new miniseries

PREGNANCY & PASSION

When four irresistible tycoons face
the consequences of temptation.

Book 1—ENTICED BY HIS FORGOTTEN LOVER

Available September 2011 from Harlequin® Desire®!

Rafael de Luca had been in bad situations before. A crowded ballroom could never make him sweat.

These people would never know that he had no memory of any of them.

He surveyed the party with grim tolerance, searching for the source of his unease.

At first his gaze flickered past her, but he yanked his attention back to a woman across the room. Her stare bored holes through him. Unflinching and steady, even when his eyes locked with hers.

Petite, even in heels, she had a creamy olive complexion. A wealth of inky-black curls cascaded over her shoulders and her eyes were equally dark.

She looked at him as if she'd already judged him and found him lacking. He'd never seen her before in his life. Or had he?

He cursed the gaping hole in his memory. He'd been diagnosed with selective amnesia after his accident four months ago. Which seemed like complete and utter bull. No one got amnesia except hysterical women in bad soap operas.

With a smile, he disengaged himself from the group

around him and made his way to the mystery woman.

She wasn't coy. She stared straight at him as he approached, her chin thrust upward in defiance.

"Excuse me, but have we met?" he asked in his smoothest voice.

His gaze moved over the generous swell of her breasts pushed up by the empire waist of her black cocktail dress.

When he glanced back up at her face, he saw fury in her eyes.

"Have we *met?*" Her voice was barely a whisper, but he felt each word like the crack of a whip.

Before he could process her response, she nailed him with a right hook. He stumbled back, holding his nose.

One of his guards stepped between Rafe and the woman, accidentally sending her to one knee. Her hand flew to the folds of her dress.

It was then, as she cupped her belly, that the realization hit him. She was pregnant.

Her eyes flashing, she turned and ran down the marble hallway.

Rafael ran after her. He burst from the hotel lobby, and saw two shoes sparkling in the moonlight, twinkling at him.

He blew out his breath in frustration and then shoved the pair of sparkly, ultrafeminine heels at his head of security.

"Find the woman who wore these shoes."

Will Rafael find his mystery woman?
Find out in Maya Banks's passionate new novel
ENTICED BY HIS FORGOTTEN LOVER
Available September 2011 from Harlequin® Desire®!

Harlequin® *Romance*

Discover small-town warmth and community spirit
in a brand-new trilogy from

PATRICIA THAYER

The Quilt Shop in **KERRY SPRINGS**

*Where dreams
are stitched...patch
by patch!*

Coming August 9, 2011.

Little Cowgirl Needs a Mom

Warm-spirited quilt shop owner Jenny Collins promises to
help little Gracie finish the quilt her late mother started,
even if it means butting heads with Gracie's father,
grumpy but gorgeous rancher Evan Rafferty....

The Lonesome Rancher
(September 13, 2011)

Tall, Dark, Texas Ranger
(October 11, 2011)

www.Harlequin.com

HRI7745

ROMANTIC
SUSPENSE

NEW YORK TIMES BESTSELLING AUTHOR

RACHEL LEE

The Rescue Pilot

Time is running out…

Desperate to help her ailing sister, Rory is determined
to get Cait the necessary treatment to help her fight
a devastating disease. A cross-country trip turns into
a fight for survival in more ways than one when their plane
encounters trouble. Can Rory trust pilot Chase Dakota
with their lives, and possibly her heart?

**Look for this heart-stopping romance in September
from *New York Times* bestselling author Rachel Lee
and Harlequin Romantic Suspense!**

Available in September wherever books are sold!

www.Harlequin.com.

RSRL27741